Good job. ...
Wishes
Darrell Egbert

the Third
Gambit

A Novel by
Darrell H. Egbert

Other Novels by
Darrell Egbert

Zachary's Gold

the Indenture of Edward St. Ives

The Secret Of Recapture Creek

the Third Gambit

A Novel by
Darrell Egbert

Publishers Place
St. George, Utah

ISBN 0-9754460-1-0
v.1

Published by Publisher's Place
St. George, Utah
www.publishersplace.com

Cover designed by Wallace Brazzeal

Printing in the United States of America
10 9 8 7 6 5 4 3 2 1

CHAPTER 1...SINGAPORE, 1973

Two young Chinese walked along the shaded side of Orchard Boulevard in metropolitan Singapore. Each was dressed in a traditional long-sleeved white shirt under a light-weight white business suit, and each was carrying a small suitcase. They looked as though they had just stepped from an airport taxi and were looking for one of the many hotels to be found near this part of the main thoroughfare.

Singapore: Garden spot of the orient, long before the Japanese incursion into Malaysia. Then, the very name conjured thoughts of intrigue and secret deals.

Singapore: A name synonymous with subterfuge and broken promises, of large sums of money paid out for intelligence and counterintelligence. And it is still the home of an enclave of secret underworld characters who freelance, and still others who have been long-time professional spies for a myriad of governments.

Singapore: City of Hindu temples, corniced with painted gods and goddesses of every hue of the rainbow.

Singapore: City of tropical rain forests and blinding sun. Where to the north lies...*the road to Mandalay, Where the flyin' fishes play, An' the dawn comes up like thunder Outer' China 'crost the bay!*

The two turned off into a side street, narrow and winding and fronted with rows of tiny, brightly painted houses. The day was seasonably warm. They were beginning to perspire in the humid tropical weather, so they stopped for a glass of sweet iced tea and a plate of cubed durian and melon, topped with a layer of shaved ice, at one of the many shaded outdoor kiosks lining the streets off Orchard.

Finished, they picked up the pace. They took a shortcut through a back ally-way, home to a number of herbal medicine doctors plying their trade from dimly lit, crowded spaces, which substituted for both home and office. Their large shingles, written in English, Chinese, and Malay, swayed in the gentle breeze. Overhanging laundry was suspended from long bamboo poles protruding from small buildings on both sides of the street. Looking up through the laundry, they could see their destination, a tall modern skyscraper in the distance. They were sweating now more than they should have been, given the walk and the ever-present humidity.

They approached the front entrance to the building. Walking across the tile entranceway, they moved through the revolving door into the welcome air-conditioning. They hurried across immaculate marble to the elevator, entered and pushed the button for the second floor.

Their final destination was a suite of offices–home to East India Trading Ltd., painted in gold letters on the upper part of a frosted glass door. Inside, three men and one woman were busily engaged in the work of the corporation.

There was a long table in the middle of one of two rooms. The table contained a number of large maps of the Far East, one of which was a blow-up of the Republic of China.

One of the men moved from the table toward the bathroom. He had been leaning over the table in his shirtsleeves studying the maps, as the two Chinese exited the elevator and walked the few yards to the plainly marked office.

They looked neither left nor right. Nor did they say anything to one another as they tried to open the door. Realizing it was locked, they stepped back. They shielded their faces from the flying glass exploding around them as the first bursts from their Russian machine pistols shattered the door.

They pushed into the inner offices, killing outright every single person in the room. The two men were sitting at desks, bent over, occupied with business papers. The woman was standing at a reproduction machine. She fell as a fusillade of slugs tore into her body. Each one died quickly in the hail of bullets that tore the office apart.

When the firing stopped, the two assailants counted the dead and then looked at each other. Without saying a word, one entered the second room being used for storage and sprayed it with a full clip before reloading. His companion moved into the bathroom and did the same thing. When they were certain no one was left alive, they walked unhurriedly toward the door and exited as they had entered.

The man who had gone to the bathroom rolled over into the tub-shower when he heard the door of the office shatter. Seconds later, he heard the bathroom door burst open. Instantly, the room filled with plaster dust as the bullets tore down the shower curtain over his head, embedding harmlessly in the wall. The shooter left coughing, half-blinded, without bending over and physically inspecting under the shower curtain for a third man.

As they walked toward the stairs at the end of the outside hall, one of them remarked to the other that there was supposed to have been three men. But clearly there were only two, and they were lying lifeless back on the floor of the office. Neither bothered to check the number of coats hanging on the rack inside the door, one of which was dark in color in a city where white was traditionally worn the year around.

Walking with suit coat in hand and covered with plaster dust, he hurried as fast as he could without drawing undue attention to himself. He moved through the streets as though he knew the city intimately. But actually he had only been down this particular street once in his life. His goal was the shop of an herbal doctor whom he had met just days before. He entered the shop and waited until a woman in her early thirties came down the stairs and moved behind the counter.

"How can I help you, *la*?" She said in perfect English.

"I would like to see the proprietor," he said, thinking how the Malay ended most sentences with the odd expression, *la*. It tended to throw off the natural flow of words and was confusing to the non-native ear. He thought it was much like the Canadian manner of beginning sentences with the word, *hey*, dropping the first letter, or the exasperating manner in which Americans with limited vocabularies used fillers such as *ya know*.

"I'm sorry, but my father is not here right now." It never occurred to her she might be telling a stranger she was there alone. She never remotely considered that she might be placing herself in danger. This was, after all, Singapore, a place known for its law and order, where spitting on the sidewalk could get you fined, where possession of illegal drugs was a capital offense.

"When will he be back?" he asked.

"He has gone to the peninsula, to Kuala Lumpur on business. And he won't be back for another week," she said. "May I ask how you know him, *la*?"

"He has a reputation for being a chess master, and I was here a week ago by invitation. We played part of a game and then I had to leave. I have some time now, so I thought perhaps we might finish the game."

She thought something was amiss. He was disheveled and she had never seen him before. And the board was set up in their parlor for a new game. He obviously knew her father, because her father was a player of some repute. But once a game began the board was seldom disturbed. Why then was this American misleading her? The fact he was American, as opposed to some other nationality, was of no consequence to her.

Other than San Francisco, Singapore is probably the most cosmopolitan city in the world. Here the races and nationalities meld together in almost perfect harmony. Here business, and not color, determines friendships. The residents had discovered decades ago that such an arrangement had resulted in mutual profits for all concerned. And except for the occasional stuffy tourist, who had brought his prejudices with him, things worked fine. And the quickest way to be singled out as a non-resident was to exhibit social preferences.

The man on the other side of the counter was not from around here. As they say in parts of New England, regardless of how long you have lived in a community, if you were not born there *you are from away*. She did not know how long he had been visiting, nor was it of any of her concern.

He was desperate. She could see it in his eyes and in the way he addressed her. Even now, he suspected he was being followed. He broke off the conversation with the younger woman and went to the open doorway. He looked up and down the narrow alleyway. He was looking for somebody who might be lurking across the narrow street. She watched him as he moved, and then listened as he spoke in a hurried manner. He was sweating, and she was convinced now more than ever that he might be in some kind of trouble. But the thought of calling the police was something that never entered her mind. The police were separated from the affairs of the general population, perhaps because even minor offenses were punishable by the harshest of sentences.

The laws were enacted and enforced by a parliamentary government, which was patterned after the British. But unlike Britain, the Prime Minister functioned more in the guise of a dictator than a leader of a constitutional monarchy. His handhold over the majority of the citizenry was through the medium of the housing permit. Housing was at a premium in Singapore, and the loss of one's housing permit resulted in your being put into the street. If you were unfortunate enough not to have relatives who would take you in, you were in danger of being hassled by the police as a vagrant. The housing authority was the Prime Minister, who gave or took away housing permits according to the willingness of the individual to comply with parliamentary dictates. Most of the housing was in the hands of the government, who used it as a *Sword of Damocles* over the heads of the citizenry. The Prime Minister and his underlings were elected officials, to be sure. But with one major difference from the English system-the Prime Minster or a member of his family selected all those on the ballot. Any interloper with the audacity to stand for election in any capacity was dealt with on a variety of trumped-up charges. The police and the judiciary appointed by the P.M., as he was called, naturally enforced the charges. It is no wonder then that the general population had long ago learned to distrust and to fear the intrusion of the law into their personal affairs.

He closed the night door and hung the closed sign on the hook provided. And then he went back to the counter, his manner now completely changed. She thought she saw something in his eyes not there before. It was a kind of animal look, a look that said he was prepared to do anything to keep from falling into the hands of his would-be assailants. He spoke to her, telling her again that he was a friend of her father.

"What is your name," he asked in Malay. He asked, not to show his proficiency in her language, which was not very much, but to allay her fears that he might be somebody from someplace else. He knew she knew he was not, but he had to make absolutely sure.

"My name is Helen Wong," she answered. And then she continued in Malay to explain that her father was Doctor Wong. And that she was of Chinese and Malay heritage.

He understood some of what she was saying. However, he was quick to point out that he was unable to carry on any kind of sustained conversation in either Malay or Chinese.

"I need to impose upon your father's hospitality for a few days," he said, in English. Before she could answer, he assured her nothing would happen to her if she cooperated. But he implied that something might if she was reluctant to do so.

"I need a place to stay until your father gets back." With that he opened his coat to reveal a pistol in a shoulder holster. She was slow to catch onto the reason. He did not want her to be a willing abettor. He wanted her to be able to tell anyone who might interrogate her with a lie detector that he had entered the shop uninvited and had threatened her.

"I want you to keep the shop closed. I want you to call as many of your friends as you think might be interested. Tell them you have been called away to join your father. You're not to leave unless I give you permission. Have you an *amah*?"

"Yes."

"How many times does she come in?"

"Every other day."

"Call her and tell her you're going to be away for a couple of weeks."

She nodded her head. But now she was afraid. Firearms were

forbidden on penalty of long prison terms. She had changed her mind. Now she was not sure this man knew her father. And if he did, she was not sure they were the friends he had made them out to be.

As he sat down in front of the now frightened woman, he saw the whole thing as one big charade. He was tired and confused and his mind was wandering. He was sweating profusely and his lips were dry, and just for a moment he thought if he stood up he might go into shock. His mind was becoming hazy, and things seemed to be moving in slow motion, as the reality of the events of the past hour began to set in. Just for a moment he had a weird feeling he might be acting out a role in a new book written by James Grady, a friend of his. He felt the need to talk to take his mind off the scene of violence he had just experienced. But his tongue was thick, and he asked her for a glass of water.

She moved quickly to the small efficiency-kitchen off the main part of the apothecary, through hanging oriental beads, to reappear only seconds later.

She had thought of asking him if he wanted a glass of iced tea; she changed her mind when she decided he was not a guest but an intruder in her home. Lacking a paper napkin, she handed him the cold water, wrapped in a small *serviette*, and sat down. She sat with her head lowered as though she considered herself to be a prisoner. Then she looked up at him with the inscrutable look Occidentals maintain Orientals reserve for them—the look that appears to hide their true thoughts, and serves to make them appear mysterious.

She did not move away from him as he took the glass. He took a long swallow and then moved closer to her, as though somebody might be listening. And then in a quiet voice, almost whispering, he said, "I have recently read a new book entitled, *The Three Days of The Condor*."

She wanted in the worst way to tell him the statement was absurd, given the situation. It was incongruent, something inconsistent with the mood, which made her for the moment question whether she was in the company of a completely rational person.

He told her a friend of his had recently asked him to read the manuscript and to check it for technical accuracy. He said his friend had already sold the movie rights, and that Robert Redford and Faye Dunaway were going to star in the picture.

He spent the next few minutes telling her about the story plot. When he was through, he said he'd told her the story to emphasize a point. He said he was in danger of being killed for what he knew, just as Robert Redford's character was. And unlike Redford in the upcoming movie, who did not know until the end who it was who wanted to kill him, he said he knew. And now, like Fay Dunaway's character, he said, she too had become a target because she was assisting him. It did not matter, he explained, that it was all happening against her will; she was a witness, and the assassins could not afford a witness to his demise.

There was another parallel, he said. If she cooperated and let him stay with her for a short time, just until he collected his wits and recovered from his recent ordeal, he would leave quietly. What he failed to mention was how the two characters in the book, after spending time with each other, eventually fell in love. And now that he had the time to study her more closely, he could see she was a very beautiful woman. And something else he noticed for the first time: she was several years younger than he was and she was not wearing a wedding ring. But age difference between couples in Singapore was never considered all that important.

CHAPTER 2 ...1972

A taxi pulled away from the train station and headed north away from the small commuter village. Within minutes it was moving through the rolling countryside of one of the more exclusive areas of New England.   Quarried stones, which substituted for cement curbing, bordered the two lanes of the asphalt road. White painted wooden fences just beyond stretched for miles in either direction. The fences, which rose and fell with the terrain in gentle arcs, were made of construction quality lumber. The top headers were oversized in width, while the cross members were doubled, not only for strength but, like the stones on the road, part of their function was to impress the passer-by with the wealth of the nearby residents.

The cab had been in route for almost twenty minutes. At the direction of the passenger, the driver made a left turn across the road and stopped in front of a large ornate iron gate, flanked by two large stone pillars. The pillars were part of the stonework that sloped down on both sides some ten yards or so to the level of the wooden fence.

The passenger emerged from the rear seat carrying an attaché case. He paid the driver, giving him a generous tip. The taxi then turned around and headed back toward the village.

He stood for a moment admiring the artistry of the gate. He had been here many times before over the years, and he was always fascinated by the entranceway to this particular estate. Not that it was all that different from the scores of others along the road. But because it always reminded him of the opening lines of *Rebecca*, where in a dream the second Mrs. DeWinter describes her return to Manderley.

He peered through the bars toward the mansion he knew was at the end of the twisting, tree-lined, gravel drive in front of him. And he imagined it was the same stark, burned-out hulk she saw, silhouetted against the dark autumn sky. And it reminded him that he, too, was homeless as she once was. But unlike the character in Daphne duMaurier's fiction, he preferred it this way.

At first glance, his attaché case and his dress might have caused him to be mistaken for a visiting professional, perhaps an attorney making a call on a wealthy client, or a professor, which might have been a second guess. Truth be told, no one was ever quite sure exactly who Herbert Rosenthal really was or what he was supposed to be doing to outwit life.

He was a scholar all right, having graduated with honors from Harvard University with degrees in English literature and foreign languages. But if you concluded liberal art was all that he was about, you would be wrong again. Herb Rosenthal was more than a doctor of philosophy of two rather scholarly disciplines; he was an authority on many other things as well. As a result, people in high places in government and in private industry wanted him to work for them. But while he would occasionally give them his opinion on one matter or another, he steadfastly refused to be tied down to any recognizable form of steady employment.

When asked from time to time if he would be interested in

a job, he would simply smile a kind of enigmatic smile, saying he was already employed. And then when he was asked for whom it was he worked, he would smile again, insinuating this information was classified. But he would always purposely leave the impression his employer was either the Central Intelligence Agency or one of its undercover contractors.

Many of his friends did not believe his insinuations. However, they swept it under the rug with a smile. They considered it to be nothing more than whimsy on his part. Just another one of his peculiarities, they said. They did not care that he may have had a penchant for embellishing the truth. To them he was a wonderful houseguest, one who raised conversation to a high intellectual level wherever he went. For this reason, he may not have needed a home. He was a bachelor and a professional guest whose company was continually sought after by the great and the near great, as well.

Herb was said to travel light. In fact, other than a small amount of money, he carried everything he owned in an attaché case that seldom left his side. It contained a few toilet articles, a change of underwear, which he washed in his guest's sink of an evening, and an extra shirt. He bought an overcoat in the fall and discarded it in the spring.

The dark-colored single-breasted lightweight suit he was wearing was the suit he always wore. He would occasionally stop at a walk-in cleaning and pressing establishment, where he would wait behind swinging doors for the operator to refurbish it again. When it started to become threadbare, he simply bought another one as close to the original as he could find. This way it looked as though he had worn the same suit for the past ten years. When he was asked why he did this, he shrugged his shoulders and mumbled something about there being no sense in changing something you liked for something you were going to have to get used too. What they thought of this eccentric behavior was of absolutely no concern to him.

Herb Rosenthal did not see himself as a freeloader. He was, of course, but he never thought of it in this way, if he thought about it at all. He lived on another plane, another level, the one inhabited by many another brilliant eccentric. And the mundane affairs of life simply were of no interest to him. If he had been poor and boring, things would have been different. But he was neither, so society allowed him to go marching unobtrusively to the beat of a different drummer with only a few objections.

Unlike many gifted eccentrics, he was gregarious. But then he only associated with those people whom he considered to be somewhere near his intellectual level. He did not suffer fools gladly. In fact, as they say, he did not suffer them at all. That is why he preferred to talk to the self-made wealthy, those who had been set apart in some way from the herd. Not that it really mattered all that much, because Herb managed to monopolize the conversation in any company he chose to keep. But those he did bestow his intellectual favors on never objected.

He was capable of remembering seemingly unlimited bits of trivia, as well as a staggering amount of serious information. He was a voracious reader who was quick to catch on to complex technical data he either read or was told about. In fact, no one, least of all Herbert Rosenthal, had any idea just how much he really knew.

Conversation with Herb was different. To be sure, he was most interested in the opinions of others. But few it was who ventured into these uncharted waters for fear of being overshadowed and thought deficient. So most of the time they just listened, nodded, and occasionally interrupted to agree with him. He usually took this to mean they were enjoying his company. If there were any who did become bored, they never said so. And, anyway, his visits were always short-lived. And his hosts from previous experience knew that, more likely then not, as soon as they turned their backs he would be gone.

One of his habits was to arrive unannounced after having been away for several months–and sometimes for years. He simply walked in and acted as though he had never left. When asked where he had been, he smiled that special smile of his and replied, "Operations." When pressed for a more definitive answer, he would continue to smile, his lips turning up at the corners ever so unobtrusively, and then he would discreetly change the subject.

When his hosts asked him how long he could stay, he would again look at him or her as though he were staring into some middle distance and reply, "It all depends." The implication was not lost on them. However, they were left on their own to determine exactly what important clandestine adventure he was about to embark on next.

When he was ready to leave after a few days, he would vanish without so much as a by your leave. His hosts may not have known for hours or for days that he had moved on. And sometimes, they would not hear from him again until he reappeared on their doorstep. But they never objected; in fact, they always gave the impression they were flattered that the great Herbert Rosenthal had condescended to spend some more of his valuable time with them. How valuable it was, however, was anybody's guess. It was just assumed it was. And his many wealthy friends and acquaintances were left to speculate as to what it was that kept him so busy.

He awakened from his reverie at the gate, leaving Mrs. DeWinter back in England. He now directed his attention to the electrically controlled lock to the side entrance, which was part of the gate. He reached into his inside jacket pocket and removed a small notebook. He looked up a number and punched the code into the lock. The solenoid on the door hummed and Herb quickly moved to enter. He walked up the road, all the while admiring the recently barbered lawn and the landscaping on both sides of him. He was thoroughly enjoying himself. He occasionally nodded or waved to the gardeners, who recognized him and allowed him to proceed unchallenged.

He rang the bell at the main house. The butler greeted him with a warm welcome, but he never commented on anything else He showed him to a guest room, and reminded him that dinner would be served at the usual time. This reminder was made more for conversation than anything else, because he knew Herb had not forgotten.

Herb had grown up in the Jewish section of Brooklyn. And while doing so, he did all the things a young man of his religion was expected to do. But it would never be said of him that he was very religious. He went to synagogue because he was expected to, and because his mother wanted him to. After she passed away, he slowly lost interest until the best that could be said of him was that he was Jewish in name only. But in any discussion of the subject, like so many others, he amazed his listener with the depth of his knowledge.

As a youngster, he had little interest in hanging out with the other kids in the neighborhood. Not, that is, until they came around to ask him if he wanted to play baseball.

It was one of his many passions. And it had been from the time he was old enough to play the game. But unlike for many of his acquaintances, it was not all-consuming; he had other interests as well. He was an outstanding player, but he did not work at becoming such. He was said to be a natural; perhaps that is why he liked it so much, as he did not have to work at it very hard to be good.

Herb would never say who contacted the scouts at Harvard University; perhaps it was his high school coach. But then again, no one could say, because Herb and the coach never saw eye to eye on much of anything.

The coach would comment later, after Herb was offered a contract, that Herb did not have the proper attitude to succeed in the major leagues. It was probably because Herb Rosenthal's personality did not sit well with the coach. He was not the stereotypical jock the coach expected him to be; he was too nonchalant. He was outside the pattern; the coach thought of him as being a smart aleck, and Herb irked him no end.

It all came so easy for him, and he completely ignored the coach's suggestions on how to improve his game. It did not need to be improved, he said. And Herb did not hesitate to let the coach know of his thoughts and feelings on the subject early on. This was the reason behind their failure to communicate.

Years later, when asked about time spent with this particular coach, he was hard put to remember anything significant about the man, other than to say he did not like him. To Herb Rosenthal, he was a non-entity, a cipher that was purposely forgotten. He was viewed by Herb as being irrelevant in the greater scheme of things.

Baseball could be said to have been good to Herb. Among other things, it provided him with an education, which could not have been obtained in any other way.

During his playing years in the majors, he was good enough to have national name recognition. But because he was somewhat eccentric, even in those days, he received more attention from sports writers than his ability warranted.

His celebrity status increased even as his playing days wound to a close. Now, he was better known for his activities off the field than on. At first he was a curiosity among the Eastern elite, more because he was a professional athlete than anything else. And then when he became better known for his mind than for his athletic ability, he was even more sought after as a party guest by up-scale party givers.

It was about this time that his name began to show up in the society columns in and around Washington and New York. Gradually, he came into close contact with congressmen, and eventually with intellectuals in the Office of Strategic Services. First it was on a social basis, and then he gave his closer associates the impression his friendship with members of the intelligence community had escalated into something more professional.

Herb liked this kind of notoriety. He liked the hubris and the secrecy, at least he gave the subtle impression he did. But whether the OSS or later the Central Intelligence Agency was ever particularly interested in him, no one ever knew. When they were asked specifically, they would neither confirm nor deny having any professional association with him.

After he left baseball, he began to drop names of people whom he knew worked in high places in the OSS. He would more and more insinuate in casual conservations how he was privy to classified information about special projects. Without saying anything explicit, he would imply that he was involved in these projects to some degree. After all, he said, the country had given him so much; now it was his turn to pay it back. And many believed the means he had chosen to do this was by serving among the shadows of the OSS.

It was all so plausible. While there were laws against impersonating commissioned officers of the armed services and agents of the FBI, there were none against spying for the government. So he was at liberty to role play to his heart's content. And because he would never personally confirm or deny the length to which he had become involved, the myth steadily grew that he was a genuine *agent provocateur*. And wherever he went, Herb Rosenthal was viewed as a man of mystery.

Herb had invested his rather meager baseball salary wisely. That is to say, it was meager when compared to the obscene salaries of today's professional athletes. But as time went by, his estate grew steadily. And because of his life style, he saved more than he spent. However, people who took an interest in such things always thought his income came from the government.

For the longest time, Herb was frequently seen around Washington. And then suddenly he was seen no more. Not that he was missed, mind you, just that he was not seen around anymore, much like television anchors who move to different markets. No one seems to miss one of them until they show up on another station in another city. That was the way it was with Herbert Rosenthal. But in his case, he was never seen again in social circles around Washington, New York, or anyplace else for that matter. It was as though he disappeared the way he had many times, without announcement. But this time he never came back.

CHAPTER 3
OVER INTERNATIONAL WATERS, 1985

My name is Chris Mayo. I just woke up. The sound of the engines had put me to sleep. I just checked my watch and it tells me we are now six or so hours into an eighteen-hour flight from Singapore to San Francisco.

I haven't had much sleep this past couple of weeks. Not since I got a three in the morning wake-up call from some joker I thought was calling me from a party somewhere.

"Hello," he said, "now don't hang up on me because I have something important to tell you." He goes on to tell me about how there's some big money to be made. He says if I'm interested I should go make a pot of coffee and drink a couple of cups. He says he'll call me back in twenty minutes or so. He didn't even ask me my name, which means he knows who I am. And he obviously knows my address and telephone number, which means he has gone to some trouble to find me.

Not that my name is a really big secret. I suppose a lot of people know me, or I should say, knew me.

Chris Mayo is not my real name, though. I changed it because the one I was born with had too many vowels for your average Anglo-Saxon tongue to handle easily. Still, I wanted one with an Italian sound, because I'm a sports writer. At least I was. I worked for a couple of papers in Chicago and New York as a stringer, which is not the same thing as having a column of your own. I write feature articles, mostly about baseball. And many of my readers are Italian. That's one of the reasons I left my name Italian when I changed it. The other is that I just liked the sound of the name, Mayo.

They ask me all the time if I am related to the actress by the name of Virginia. You know the good-looking blond who played the floozy in the award winner, *The Best Years of Our Lives*? You know, it starred Fredrick March and Dana Andrews, along with Myrna Loy and Joan Leslie? The answer I give them usually depends on how much I've had to drink. I have even been known to tell them she is my ex-wife, just to watch the expressions on their faces.

I got up and had a shot of Jack Daniels instead of coffee. By the time he did call back, my head was clear and I was ready to listen. I thought the whole thing was some kind of a practical joke. But I didn't go back to sleep after his first call, because I more than half-way expected to be awakened again if I did.

"Chris," he said, "you know me. My name is Herb Rosenthal. I played ball back in the old days. You interviewed me a few times before and after I left the game."

If it was the Herb Rosenthal I knew, he would be about my age, somewhere in his sixties. I remembered he was noted for being a sharp cookie more than he was for his ability to hit a fast ball down and out.

"I want you to write a book for me," he said.

"Why don't you write it yourself?" I asked him.

"Because, I'd just as soon not let certain people know I'm

still around and kicking." he said. "The book is an expose type thing."

"An expose of whom or what?" I asked him.

"Look, I want you to meet me in Singapore…"

"Singapore, are you nuts…?"

"It's got to be Singapore. I'm going to make it worth your while. Meet me there and I'll tell you all you need to know. I'll give you all the information you'll need at that time. Before you turn me away, though, let me tell you that, if you do agree, a messenger will bring you an envelope in the morning. It will contain some earnest money, so to speak. I rather suspect it will be enough to get you interested."

He went on to tell me about myself, and he knew quite a lot. For instance, he knew I had not exactly set the world on fire with either of my two novels, which I wrote after I left the newspaper business. And he knew I was all but broke. If he knew my address, he would have known that. There is no doubt about it, he had done his homework. And anybody who had gone to this kind of trouble to locate me must really be on the level. I don't see it any other way.

We talked another few minutes before he hung up. During our conversation, he must have repeated it several times. He wanted me to be sure I didn't tell anybody what I was doing. He said both of our lives could be in danger if I started checking around trying to find out something more about him than he had already told me. He reiterated the part about the messenger and the instructions about what he wanted me to do. And he emphasized the amount of money he was going to pay me up-front. And he told me again about how I was going to make some real money when it was published. He said I didn't have to worry about finding a publisher. He said he had connections. All I had to do now was show up at the place and date contained in the instructions.

I wanted to talk some more but he was real hush-hush about the whole thing, like he expected the call might be monitored or something.

I had some more Jack Daniels before I went back to bed. I lay there trying to remember what I knew about this Herb Rosenthal. Not much I'm afraid, except for the fact that he was known as some kind of an intellectual, which in itself is different for a baseball player. And it also came to me while staring at the ceiling that he was some kind of a character who went around playing like he was some kind of spy or something.

The next morning the messenger showed up on time. Of course, I agreed to do it. Why wouldn't I? I had nothing else to do, and my curiosity was starting to drive me crazy. Then there was the money thing. I hoped it was enough to pay my rent and to get me some decent clothes.

The money was a lot more than I expected. This Herb Rosenthal seemed to be doing quite well for himself, quite well indeed. I wondered if it had anything to do with his sudden disappearance years ago.

The envelope contained details about what he wanted me to do. There was also a prepaid round-trip ticket to Singapore on Singapore Airlines, and a reservation at the Raffles Hotel for two weeks. What I was going to do for those two weeks, I had no idea.

As I think about the Raffles now, it all seems to fit. Herb Rosenthal was a romantic as much as he was anything else. How much of his choice can be attributed to romance, and how much was because it was just a good hotel and he wanted to impress me, I don't know. But the Raffles is the one he chose, and that's where I ended up. Thinking about the last two weeks though, what transpired between the two of us was certainly in keeping with the history of the place. Let me explain this last statement:

Raffles was not named after the famous English second story-man. It was named after some English nobleman who helped settle the place for English colonialism. It has always been a five-star layout; maybe that's why people on government expense accounts usually stayed there. I'm talking about spies. These guys congregated there from all over the world before the Japanese onslaught into Malaysia. Remember how they spread the baloney about how good they were going to make it for the brown-skinned Malay. They said the same thing to the poor Chinese, just before they slaughtered them by the tens of thousands. And then after the War they lied about it. And they are still doing it.

Anyway, this hotel was the mingling place for many characters who would now be referred to as *members of the intelligence community*. In those days they were simply known as spies. Singapore was something like Lisbon during the War or Tangiers to a lesser degree. And I guess there was more than one notorious hotel in those cities as well.

This spy business and the Raffles never ended with World War Two. During the Vietnamese War it was the scene of more than a few deals involving the CIA. Before I left Herb at the Raffles, he gave me a healthy advance on our new book. I keep calling it a book since it is about ninety percent factual. But he said we should call it a novel because people nowadays prefer to read novels. He says they have a real low attention span. That is most of them do, not like him. You can't compare anybody with him. But he does it all the time. And he says when they get to the part about some of the under-the-table dealings involving the

CIA, they will be able to recognize the truth, whether it's a novel or not.

He gave me a suitcase full of material. A week later, I looked for him; he had disappeared. However, he left a note saying he would contact me in a few weeks and then we would go over the outline. That's what I was doing, writing the outline, when I fell asleep.

CHAPTER 4…SYDNEY, AUSTRALIA, 1979

The police approached a late model Mercedes that was pulled off a back road a short distance from the town of Lithgow, about ninety miles outside of Sydney. What they saw inside the car, slumped over the wheel and shot in the head with a hunting rifle, would have far ranging effects throughout the United States.

One, Frank Nugan had committed suicide. That was the official cause of his death, at any rate. That was what was stated on the coroner's report. But there were a number of investigators, other than the coroner, who believed it could not have happened that way. The distance from the trigger to the end of the barrel was too long for him to have used one of his fingers. And his shoes and stockings were still on his feet. They believed he had been assassinated because of what he knew, and because of what he might have done with this information. Then too, the affairs of his bank, which was on the verge of bankruptcy, would have become public had he been forced to later testify.

Nugan's business partner, Michael Hand, was a former decorated Green Beret who had distinguished himself in combat in Vietnam. While serving there he developed CIA contacts, which would later be used to establish the Nugan Hand Merchants Bank of Sydney.

Mike Hand stayed in Australia after he left the service. In a short time, he and Nugan were said to have made a small fortune selling coastal real estate. They were helped in this endeavor by the singer Pat Boone, whose name they had been authorized to use as an interested investor. To what degree the popular revivalist participated in this endeavor, or whether he did at all, is unknown. But he was interested enough to journey this long distance to meet and talk with the two entrepreneurs.

There were other monies and support from high-ranking members of the government as well. And no less than the head of the CIA himself turned up on a list of friends of Frank Nugan. And this same CIA official had been the boss of Michael Hand during the War. He would later be promoted to head of the Agency before being fired by President Gerald Ford for suspected complicity in another matter.

This was the beginning of the Nugan Hand Bank, which would find itself moving further and further into the area of shady finance and money laundering. There are those who believed the bank was a legitimate for profit set-up. But this would come into question, as the bank would be later charged with money laundering and with acting as a fiduciary in the handling of money and property investments of the military and the CIA in the Far East. The officers of the bank would be accused in a far-reaching scandal, which would shake the offices of corporate industry and the Pentagon. The bank would become synonymous with drugs and illicit acquisition of stolen military property.

One frequent visitor to the newly acquired estate of Frank Nugan's partner was Herbert Rosenthal. Where he came from or what he was doing in Australia was unknown to Michael Hand. But Hand was soon to find that Herb Rosenthal was most knowledgeable in the intricacies of the banking business. And Rosenthal was quick to imply that he spoke for certain elements in the government who wanted the bank to succeed. These people were willing to furnish Hand with expertise and contacts, according to Rosenthal. Furthermore, he led Hand to believe that he, Rosenthal, was authorized by the government, the director of the CIA to be exact, to assist him in any way he could. He also told him he was willing to move into his home and to stay as long as he was needed.

Michael Hand was impressed with Herb Rosenthal, and he considered his offer to be both genuine and considerate. He was also flattered at the attention he was getting. But above all he was elated at the prospects of becoming rich, and for the high-level cover and support for the illegal operations he and Nugan were contemplating. Whether Rosenthal, at this point, was knowledgeable of Nugan and Hand's long-range plans would be a subject for discussion at the highest levels at Langley for some time to come.

With the death of Frank Nugen, the bank moved into receivership. It was the end of a banking era that began with Frank Nugen writing a check in the millions and then depositing it in the bank, which had begun with a mere eighty dollars. He promptly withdrew the money, but he would later claim the bank had recently had a working capital of millions of dollars.

Immediately, they began to launder drug money, and to act as a dispersing center for millions more of the CIA's money used to fund various operations during the War.

Nugent's death threw the whole operation into turmoil. And once the can of worms was opened, it spelled disgrace and possible prosecution for many high ranking military officers who had been hired by Michael Hand. Most of them quit when they discovered exactly what the bank was doing, but by that time their reputations were ruined.

To make doubly sure he was not the only one at fault, Frank Nugan may or may not have been responsible for a blood-soaked Bible left by his side that fateful morning. In it were listed the names of a dozen others whom he claimed were responsible for the entire affair.

Nugen had in his last days, when he saw the house of cards he had helped create about to tumble, professed he had been an innocent bystander. He said he did not have the financial know-how to establish such a large and complicated organization. He maintained he was merely a pawn in the hands of the CIA and other special interests. Among the names listed was Herbert Rosenthal's, with a comment that he was one of the main representatives from the CIA. But these names never saw the light of day, nor were any of the bank's officers prosecuted for fraud. When the story of Nugan's death reached Washington circles, the CIA stepped in and stopped the investigation by the State Department.

But Herb Rosenthal knew who the players were; and the hierarchy of the Agency was ill at ease, and would remain so as long as Rosenthal remained outside the inner circle.

When the scandal broke and the heads of the Australian government became aware a friendly nation had been operating illegally on Australian soil, they too became critics. At one point they went so far as to threaten the United States with refusal to cooperate in any further joint world banking ventures. But this was an idle threat, made by someone who did not understand the ramifications of world finance. Australia, later realizing what a disaster it would be if they did this, and not really wanting to detach themselves financially from the West, withdrew their formal statement. But they were smarting from the slight and what they considered the utter disregard for their sovereignty by a respected ally. And the resulting letters passed by their respective ambassadors received attention at the highest levels in the White House. And for a short time anyway, the name of Herbert Rosenthal was on the lips of the President and several members of his Cabinet. And none of their subsequent comments about him were favorable.

CHAPTER 5
NEW YORK, DECEMBER 10, 1942

Two FBI agents sat in a parked car, down the road about a half mile from one of the large estates in East Hampton, New York.

"Who is this guy? I mean, outside of baseball who is he really," one of them asked the other. The one who was asked the question was the senior agent. He was pouring a cup of coffee from a thermos and was hesitant to look up.

"You know it's none of our business who he is" was his reply.

"Come on, Jim," the other one said. "I'm not looking for any secrets. You know that. I'm just curious about what I'm doing out here in the middle of the night tailing some obscure baseball player."

Thinking he might hurt his friend's feelings and wanting to talk about something to stay awake, Jim replied. "I don't know too much about him. But I will tell you this, he is no ordinary guy. Hopefully, he's going to meet with the Director tomorrow."

"Nobody told me."

"Who said you were supposed to know?"

"Nobody, I guess. But if you want my opinion, these are sure screwy times. Baseball players meeting with J. Edgar Hoover. The Bureau is going to pot, in my estimation"

"Well, buddy," Jim said good-naturedly, "there's always the Army." Both of them were of draft age, and had they not been in essential government service there is no doubt they would have been classified 1-A and drafted a long time before this.

Their conversation changed at Jim's insistence. He had received only the very briefest of instructions, and his companion was told nothing at all; there had not been time.

Apparently the special agent in charge of one of the New York offices had received a call from Mr. Hoover's assistant yesterday morning. He was told another agent was flying in from Washington and that he would arrive as soon as he could get there. He was carrying a personal letter from Mr. Hoover to a Herbert Rosenthal. The letter requested an immediate appointment. It was to be delivered to Rosenthal by one of the resident agents, which as it turned out was Jim Larson.

The Washington agent had been given verbal instructions of the highest classification. These instructions were to be passed on to the agent assigned the detail, along with the letter from Mr. Hoover. Also, Rosenthal was to be told that Mr. Hoover wanted to meet with him near the campus of Princeton University the afternoon of the next day.

The agent running the two-man detail was supposed to contact the subject individual, who was a guest at the address they were staking out.

Jim Larson and his partner were to tail Rosenthal and then approach him in some discreet locale of their own choosing. They were not to be seen by anybody, whomsoever, when they approached him. They were to give him the letter and then wait until he had read it and acknowledged he understood it. They were not to question him about the contents, but they were simply to ask him to reply to one question: yes or no?

How much Larson chose to tell his companion about all of this was being left up to him. But he was advised to treat the matter with the utmost secrecy.

Larson had told his partner very little of consequence so far, except for the name of the limo passenger they planned to apprehend, that he used to be a baseball player, and a few incidentals about his background.

Larson had been told that a limo could be expected to emerge from the estate at any time before dawn. They were not going to arrest the passenger, he told his friend, but were simply going to stop him someplace and ask him to read the letter. The reading must be out of sight of the limo driver. Grand Central Station seemed a good choice, the place the Bureau thought he might be headed.

"Jim, why do you suppose they always send out two agents at a time when only one is needed? I don't see why I'm necessary tonight if no one sees fit to let me know what's going on."

Larson looked at his friend in the dark and laughingly replied. "Because I need someone to keep me awake."

It was well after midnight now and still no sign of the limousine. They both hated stakeout detail. After a few hours you were all talked out. And the cigarettes made your mouth taste like the inside of a Turkish wrestler's jock-strap. And the coffee was cold, and you were on edge because of all the caffeine. You wanted to go to sleep but you could not. You were both afraid if you let your guard down the least little bit, something was going to happen. But you knew it would be unlikely—not until after the sun came up, anyway.

Still, you sat and tried to make small talk while you fought to stay awake. Bureau gossip was usually the preferred subject at times like this: what happened to so and so, and who do you think is going to replace such and such a friend who is being transferred.

After a while they began talking about the subject, the one that was occupying the minds of most people these days. The one about the Army, and who was in it and who was going to be drafted next, mutual friends mostly from school. And then it shifted again to mutual friends who were in the Bureau, and then to a discussion about where they were working.

They had both decided they were in the right spot. They were far enough away from Headquarters, and the all-seeing, all-knowing eyes of Mr. Hoover, yet close enough to get into any real action if there was to be any. So far though, they had spent most of their time investigating defense contractor personnel, and officers in the military being trained for classified projects.

"Jim, do you suppose this guy Rosenthal is as smart as they say he is?" He put up his hand in the dark as if to feign off an expected swat across his head. "Ah, come on," he said, as his friend gave him yet another dirty look. "You said he speaks a hundred or so languages. And you said it's no secret he is supposed to go around talking in Latin or Sanskrit, which might be Yiddish as far as anybody knows. I mean do you suppose the Director wants to see him because he's some kind of an Ivy League brain?"

"How should I know," was the reply from the dark. But Jim Larson, who was smoking yet another bitter cigarette, knew. And the other agent knew he knew.

"Wait until after this job is over, and I'll tell you what I do know as long as it isn't classified. I know you're cleared, of course, but there's something about this guy and this job that doesn't sit right, somehow. But you can take it as a given that if the Director has a personal interest in him it's not a good idea to ask too many questions."

They had changed the subject again, and again they were making small talk to keep awake when Jim interrupted the conversation.

"Look, I see headlights. Start the engine but don't turn on our lights. Wait until he is about a half mile farther down the road."

His friend looked over at him with a frown as if to tell him *blow it out your barracks bag*. Of course, Jim might not know exactly what that meant. His friend had heard the saying from his young son. He guessed someone's older brother had brought it back from Army Basic Training, and it had been picked up by the kids. It was an innocuous put-down, and he had been wanting to tell Jim something like this for some time now. He wanted him to quit patronizing him. But he figured this was not the time or the place. Anyway, Jim Larson was now all business, and he figured Jim would not have been the least bit interested in any of his friends personal problems.

Just as headquarters had predicted, the limo turned in at Grand Central. Larson wondered, without saying anything, whether Mr. Hoover was right in his judgment of this brainy guy. He seemed too predictable, too easy to figure. If he really was some kind of a shady character, as he was making himself out to be, then he was going about it all wrong. He thought he should have taken a subway or gone to the bus station, something other than what he did. If the Bureau was going to hire some guy off the street, or off the ball diamond, they should at least have gotten one with a little more street smarts and a little less book smarts. Anyway, that was his opinion, which he kept to himself.

The government vehicle pulled into the rear of a Safeway

parking lot. It slowed and then parked about fifty feet away from a newly waxed Buick. Herbert Rosenthal was escorted toward the other automobile. A chauffeur disembarked from the Buick and opened the rear passenger door. Herb was invited to enter. Sitting in the rear seat was a heavy-set man who was smoking a cigar. In the passenger seat was another middle-aged individual, dressed in an almost identical suit.

The two agents and the chauffer then turned and hurried back toward the first car, entered and sat down. Rosenthal watched what appeared to him to be rehearsed choreography, thinking it might be a bit overdone. But later he would realize they had been instructed to get out of sight and to remain as inconspicuous as possible.

"Mr. Rosenthal, my name is Hoover. I am the director of the FBI and this is my friend and colleague Colonel William Donovan, director of the Office of Strategic Services, better known as the OSS."

A brief handshake was offered all around, and then Hoover said, "Do you recognize either one of us?"

"I have seen both of your pictures in the newspapers and in magazines," Rosenthal replied.

"Good, then that takes care of one of the formalities. Can you swear then that you know who I am. I want you to tell the Colonel for the record that I am J. Edgar Hoover. I want to hear you say you are entering into this conversation of your own free will, and that neither of us has coerced you in any way."

When Herb had replied as directed, Mr. Hoover reached into his pocket and pulled out a one dollar bill. He handed the money to Herb with a short speech, the jist of which was that he was now officially a Dollar a Year Man.

Herb knew what the term meant without being told. There were only a few of these people who had been designated by the

President, usually men of social position, and usually of considerable wealth. They were asked to serve their government for the duration of hostilities. And to serve without pay. The dollar was symbolic as well as a way to satisfy the clause in most contractual agreements, which stated *for the sum of one dollar and other considerations.* The other considerations would be in the form of personal satisfaction, adulation, and the respect of his fellow countrymen for the valuable services rendered the nation.

"I must advise you at this time, Mr. Rosenthal...."

"Call me Herb, please...."

"Herb," he started again, "I must advise you that in your case the consideration spoken of in the contract, the one I want you to sign in a minute, cannot be bestowed on you until well after the War is over. And I am obliged to tell you now before we proceed any further that you now come under the Official Secrets Act. If you divulge any part of what you hear here in the next half hour; or if you repeat anything to anybody not associated with this project, unless you are given written permission by me, it will result in your being summarily shot.

Herb was a little sleepy. He had been put up in a hotel room for what remained of the night, and then he was rooted out to dress and shave in preparation for this meeting. He was beginning to drowse as the Director droned on in a lawyer like manner. He thought if Hoover kept on, he might nod off. But then he thought again, and decided it was impossible because of the thick cigar smoke in the car. But if he had any further worry about getting drowsy again, he had forgotten about it. The Director had his full attention now. And Herb was not the least bit hesitant to ask him if he really meant to shoot him. The answer was in the affirmative. But it was proffered with one of Hoover's rarely seen smiles.

"Don't worry about it," he said. "I had to tell you this for the record. Of course, there is nothing in the Secrets Act that is going to allow me to shoot you. But this is war, and we do things a little differently now. Yes, I will have you shot. But when you come to realize how serious this matter is, I don't think you will blame me." With that he smiled again, as did Colonel Donovan from the front seat.

"What do you know about atomic energy?" Hoover asked him. "I mean what do you know about the atom? Don't be bashful about it. I confess, up until a few months ago, I didn't know anything. I studied law in school, and I really only had a passing acquaintance with the sciences.

"It's a new field," Hoover said. "It's so new that most people don't know much more about it than what they learned in high school physics and chemistry. Now we're going to ask you to go back to school. We're going to ask you to learn more in the next few days than most undergraduate college majors know. Sound impossible? Some people think so. But others who know you don't agree. They seem to think you're some kind of a whiz-bang who can learn or memorize anything on short notice. If that's so, then we're going to find out.

"There's a new physics rambling around the halls of ivy these days." Mr. Hoover was off and running again, this time at an increased speed. "It's called theoretical physics. It's also known by another name: it is called Quantum Mechanics. It is radical in its scope and radical in its application.

"You see, Herb, this country has recently embarked on a Herculean project. It's going to be the biggest industrial undertaking in the history of mankind, to date.

"Herb," the director paused for effect before he continued, "as of last week we can say we have harnessed the atom. We're planning to build an atom bomb. And you're going to play a major role in the building of this thing. What this new physics has to do with atom bombs, I am not qualified to say, but why we bring the subject up at all will become apparent to you in a few minutes.

"It's not my intention now to give you a course in how to build a bomb or even how to bring about nuclear fission. I'll leave that up to the colonel here, and the professors whom you'll meet directly. But I do need to tell you what I know. I need to put you far enough into the picture for you to make an intelligent decision as to what you want to do. I don't want to down-play the danger involved in the task we are going to ask you to perform. We have been over the plan carefully. And with British support, I think we can pull it off.

"I need to know whether you're prepared to risk your life to keep the world free, and to prevent the extermination of your race. And I'm afraid I need to know soon. Mind you, I said your race, not our race. Adolph Hitler and his minions are dedicated to extinguishing the Jewish race. And if they succeed in building a bomb before we do, they're going to do just that."

Hoover was a crafty one, Donovan thought. He could see he was not above using any tool he had at his disposal. He was going to appeal to Rosenthal's patriotism, God, or anything else that came into his mind. Hoover had convinced Donovan that Herb Rosenthal was essential to his plan, and he was not going to settle for anybody else.

Hoover went on to tell Rosenthal what Col. Donovan already knew; Germany once had a heavy water plant in Norway. And worse yet, they had been experimenting with it as well as producing this product since 1934.

"Do you know what *heavy water* is and what it is used for?" Hoover asked Rosenthal.

"I know it's an isotope of hydrogen," was his reply.

Hoover was taken aback by his answer. He looked at

Donovan as if to say, *I believe we have a keeper here.* Donovan just smiled a smile of approval at the two of them.

"What is it used for?" Hoover asked Rosenthal as a kind of test to see whether he could ascertain just how much he did know.

"What little I know is it is being used for nuclear fission experiments. It is more stable than water, and it is used to slow down the neutrons in an atomic pile."

"Where did you hear that?" Hoover wanted to know.

"I didn't hear it anywhere, I read it in a German physics publication some years ago."

"Do you know who wrote the article?" he asked.

"Not really, but probably the Danish scientist, Niels Bohr, or a German by the name of Werner Heisenberg. They're both pre-eminent in the field. Those two were the principles at a symposium in Copenhagen some time ago. They wanted to agree once and for all whether light was a wave or a particle, something like that. I don't know whether this was before or after Heisenberg got into quantum mechanics."

"It was before," volunteered Col. Donovan, not wanting to have the two of them continuing to think he was some kind of a dummy, just sitting there and saying nothing. However, he wished he had thought about it a little longer before popping off from the top of his head. Rosenthal looked at him kind of funny, so he guessed he had it wrong. Still he had a fifty percent chance of being right going in, and he did not expect either one of them to know the answer. Now he was not so sure Rosenthal had not had second thoughts about contradicting him. He thought he could tell by the way he glanced his way. But Herb said nothing to the contrary, and Donovan recognized a gentleman of the old school when he saw one. It was obvious   Rosenthal was not going to embarrass him.

"I wish I had time to talk to you at length," Hoover said. "You're one interesting guy, I can tell that.

"Well, there is a lot more to it," Hoover went on. "The people here at Princeton are going to give you the quickest most detailed course in nuclear physics that has ever been given to anybody. Then I want you to board a B-17 bomber headed for England. We want you to meet with Werner Heisenberg in Germany. The details of your mission are going to be furnished you step by step. But right now, I want Colonel Donovan to go through the plan on the surface. You need to know much more before you are in a position to say whether you are in or out. But whichever way it is, this meeting never happened. Understood?

"Now I am going to have to run. Colonel Donovan will be in touch with me.

"I'll take the other car and my people. I'll leave this machine and the chauffer with you and the Colonel. You'll be quartered in student housing in a private room. We have already registered you as a graduate student in physics, so your presence in the building will not be too suspect. I will see you before you leave for Europe.

"Oh, one more thing I forgot to mention," he said, as he exited the car. It was obvious he had waited until the last minute for dramatic effect. "If your in, and I assume you will be, if you determine Heisenberg is further along with his nuclear fission program than we are, and if you determine that Germany has the capability to build a weapon before we do, I want you to kill Heisenberg."

The two of them watched the FBI director enter the other car and drive away. Donovan turned to Herb in the back seat and said, "Herb, my job is to get you to Heisenberg in order for you to make your determination. This is the way we see it. Please hold your questions for a few minutes, and maybe they'll be answered. Our plan goes something like this:

"Werner Heisenberg is giving a lecture about the role heavy water plays in nuclear physics. It will take place at the University of Leipzig the middle of next month, so time is of the essence. He will also talk about the role quantum mechanics plays in his new physics. Thus far, traditional German scientists have down-played quantum mechanics as not having too much importance in anything. Over there they call it Jewish physics. It sounds to me like they're jealous of Heisenberg and his team, which is comprised of several of his colleagues, as well as several gradu-ate students. Incidentally, they all just happen to be Jewish, and the other guys are Nazis.

"The reason these Jews are not all in concentration camps is because of Heinrich Himmler's intervention with Hitler. He, Himmler, is head of the Gestapo. And he doesn't think all that much of Hitler's so-called Secret Weapon's Program, which Hitler believes is going to help Germany. In the beginning, Hitler was all in favor of going for a nuclear bomb. You may or may not know that Heisenberg and his team was the first to split an atom. This happened several years ago. But we don't think he was ever able to sustain a reaction, which I understand is the most impor-tant part. However, we have lost track of what he has been doing lately, and we may wake up to find out we are in big trouble. As I was saying, in the beginning Hitler figured a bomb was the answer. But now we think he's sort of cooled off in favor of some of his other monster projects. He realizes a bomb is going to cost him far more than he can afford. Himmler, on the other hand, wants to pool most of their resources behind a nuclear bomb of some kind, and then use it to somehow get Britain to surrender. So he hasn't given up, and that's why Heisenberg is still around. We think what's going to eventually happen will depend on their continuing progress. And that will depend largely on their continuing supply of heavy water."

"Tell me some more about this stuff," Herb said.

"I don't know all that much about the details, even though I have studied the subject and I have been briefed twice by British Intelligence. Donovan, said.

"What I do know about it is this: this so called heavy water is necessary as a moderator to slowdown the emitted neutrons in an atomic reaction. This neutron slow down increases the fission reaction rate, which enables them to acquire a sustained chain reaction. Without this water, I suppose you wouldn't even get a poof out of it."

"Tell me some more." Herb looked anxiously at him. Here for the first time in a long time he had met somebody he suspected knew more about something than he did, and as tired as he was, he was beginning to enjoy himself.

"Well, it may be possible with this heavy water to use natural uranium to get a reaction. The big problem is that, without this magic water, you have to enrich natural uranium to make it work. This enrichment takes real big bucks and a lot of time, both of which they are growing short of. But if somehow they can get enough of this special water, they can use the untreated uranium; then maybe they have a chance to beat us."

Herb asked him what else he knew about it.

Donovan replied: "Well, first of all they don't make this stuff. Molecules of deuterium are to be found in plain everyday water, but it is in very small quantities. They first separate the hydrogen in water from oxygen using electrolysis. Then they liquefy the hydrogen and distill the liquid to acquire the small amount of deuterium remaining. And then they remix this deuterium with oxygen to form heavy water. I understand there is more than one way, or a combination of ways they are using to bring this about.

To tell you the truth we don't know. And the problem of finding out is not so simple, because they have moved their production facilities from Norway back to Germany. As you told Mr. Hoover, heavy water is used as a moderator to slow down the reaction in an atomic pile. However, I should point out that we never used any of this water at Chicago last week. Instead, we used graphite as the moderator." Donovan was prepared to engage in a more lengthy discussion with Herb but changed his mind. Instead, he handed him a pamphlet which Herb guessed contained the details of the methodologies involved.

"Why, exactly, can't they use regular water as a moderator? It has all the orbiting electrons except one, unless I missed something," Herb said.

"Good question, I guess," said Donovan. "As I understand it, regular water won't work because it absorbs neutrons too fast, and it brings the reaction to a halt before it ever really gets started."

Herb's mind had now shifted into high gear, and Donovan, who himself was not in the habit of riding around on turnip trucks, was beginning to marvel at the intelligence of the man. Donovan had studied the subject quite extensively in order to adequately supervise covert operations in which his people might be engaged. And he had also studied a special brochure, which had been prepared for him hours before he set out from Washington. But now this guy, whom he thought had never heard of the subject, was apparently way ahead of him, and he suspected he had been all along. Donovan stopped talking and watched the wheels turn in Herb's head. He watched for a full ten seconds as Herb looked off into space, and then Herb began to speak:

"You know something," he said, not expecting an answer. "If they ever use this stuff to heat water to make steam to power turbines, they are going to find it is more practical to use enriched fuel. They can use regular water for cooling the engine, but they're going to have to have vast amounts of it. And you know something else, they're going to end up having to enrich this uranium. Do you suppose they know this now? Are we working on heavy water or are we trying to figure out a way to enrich uranium for a bomb, and then use the same method later for commercial purposes?"

And that, thought Donovan, *is why this guy is here and not somebody else. And that's why he is going to be able to understand Heisenberg's lecture and then make an accurate determination of how far along he is. And I guess it doesn't hurt that he is supposed to speak fluent German.*

"All of this is good background," Herb remarked. "But where are the Germans making this stuff? And what are you doing about getting rid of it? Obviously, if they're going to use this altered water then they're going nowhere without it."

"Right," Donovan replied. "We blew up one of their plants, and we sunk a ferry with enough production on board to build at least a half dozen bombs. We think Norwegian commandos, along with the help of a few British, have managed to put a real dent in their supply.

"The Germans had a plant outside Tellemark in southern Norway. They sent in some of these fellows who lived back in the mountains, living on reindeer most of the time. When they were ready, they got into the factory somehow. And because of the noise of the electrical turbines, they pretty easily got around where they wanted to go. They dressed like workman and planted dynamite bombs all over the place. It was a hairy operation, to say the least, but they pulled it off.

"But as of now," he continued, "we don't know whether the Germans are back at it or how far they have progressed if they are. And the big question is: What has this Herr Professor

Heisenberg been doing, lately? You know, Herb, if he could make just one bomb, and if he made us all believe he had more, we might all throw in the towel. One of these babies is expected to blow up a lot of city. There are too many unknowns, so we figure it is easier in the long run to just cut off the head of the snake that's causing us the problem. And that head right now rests on the shoulders of Werner Heisenberg."

CHAPTER 6...PRINCETON UNIVERSITY, 1942

The FBI had run a hurried clearance on Herb Rosenthal. Mr. Hoover had directed it be done post-haste, and all field offices involved made a maximum effort to comply. The word came down on the third day of his stay at Princeton: Go ahead. It meant he was to be given access to all available material on the subject of atomic energy.

Time was of the essence. Hoover knew if they procrastinated they were going to miss Heisenberg at Leipzig.

Up to this point, Rosenthal had been tutored almost around the clock in theory. Now he was to be taught by one of the scientists who had been working directly with Enrico Fermi at The University of Chicago.

In fact, that very morning, Walter Zinn had arrived under the guise of being a guest lecturer. Zinn was considered to be the number one assistant to Fermi in the construction of the first workable atomic pile.

Columbia had been home to Zinn for several years before he left for Chicago. There he had worked with Leo Szilard in the Office of Scientific Research and Development in its chain reactor program. Soon after it was moved from Princeton and Columbia to Chicago, due in part to an advanced metallurgical laboratory at Chicago, which was necessary for the research of the blocks for the atomic pile, both Zinn and Szilard moved as well.

Zinn had been with Fermi's team for the past year. Fermi thought so highly of him that he had put him in charge of designing and manufacturing the graphite and fissionable blocks of the atomic pile. This was considered to be the most important of the manufacturing projects leading up to the recently celebrated experiment in the squash court at Chicago.

Zinn lost no time after arriving at Princeton. He taught one class of graduate students for show, and then he was introduced to Rosenthal.

"Doctor Rosenthal, I have been brought here, as I understand it, to tell you what I know so that you can kill one of my colleagues." It could be said of Zinn, if he was not actually acerbic, he was certainly known for getting readily to the point.

"Putting it another way," he went on to say, "I'm supposed to teach you enough about nuclear physics that you can carry on an intelligent conversation with one of the great minds of this century. Not only is he a genius, but he has been the acknowledged authority on this particular subject since any of us can remember. Apparently, his life rests on your judgment as to whether his program in Germany is equal to ours or has surpassed us, in other words, whether he is a threat to build a bomb before we do. Quite frankly, I don't believe anybody can teach anybody enough about physics in a year to make an intelligent determination about what that man knows or what he is doing. And we have been given only days. It follows: if you don't understand him, you may conclude in error that he is further along than we are and then do away with him needlessly. This puts a tremendous burden on my shoulders to somehow find a way to teach you what you need to know. I feel as inadequate as a teacher as I suspect you are a pupil. And because of both of our inadequacies, and the Herculean task before us, a great man is going to lose his life."

Strange man thought Herb. *He does not see Heisenberg as an enemy, but as a friend who is temporarily working on the wrong side. How can he make a distinction between Werner Heisenberg and any other soldier, who by doing his duty, is a threat to my life?*

When they were first introduced, Zinn referred to him as doctor, as if his scholastic title would somehow make things easier. It was customary to do this among Zinn's colleagues when first they met and, thereafter, to refer to each other by their first or last names. In the case of Fermi, they made an exception and simply called him professor or doctor. No one presumed to know him well enough to call him Enrico.

"I have asked and have been told the reason why we are being pushed for time. It's because Doctor Heisenberg is going to be lecturing at Leipzig in a few weeks."

This last statement of Zinn's was well received by Rosenthal. Frankly Zinn's attitude when he first met him had surprised Herb. Herb was almost convinced they had chosen the wrong man. His apparent reluctance to cooperate and his gruffness were now seen by Rosenthal as being his way of expressing his dissatisfaction at having been chosen as the one to tutor him. Then too, Zinn had not fully come to terms with the need to eliminate Heisenberg as the only viable solution to the problem facing them all. Herb thought Zinn knew it was obvious, he was just reluctant to come to grips with what was a very disagreeable situation.

Zinn continued: "I have also been told this lecture presents the only window of opportunity available to us. I don't like any part of it, but in a sense I'm a soldier, just as you are, and I will do as I am directed." The way he was looking at Herb now reminded Herb of the way his fourth grade teacher often looked over her glasses at a struggling student. The look was often interpreted by Herb to mean, *What am I doing here among these young idiots?*

The fact that Herb had come to him as a student of the Muses, so to speak, with no apparent grounding in the sciences, displeased Zinn no end. But he was fully prepared to spend a few hours with him, pointing out his inadequacies, and then declare him incapable of learning anything of any practical value. In the worst way, he wanted the authorities to realize this project was hopeless. Zinn was of the strong opinion that not only might Heisenberg needlessly lose his life, but the most unprepared student he ever taught might lose his as well.

After a few days of tutoring, Zinn began to suspect he had not been saddled with an absolute dolt. It was when they began to explore the mathematical relationships between different sized piles of varying fissionable materials that Zinn became impressed with Rosenthal's knowledge of mathematics. He knew he had been crash-tutored in physics for the past few days, but he also knew you cannot teach someone advanced mathematics that easily.

"I was under the impression you had no formal training in college algebra and calculus," he said to Rosenthal.

"I haven't had any training. What I know I have taught myself."

Zinn was impressed, and for the first time he began to believe they had a chance to pull it off. But they had to fool Heisenberg into thinking Rosenthal was a graduate student. Not just a run-of-the-mill student, either, but one in whom Niels Bohr had taken a special interest.

This led to a lengthy conversation about how willing Bohr might be to help them get Herb into Heisenberg's lecture and into a private meeting afterward. And whether Heisenberg would still be angry enough to turn Rosenthal away when he was informed he was carrying a letter of introduction from Bohr.

"What do you think was the cause of the controversy between the two of them, the one that arose from their last meeting?" Rosenthal asked him.

"I've heard the story, but I can't honestly say. What I can say is, I'm impressed with your knowledge of the inside details of such things as this. Where did you hear about it?"

"I don't remember. There's a lot I don't know. I probably read about it, but I can't say for sure. I do know there were some hard feelings between the two when last they parted. I also know it first started when Heisenberg showed up at Bohr's doorstep. Bohr was ill at ease when it happened. Bohr didn't want to be seen in Heisenberg's company. He long believed the Gestapo, as well as British MI-6, had them both under surveillance. He thought he was going to be seen by the Allies, and by his own people, as a Danish scientist who was helping a German in what many people would view as an undercover effort to assist the Germans in bringing about nuclear fission."

Rosenthal went on to tell Zinn what the scientist already knew–that Bohr was angry before they ever began to talk: "The first subject they chose to discuss was divisive. It didn't help matters any when Heisenberg began by asking him his opinion as to how far he thought science should be prepared to go in wartime in helping to build an atomic bomb."

Zinn had not talked this way with anybody other than his colleagues before. He surprised himself now. But he had been slowly gaining respect for Rosenthal, who seemed to be knowledgeable on a number of diversified subjects.

Zinn at first was admittedly stiff, and he felt ill at ease talking about this particular subject with someone who only a few days ago was a stranger, one outside the scientific community. But now he felt better and somewhat more relaxed with Rosenthal, whom he was coming to accept as more of an equal. He was feeling more at ease; he was beginning to like Herb, and he was now genuinely interested in contributing to the conversation.

Zinn said: "Both Heisenberg and Bohr knew it was possible to make an atom bomb. But whether Bohr thought they should be doing it at all was the question Heisenberg put to him. Bohr believed it involved more than an academic discussion of morals and philosophy. He believed Heisenberg deliberately asked him in such a way that he, Bohr, could only presume the Germans were ahead of the Allies in building a bomb. And furthermore, Bohr believed it was calculated to give the impression that Heisenberg had inside information, which he knew would mislead him into believing the Germans were going to win the War, and the world was soon going to be German. And if Bohr was smart, Heisenberg implied, he should get on the band-wagon now rather than later.

"In my opinion," Zinn continued, "Heisenberg wanted Bohr to see his visit as being perfectly natural. Here was an old student, coming to pay his mentor a friendly visit, and maybe at the same time to let him in on some inside information, which was going to immensely benefit him for the rest of his life."

"I agree with you," said Rosenthal. "But Bohr didn't see it that way if, indeed, that is the way it was meant. The thing that angered him more than anything else was that Bohr knew his information and purpose were misleading and false. That's the crux of the whole thing, in my opinion."

Heisenberg would later deny he had said anything of the kind. And he maintained it was all a mistake. They parted with Bohr still angry, because he knew Germany was not in the advanced position Heisenberg had tried to lead him into believing they were in. Bohr thought it was a back-door way of winning him over to the German side. If he had been taken in and had actually joined the German program, it would have impressed Himmler no end. And it would have guaranteed Heisenberg a certain security, which might have lasted him through the War.

Bohr was already angry with Heisenberg for what he saw was Jews working with a monster enemy, whose national goal was the elimination of world Jewry. Bohr had lost his trust in Heisenberg, and Heisenberg had come to suspect he had. And this caused a good deal of resentment on the part of Heisenberg.

"Do you think Bohr will write me a letter"? Rosenthal asked Zinn. "How fractured do you believe their friendship to be? Maybe, more to the point: Will Heisenberg see me even if I have a letter? We both know there'll be dozens of people wanting to talk to him privately after his speeches. And we both know the only way I'm going to get in is with a letter of introduction from Bohr. How will Heisenberg take this letter, which is obviously going to be one of reconciliation? Maybe it's best worded as though nothing happened between them. Maybe I'm going to risk my life getting into Denmark only to find I have no chance of getting a letter of introduction. Equally obvious, I'm going to have to be alone with Heisenberg. I may need further clarification on some point; or I may have made up my mind before I talk to him. In either case, I'll need a private audience. I can't shoot him with a bunch of people standing around who might stop me or who can identify me."

"I don't think you're going to have any trouble with Bohr writing you a letter," Zinn said. "If he doesn't, he is unlikely to get the cooperation of either this country or Britain in his effort to get out of Denmark and over here to work with us. Einstein sent him a note saying we had been successful in sustaining a nuclear reaction. Yet, if I were he, I would really be worried."

"What about?"

"Well, if he writes the letter, which is essential for you to get a private audience with Heisenberg, and then if you do decide to shoot him, they are going to trace the whole thing right back to Bohr."

"I know that," Rosenthal said, with a look on his face and a tone in his voice that indicated Zinn was patronizing him; something that Zinn was not used to… It meant that he, Rosenthal, should be given some credit for having some smarts. "He can rest assured, I will take all precautions necessary to keep him out of it," Herb said.

"I know you will, but the person you have to convince is Bohr and not me," Zinn remarked, with a look that meant he had taken no offense. "All I'm trying to say is, it might not be so easy. But then again, Bohr is between a rock and a hard spot. In the end, I think he is going to have to commit himself to our cause, in spite of the danger he may face. What you need to do is get with your Colonel Donovan and arrange to have him standing by to move Bohr, if you decide to do away with Heisenberg. And you need to convince Bohr you have a workable plan to do just that."

CHAPTER 7...January, 1943

The new B-17 Flying Fortress took-off from Boeing Field, Seattle, and climbed to a cruising altitude of fifteen thousand feet. The co-pilot, who was acting as navigator, gave the pilot a heading of 150 degrees. They intended to land at Mountain Home, Idaho. They would relax for an hour while taking on additional fuel for the flight to Salt lake City. There, the women WASP ferry pilots would turn the aircraft over to a combat crew who would take it on to England the following morning.

The year before, the fairgrounds at Salt Lake had been converted into a housing area, and the adjacent commercial field had been used for training of air crews in transition to combat readiness. Prior to this, the field had been the sole domain of the Seventh Bombardment Group. They had been recently stationed at March Field, California, and now they were housed at Fort Douglas, to the east of the city. But the Army Air Force was expanding. And this facility at the fairgrounds, like many others throughout the nation, had been pressed into temporary service.

Several hours later, the bomber touched down at Offutt Army Airbase in Omaha and taxied in front of base operations. The crew of three officers walked the few yards to a small cafeteria in the same wooden building and sat down. Each ordered a hamburger and a cup of coffee. Even before they had given the counter girl their orders, the fuel truck was pulling up alongside their aircraft and the tanks were being refilled. The pilot remarked to the others about what fast service they were receiving, something they had not been accustomed to at the few transient bases they had visited.

The pilot had been commissioned the longest of any of them, some eighteen months, and it had been just weeks since he had been promoted to first lieutenant. This was the subject for some comment about fuel service, and now that he had been promoted, they could expect the same treatment in the future. After all, one of them remarked, rank did have its privileges.

Just before boarding, thirty minutes later, they were briefed by a maintenance sergeant on the status of the aircraft, and then they were off again.

They landed at Andrews, Washington, late in the evening. But instead of being taken to the Transient Officers Quarters, where they expected to stay overnight before pressing on to England, they were taken to a hotel in the city. They stayed in the hotel for two days before they were taken back to Andrews and then flown back to Salt Lake City on a transport. There was no explanation for the deviation in plans, and nobody seemed to know why.

As they were boarding the transport, they noticed two staff cars parked alongside their bomber. There was another crew performing the pre-flight, while a group of three civilians were observed to be standing at the waist door conversing.

One of the civilians was Herbert Rosenthal. One of the other two was Colonel Donovan, and the third was an agent of the OSS. The newcomer was to be Rosenthal's companion, and soon to be friend, for the next few weeks. He would accompany him on this flight overseas and then stay with him until the operation was completed. His cover story would change as Donovan's plan progressed. At this point, however, he was a writer for a magazine. He was supposed to be doing a story about bombers being ferried to England for use by the British, as well as replacements for combat groups stationed near London.

The new crew was older and apparently more experienced. But still, although they were all higher in rank than the crew they had replaced, the oldest of them was only twenty-five.

The flight plan called for a great circle flight over Presque Isle; Goose Bay, Labrador; Narsarsuaq, Greenland; and finally landing at Burtonwood, which was a depot-base on the outskirts of London. The next day, the airplane would be flown the short distance to one of the American bomber bases near London by yet another crew, who were presently on leave in the city. None of the disembarking members of the incoming flight would see the new crew.

From Burtonwood, a staff car drove the two bomber passengers through the ruined parts of London to Liverpool. Then in the dead of night, they were whisked aboard a Swedish fishing trawler, which hastily pulled out into the channel.

The trawler hugged the English coast, avoiding any prowling German E-boats, although neither of the Americans was aware of any such danger. The trawler had been flying the British flag, but a few hours from their destination, a Swedish seaside fishing port, they hoisted the Swedish flag. Because of the way they went about their work, and in view of the risks they were taking as neutrals, Rosenthal suspected they might be full time members of Colonel Donovan's organization.

They were given one day to rest and to get over their seasickness, and then they were placed on a train to Uppsala University. There they were given still another briefing by a person who spoke English with a Swedish accent. They were both given student status, complete with a fake transcript of grades and student credentials. They stayed in the dormitory one night for the purpose of being able to answer any questions that might later be asked by any German interrogator; then they were familiarized with the rest of the campus and all the physical aspects of the science departments. They met and talked to several physics and mathematics professors. They were told to memorize their names and where they lived. They were then given complete picture layouts of their homes and told to memorize not only the inside of their homes but the pictures of their wives and children, as well.

Post-doctoral graduates, being groomed for teaching careers at this Swedish university, would be expected to have dined at the homes of each of the faculty members at one time or another. And since they were posing as graduate students in physics, the Gestapo was expected to grill them both on many aspects of their schooling, and on their close associations with faculty families.

Two days later, they were on a train to Copenhagen. Legitimate looking papers had been provided them; otherwise no special precautions were taken. Herb simply maintained they were graduate students in physics   from Uppsala who were students of Niels Bohr while the two of them were on their way to visit with Doctor Heisenberg. Twice they were brought before Gestapo officers demanding to see their papers. Each time they did not hesitate in presenting their fake invitations from Heisenberg and the letter written in German from Niels Bohr. The mention of Himmler's name, and the presentation of fake invitations inviting them to Germany to attend Heisenberg's lecture, were all that was required. In both instances, Herb told them in perfect German that he was a Jew who had been permitted to leave Germany for permanent residence in Sweden and who was returning at Heisenberg's request. His companion was a student, too. But his main function, according to Herb, was to act as his secretary and interpreter. The university wanted a full report of the meetings in Swedish, he told them, and Herb's knowledge of the language was less then perfect.

The forthcoming lecture at Leipzig was a little less than one week away and was a matter of record. Rosenthal brazenly challenged them to check it out. Then without losing his composure, he inferred there would be dire consequences if they were held up and missed out on the lecture and the personal conference scheduled immediately thereafter. He was also quick to tell them to check with Himmler's office if their orders so required.

Prior to 1942, Jews were encouraged to leave Germany if they had the funds and a place to go. Subsequent to a conference held at Wannsee near Berlin in early 1942 to discuss *the final solution to the Jewish problem*, they were no longer allowed to leave. All those who were in Germany following this meeting were subject to *transportation* to concentration camps, where they were murdered in the millions by various means.

The conference was chaired by one, *SS* General Reinhardt Heydrich, who was known as the Butcher of Prague and Europe's Hangman. His able assistant was the infamous Adolph Eichmman, who would later be charged with and hung for the deaths of several million Jews.

Being a returning Jew was a highly believable scenario, put together by Donovan's people. And as long as Rosenthal stuck to his rehearsed story without becoming overly nervous, Donovan knew he was in no real danger.

Rosenthal had things pretty well figured out for himself on the eve of his arrival in Denmark. He believed Heisenberg had come to Denmark to convince Bohr he was on the losing side. He wanted Bohr to join him in Germany and to play an active role in the victory to come. Then the two old friends would be given unlimited funds and facilities for their ongoing nuclear experiments, ushering in a brave new world of prosperity through the use of atomic power. But their meeting had not gone well, and Heisenberg's goal was not realized. Instead, he alienated Bohr, and their close friendship really ceased at that point.

Herb Rosenthal sat listening to Heisenberg, the great scholar and pre-eminent scientist, expound on his version of quantum mechanics, or the structure of the world at the sub-atomic level. If he had been apprehensive about being intimidated by Heisenberg's knowledge and experience, he need not have worried. Several times he wanted to raise his hand to tell him his concept of certain things was right in theory, but recent experiments at Chicago had not proven accepted theory to be entirely correct. But of course he did not.

The first day of a two-day lecture series had gone well. He sat in the front row with a briefcase at his side. The case did not contain books or notes, or anything of the sort. It contained a .45 cal. Colt automatic, Army issue pistol and two American-made hand grenades.

Herb had hastily put together an on-the-spot plan: not only would it be easy to do away with Heisenberg, but he could do away with many of his constituents at the same time.

His orders from Mr. Hoover did not require him to kill all of them. But the more he mingled with Jews who were working toward the killing of other Jews, the angrier he became. Heretofore, his interest had been literally academic. But this changed once he crossed the border into Nazi Germany. Now things were more real, and not what he had expected at all. The depth of his feelings toward Hitler and Heisenberg surprised him. He had become personally involved, something he had been warned not to do. But he could not help himself. He was a competitor. And overnight, he had worked up a strong dislike for the other side.

The lecture hall at Leipzig was of the theater type. Although somewhat larger than most schools, it was constructed about the same. It was located on the ground floor in one of the School of Science buildings.

Rosenthal and his companion had taken a taxi from the train station the night before and another to the university that morning. They left the hotel early to make sure they were there on time. The last thing they wanted was to show up late. Herb had been cautioned about this. He was told the doors would be locked a few minutes before starting time to ensure all attendees were seated before Heisenberg entered.

He and his companion moved toward the lecture hall, crowded together with the usual crush of students and faculty, with a sprinkling of what he guessed were distinguished visitors.

Due to the sensitivity of the subject and the prominence of the guest speaker, they both suspected the Gestapo was also mingling with the crowd in force. They both found themselves looking around at the milling students inside the large lecture room. They were looking for some of those whom they thought might be Gestapo agents. They were not sure whether they had anything to worry about. They had not heard a word from anybody about whether they were welcome or not. And then they heard a voice directly behind them.

"Du tala Sevenska, Svede?"

"Hej. Jah taler. Hur sta:r det till?" Lindquist replied with a smile on his face. The mild put-down was directed at Lars Lindquist, his bodyguard. At least he thought this was his main function—this and being his interpreter.

Colonel Donovan had seen to everything so far. How was Rosenthal able to pass himself off as a Swedish student if he could not speak Swedish? Lindquist was primarily a bodyguard who had not been allowed to carry a weapon, which made Rosenthal wonder if he was much of a bodyguard at all. But he was also there to speak up if they were addressed in Swedish.

The off-hand greeting was obviously meant to put them at ease, while letting them know somebody behind them was wanting to make contact. This person with the whimsical voice and the playful manner could be anybody. But Rosenthal suspected he was an agent of some sort. He hoped he was not Gestapo, who had a reputation for toying with their victims like cats play with mice.

"Verifran ar du?" Lindquist, asked him. *"Vilkenstad borni i?"*

But the messenger, if that is what he was, did not care to talk further in Swedish. Instead, he moved to Rosenthal's side, as the three of them edged   their way inside the door. He spoke softly but distinctly to them, telling them in German they had left their attaché cases in the taxi. With that he handed one to Rosenthal and an identical one to Lindquist. Then he stopped and let the crowd walk around him as they wandered around looking for their reserved seats.

A speaker stepped to the microphone on the lectern and made the usual test. He called for their attention and then informed them they could take notes. But the notes, he said, and their briefcases must be locked in the room until tomorrow morning. Security seals were available for anyone wanting one, he told them. If his newly acquired attaché case contained what Rosenthal was thinking it did, then he most assuredly was going to need a seal.

They sat down in adjacent seats in the front row, directly in front of the lectern. This was a good sign, thought Rosenthal. They were reserved, and the best seats in the house. And obviously they had been arranged for by somebody–maybe Heisenberg himself or one of Himmler's aides. This was a small thing, but seen as being significant. To him, it meant somebody close to Heisenberg knew he was there. In all probability the treatment they were receiving meant the Gestapo had been talking to Heisenberg, and they knew Rosenthal had been talking to Bohr. But whether Heisenberg knew Rosenthal was in possession of an introduction letter from Bohr, he had no way of knowing. But Rosenthal would have bet he did.

Lectures were scheduled to last over two days. Partway through the series of three one-hour talks on the second day, Herb shook his head in the negative at Lindquist, meaning Heisenberg knew nothing important about atomic reactors.

The Swede, if that is what he was, was becoming a problem. He had made an outlandish statement at dinner the night before. He said that if it were up to him he would grenade them all. He spoke the obvious when he told Herb the best and surest way of stopping Germany's nuclear bomb project was to eliminate them all right there and now and be done with it.

"Look, Lars," Rosenthal said, "you and I have become good friends during the past couple of weeks. But the last thing I need right now is a runaway train like you. I have thought about what you want to do, and at first I felt the same way. But I have changed my mind. I have been thinking about something else, which is really too complicated to explain. And I'm not sure I have the authority to explain it to you, anyway. But suffice to say, they are not making much progress toward building a bomb. Now, that's not to say they couldn't if they got an infusion of money and if they were sure of a steady supply of heavy water. But there's another key ingredient to the making of a sustained reactor-one that is most essential–and in all likelihood is not well understood by Heisenberg or any of his people. This essential has not been mentioned yet by Heisenberg, and in my opinion he is going to keep it to himself, because he doesn't understand. And of course, he doesn't want anyone else to know he doesn't. If Himmler ever finds out what Heisenberg doesn't know, he and many of the people in attendance here today will be headed to a concentration camp; it is that important. This thing I'm talking about must remain between Heisenberg and myself. I can't even discuss it with you. All you need to know is that Germany has no viable bomb program right now. Their atoms are not a threat to anybody. If you kill these people, you are killing just so many non-essentials. They're working hard, spending money, and going nowhere. Do you understand me?

"Revenge for what is bothering you is not a good reason to do what you have in mind, especially when I tell you I can use Heisenberg and the others to our decided advantage. As I have said, I don't want to discuss it with you further. I'm going to talk about some specifics with Heisenberg tomorrow. But I'm sure he won't have anything to say that is going to change my mind. I appreciate your position. I feel the same way you do. Maybe being a Jew gives me the right to be angrier than you are. I don't know. But take it from me, you're not in the know. You have no idea what you might actually be doing."

"What do you mean?"

"Just that I can't tell you. Trust me on this. I think we can use this Nazi and all his buddies to our advantage. You'll have gained very little if you do them in now. That's all I care to tell you. But Lars, you may be becoming a problem. And if you think I'm overstating the importance of this thing, you should think again. And please don't underestimate my resolve. Because if you do, it will cost you your life. You may kill them all. I can't stop you from doing so. But if you do, rest assured, you're going to die with them."

Lindquist looked at him with a pained expression on his face before he asked him for an explanation of his last statement.

Rosenthal replied: "Lars, if you make one move I don't approve of, I'm going to shoot you before I do him."

The next afternoon, Heisenberg dismissed the assembly to a round of sustained applause. Most of those assembled were Nazis, and the few remaining were strong sympathizers. They had been listening mesmerized to the scientific details of Germany's effort to defeat Britain and Russia using nuclear energy. If anybody there had been in doubt as to the future outcome of the War, they were not now. Heisenberg had put their minds to rest about nuclear fission being a reality. And to them, Heisenberg and company were the leading authorities of the world.

They were like Teutonic knights of old, carrying the sword of invincibility. Heisenberg was their new champion, cast in the mold of a Richard Wagner character. A hero of a different sort, but a conqueror nevertheless in the ancient tradition. They believed he was destined to make *Deutschland, uber alles*, a virtual reality.

It was no wonder everyone arose and gave him a standing ovation. It was almost surreal; almost like the torchlight ceremonies of a few years past–the ones with spiritual overtones–the ones that were deeply rooted in the German psyche. It was like a miniature mass assembly at Nuremberg, where the night was charged with the electricity of Germany's burgeoning new Nationalism, the special spectacles that took hours for torch-bearing uniformed men to march onto the field. And by the time that all was in readiness, and the Fuhrer strode to the podium, the ear-splitting shouts of *Seig, Heil* rent the air with the impact of an explosion. The masses at Nuremberg, who had been worked into an emotional frenzy, were prepared to hinge on his every word. Not necessarily because he spoke about the *leiberstrum* of a greater Germany, because they had heard this message many times before, and they never tired of it; but because they saw in him still another champion of the downtrodden Fatherland. And everybody was mesmerized. Young women were held in thrall, wanting to kneel to touch his uniform; and grown men were seen openly weeping as he started to speak. This is what it was like at Nuremberg during the birth of National Socialism. And now there was another national champion, and his name was Werner Heisenberg.

It was no wonder everyone wanted to shake his hand, to go on record as one who offered him encouragement at this critical point in history. And of course, by doing so, they identified by association with his acknowledged scientific accomplishments.

Heisenberg accepted the accolades, reveling in the literal adoration proffered him. He was still basking in the light of his newly bestowed status of Nobel Laureate in physics. He had published what was recognized as the *Heisenberg Uncertainty Principle*, which simply states: it is impossible to measure both the exact position and the exact momentum of any subatomic particle at any given time. The more precisely one of the quantities is measured, the less precisely the other is known. There is a difference between admiration and adoration; and Heisenberg was not new to either. He was more or less used to it, if large egos ever become used to such things. And Heisenberg had a large ego; Rosenthal would attest to that, it might even be as big as Herb's own, which was something Rosenthal might not have cared to discuss.

As the upper tiers began filing down, Hiesenberg took the time to glance down at Rosenthal. It was at this point that

Herb stood-up, clapping. He approached the lectern and handed Heisenberg the letter from Niels Bohr. The envelope was sealed. But Heisenberg took a quick look at the writing on the back of the envelope. It read in German script, From Niels to Werner.

He stared at Herb for a few seconds, and then spoke, telling Herb he would be with him in a few minutes.

The two visitors sat back down, watching the passing parade. Lindquist was becoming more and more agitated, as though he had a special interest in what was going on. His attitude had not changed since Herb had spoken to him. Now, he was becoming even more nervous and unpredictable, if that were possible. As for Rosenthal, he could not remember when he had ever been so ill at ease. He was angrier than he had ever been in his life, and disgusted at the scene playing out before him. It was hard to say whether he was angrier than he was disgusted as he watched them begin to file out of the room.

Then, as he glanced again at Lindquist, who was still staring daggers at the participants, it dawned on him that Lindquist might have blown this whole lecture thing out of proportion. Rosenthal, early on, had seen it as completely meaningless in the nuclear scheme of things. Nothing had been said that was of any real consequence. What had not been said told it all. True, Rosenthal was angry at the display of Teutonic hero worship shown Heisenberg, knowing that many of his supplicants were fellow Jews. But Herb had concluded early on that Heisenberg's message was just so much rhetoric. Lindquist, on the other hand, had no way of knowing what was going on. He just knew from their looks, and from the exuberance of the crowd around him, that big things were afoot that would not bode well for Britain.

If Rosenthal was correct in his supposition, Lars Lindquist was not a neutral Swede. He was with M1-6. He was an

Englishman, who in all likelihood had been in London during the Blitz. And Rosenthal and his threats were not going to stop him. As Herb watched the informal reception line file slowly across the large room and out the door, he silently urged them on. If there was no one left in the room, perhaps Lindquist, would settle down and give him a chance to implement his new plan.

CHAPTER 8...DREXEL, UNIVERSITY, 1950

Donald Eckert was walking across the campus of Drexel University. He had spent most of the afternoon in the library studying for an examination in political science. Some of the assigned reading material was *Mien Kampf* and the *Communist Manifesto*. These were two highly charged texts, which were apparently on some FBI index.

He noticed that someone was walking close behind him. He shortened his stride to let whomever it was pass on the narrow sidewalk. As he did, the person pulled alongside him and addressed him by name.

"Mr. Eckert, could I have a word with you," he said.

"What about," Eckert replied, surprised at the formal use of his name. On closer inspection, he realized the speaker was wearing a coat and tie beneath his overcoat. His first thought was that he was a professor. But what was a professor doing wanting to talk with him? Then he noticed that the man might be too young to be a professor; perhaps he was a teaching assistant. Before he could wonder much longer, the speaker asked him if he had checked out the two books he had been reading in the library, and if he had, how often had he done so.

The first thing coming to Eckert's mind was, Who wants to know? He was about to tell him it was none of his business and that he would read anything he chose. But before he did, the man apologized for the intrusion and asked for his cooperation. The stranger acted as though he had no business asking. But it was his job, he said, and he had to do his job. He asked in such a condescending manner that it threw Eckert off guard, and his blood pressure began to return to normal.

"May I ask you why you're reading those books?"

Eckert thought about saying, of course you may. Then he thought about ignoring him completely while he continued to walk toward his car parked a few blocks away. But he did not. He did what most people under the circumstances would do when confronted with perceived authority. He did his best to cooperate.

"I take a class in *Recent Political Thought*, and they are required reading. Why do you ask?" He said it with a kind of edge to his voice that the questioner seemed quite prepared to ignore. It was as though he expected the reply he received.

"I assure you I have a need to know," he said, "but I prefer not to say who I am unless you insist."

Eckert did not have to ask. He knew. The stranger was with the FBI or the new offspring from the OSS, the CIA. But more than likely the FBI, he thought. And if he was with either of these agencies, then he knew more about Eckert than he was letting on. And any show of antagonism on Eckert's part would open him up for further investigation. Still, he wondered, Why the interrogation, such as it was? After all, he was not a member of any campus clubs that were getting a lot of press throughout the country, the ones whose members were being referred to as left wingers, whatever that meant. But they were becoming the talk of many students in the plaza and in the off campus beer halls.

The movement was called *Students for a Democratic Society*. It had started at Berkeley, where one Mario Savio had whipped students into some kind of a rebellious fray, for what reason no one was quite sure. But the more Eckert learned about Savio and his activities, the more he suspected Savio might be associated with a Communist-front organization. How, he wondered, was Savio able to find the time for these kinds of things? He personally had to study just about every spare minute he was not working. And why would anybody want to question his or her school, to challenge the regents to endless debate on the grounds the curriculum being taught was, somehow, irrelevant to the needs of society? Eckert tried to purge what he knew about the Berkeley thing from his mind. He told himself that the students involved were probably crackpots who needed to get a life.

But he was glad he had reacted to the first questions the way he had. Whoever he was, the man who was walking with him continued to ask him several more questions. He wanted to know about his schooling and about his goals in life. Eckert thought he was just making small talk, trying to exit gracefully after deciding he had a legitimate reason for reading the books. But the questions continued for longer than was appropriate for small talk, and Eckert was beginning to grow apprehensive.

"I understand you are enrolled in the ROTC program," he said. "Are you planning on a career in the military?"

Ah, he thought to himself, *that's why he's checking me out. He wants to know why a future officer is reading what to him sounds like reactionary trash.*

Eckert's answer was in the affirmative, which ended the conversation on this subject. Then after some more small talk, satisfied that Eckert was not associated with any on-campus seditious group, he bid him good day.

The stranger turned and walked away. Taking a right turn at the corner, he was never seen or heard from again. But Eckert couldn't help but wonder why he had been singled out for questioning when no other students taking the class had been. Then it came to him, and before he reached his car he knew why, and he approved. And he would have cause to remember this conversation for years to come.

CHAPTER 9...SAN BERNARDINO, 1951

Eugene Ravigno was bored and had decided to walk the few hundred yards from his on-base quarters to the officer's club.

He walked into the dining room for want of someplace to go. He stood waiting to be seated. He wished there were another place he could get a cup of coffee without having to sit down in the formal dining room, where he knew the tablecloth would be changed when he left. All he wanted was coffee, but he knew somebody would be put to a lot of trouble for very little reason, and it bothered him. But then, that is the way he was.

Ravigno had the distinguished reputation of serving in the 100th Bomb Group during the War. A former Marine, he was the chief of maintenance of the unit sustaining the highest casualty rate in the Eighth Air Force.

While he waited for the waiter to take his order, he began watching a table to his left, where four junior officers were just finishing dinner. One of them was a second lieutenant in his aircraft maintenance organization. When the lieutenant passed his table he greeted the Colonel with a polite, "Good evening sir." Ravigno nodded in acknowledgement and then, calling him back by name, he asked him if he had anything pressing to do. When Ravigno was sure he did not, he asked him to go for a ride.

"I have this new car and I'm not satisfied with the way the front end sounds. I keep hearing what I think are funny noises. Then too, one of the front wheels might be out of balance. I need your young ears to tell me if I ought to take it back for a check-up?"

Don Eckert was surprised Ravigno remembered his name. He had been formally introduced two months before when he reported in, but he hardly expected the colonel to remember who he was.

They walked back, the two of them, to the colonel's quarters. The colonel excused himself for a moment to tell his wife where he was going and to tell her he would not be gone for very long. He backed his new Packard touring sedan from the garage. He waited for Eckert to open the passenger door and climb in. The car had a spacious front seat, capable of seating three people, four in an emergency, without cramping the driver too much.

They left the air base at San Bernardino and pulled smoothly onto an open road leading to Riverside. When they were clear of traffic, the director of maintenance at the depot cocked his ear. He was listening for the noise he thought he had heard the day before.

"Do you hear that?" he asked. "Listen. There it is again."

Lt. Eckert strained his ears. First, for any strange noise coming from the engine and then from the transmission. He heard nothing that was not part of the expected sound of quality machinery working at normal speeds.

"I can't hear anything, sir," he said.

"Maybe it's the tires or the wheels? Maybe it's a wheel bearing?" Ravigno phrased his comments as though they were a question. Eckert could tell he was making conversation, and he was not really listening as intently as he had been before.

Eckert glanced his way with a kind of quizzical expression on his face that Ravigno could not see. Satisfied the noise was not coming from the running gear, he shifted his concentration to the tires and wheels as he was asked to do. After all, there was a reason for his being here. Colonels did not, as a rule, ask second lieutenants to go for a ride in their cars. Not even if they had just purchased a new prestigious Packard and they wanted to show it off.

When Eckert answered in the negative, telling him there was nothing wrong with the wheels that he could tell, the colonel changed the subject as though he knew it all along. Eckert was sure now there was something more on the colonel's mind than a cantankerous automobile.

"Well, I'm glad of that." Ravigno said. "Anyway, this trip is not wasted. I have wanted to talk to you. What I have to say must be said in private, and asking you to come into my office tomorrow might be a little awkward."

Eckert understood what he meant. It was not a good place to discuss anything private. He had a civilian assistant who shared his office, and he was usually there most of the time. It would have been necessary to ask him to leave, in view of what Ravigno said next. Such a request would have made his visit seem even more out of the ordinary.

"Tell me about yourself," the colonel said, as the two of them drove down the darkened highway. "I'm not sure I know what's going on. First, I get a call from a captain in the Office of Special Investigations here on the base a few weeks ago. He told me he had been directed to perform a special background investigation on you. He said it was a local thing. He said it was in addition to the regular Top Secret clearance investigation the FBI and OSI are doing back in your home state. In case you didn't know, it is a routine procedure for all new officers. I didn't pay too much attention to what he was saying. What good would it have done, anyway? If they decide to investigate you for something else, they don't need my permission." He glanced over at Eckert in the semi-darkness, adding his observation as an afterthought.

"Anyway, I didn't bring you out here in the boonies to talk about clearances. That's one thing I don't normally have to worry about. But what I would like to know is whether you have at some time made application to join another government agency, I mean before you came into the Air Force, one that might require an additional clearance?"

Eckert was surprised at the question. His answer was in the negative, which did not surprise the colonel.

"Then you have no knowledge of what I'm talking about?" He paused and then said, "I figured as much."

"To get to the point," the colonel said, "I want you to go by my adjutant's office in the morning and check out a classified packet he has waiting for you. Read what's in it and then memorize it. Then bring it back to him with the cover letter of instructions. I won't go into it now, but from what I gather from reading the unclassified part of the correspondence, I don't believe you are going to Morocco with the Air Depot Wing we are forming here at Norton. I expect to be losing you, and that's a shame.

"When you think you have the instructions down pat, check it back in and collect a set of orders he has waiting for you. There's no need for us to meet again on this matter. If it's what I think it is, you'll be expected to disappear as quietly as possible. Your cover story is that you have been assigned to a special team to look into areas in Morocco where we want to build aircraft control and warning sites. These sites are part of our overall plans for some of the semi-permanent bases we've built over there. There are four of them planned, two actually are soon to be operational. One is an aircraft maintenance depot. That's why you're here now, to get some training in how an overhaul facility is supposed to operate. The other is going to be used by one or more of the combat commands as a staging base.

"Your personnel file says you majored in geology. According to the cover letter, you've been assigned to this radar team for that reason. Apparently they need to know something about the kinds of soil they're going to be building those sites on. I'm guessing they chose you for this reason. But beginning right now, according to the letter, you're to tell people a cover story. I mean, of course, the ones who ask you where you're going and what you're going to be doing. The story I just told you about Morocco and the radar site is it. I don't know whether that's really what you're going to be doing or not. To tell you the truth, I'm afraid I don't know much more about it than what I've told you."

Eckert landed at Andrews Air Force Base and rode into the city on the shuttle. From the dispersal point he caught a taxi for the remaining few miles it took to get to the State Department building. Upon his arrival, he checked with the information booth on the first floor. He inquired of one of the people manning the booth as to the location of the Dulles Annex. An hour later, and what seemed to be dozens of twists and turns, which often led to dead ends, he arrived at an unmarked office in the basement of the Annex. After several inquiries, he found the desk of the officer he was supposed to report to.

"My name is Major Swanson." he said to Eckert. "Although I'm wearing civilian clothes, I'm in the Air Force the same as you are. However, I am on detached duty with a government agency. I won't go into the details now about what it is or what it does. But suffice it to say it is not well known. It is relatively new, although it's been around for about four years. There are about fifty of us so far who are serving in this organization, with more to follow. If you decide to join up you'll make it fifty-one." He said this with a kind of a smile on his face; up to now he had been all business.

He leaned back in his chair and said, "Not a good idea to ask me any questions. You're going to be told everything we want you to know tomorrow. All of your questions will be answered then. That goes for the briefing, and anything else occurring from here on out. You need to understand this. I want you to sign this piece of paper saying you have been briefed on the security of your visit here. We want to be perfectly sure you understand."

He handed him another piece of paper saying, "give this chit to the transportation people and they'll take you to a hotel. They'll pick you up in the morning. Spend some time memorizing how to get back to this office from the underground parking garage. They'll bring you back there in the morning. There will be an orientation briefing at 0900. Be prompt. Don't mess around eating breakfast and fail to make contact with your driver, who will pick you up at 0800 in front of your hotel. There'll be coffee and doughnuts served at the meeting."

With that the major stood up and shook hands instead of returning Eckert's salute. "Not in civilian clothes," he said. Eckert imagined what he must have been thinking about the level of training in the ROTC these days. He knew better than to salute; it was just that things were happening too fast and he had not stopped to think.

As the staff car assigned to take him the few miles to his hotel pulled into traffic, Lieutenant Donald Eckert leaned back in his seat and relaxed. But he would not have been so at ease and so at peace with the world, if he could have seen into the future a few years. For instead of enhancing his career in the service, he had just taken the first step required to join the new Central Intelligence Agency. And it would be responsible for getting him killed.

He sat watching the scenery as the shuttle turned down Devilin Street and headed toward the flight line at Nellis Air Force Base. It turned left and then made a right turn as it entered the highway and headed east; and then it turned left again, making its way north into the desert. Its destination was Groom Lake, which was located in Area 51, about two and a half hour's to the north. The bus shuttle alternated with air transport to and from Area 51 when the Janet flights were temporarily grounded for maintenance. Some of the flights to Groom originated at Nellis and some at McCarren Field, the commercial airport just south of the city of Las Vegas.

Eckert would make many trips to and from Area 51 over the next three months, some by shuttle bus and some by Janet flights. He would come to realize security was a way of life in the new CIA. Even shuttle flights had code names. And regardless of who you were, it was necessary to hide your identity at Area 51, if you were involved with any ongoing covert activity. In point of fact, the terms Groom Lake and Area 51 were classified. Officially, the base did not exist. All projects there were known as black, meaning they could not be seen, and all operational funding was referred to by the same term, meaning it was hidden away inside the CIA budget and was not monitored by any government accounting authority. How could it, if it did not exist?

This was his first trip by bus, and to say he was remotely interested in the scenery would be an overstatement. The noticeable thing about the scenery was that there was no scenery to be seen. The countryside was the first cousin to the moon. It was stark, more stark than anyplace he had ever been in his life. Why people would want to live in a place like this was more than he could understand. But it was not going to be too bad. He was not going to have to stay that long. And it was winter, and the hot weather was some months away. This was one of the things he liked about the service. You were never in an undesirable place very long. No matter how much you disliked your surroundings, you knew it was only temporary.

He had been told in Washington that he would be schooled on several items of classified equipment, and then he would be off somewhere on an assignment. His final destination was still classified, although Ravigno appeared to have known. He asked once, when he was in Washington, and they told him he would find out–all in good time.

Nellis is mapped off into areas. Much of what goes on in one area has little to do with the others. Where he was going was called Area 51, and sometimes Groom Lake by people who were cleared to discuss the subject. And from what he had heard, whatever it was that went on at Groom had nothing to do with any other activity going on in any other area. Maybe it wasn't related to anything going on anywhere else in the Air Force.

How long this special area had been in existence no one really knew. It was started in the early forties, according to rumors. But the briefer, back in Washington, said it was much later. In fact, he said, it was quite new. Tony LeVier, the famous Lockheed test pilot, had chosen the site. Lockheed had a top secret airplane they were going to test, and this location was thought to be ideal. This airplane had been manufactured at the Lockheed factory in Burbank. It was the product of a super-secret factory known as the *Skunk Works*, which was inside a secret factory. When it was finished, they had trucked it to Groom, where it had been assembled.

Eckert had been told to expect an increase in security when riding the bus. He wondered, rather irreverently, what they could be so proud of. And what could be so secret about a place like this?

About ten miles from the entrance to Groom, the bus picked

up an armed escort. Eckert wondered where it came from. But it was an escort for a reason. Any deviation from the bus's regular route or usual activity would be promptly investigated. Any passenger attempting to disembark between here and the base proper would be arrested at gun-point; there were to be no exceptions.

The jeep behind them had pulled up to within several yards of the bus. Eckert, looking out the back window, could see a helmeted soldier. He was manning a .30 cal. machine gun, which was mounted on a swivel, and the machine gun was pointed at the back of the bus.

The bus stopped in front of the main gate. The lieutenant noticed with increasing interest as special security people went about their business of ensuring that no unauthorized personnel entered the base via the bus. Then the door opened, and two guards entered. Both carried slung carbines as well as side arms. The few passengers aboard were asked to don their special identification badges. Satisfied everything was in order, the guards disembarked and a third guard waved the vehicle through the gate.

He was beginning to suspect this base was more important to the Air Force than he had originally thought. But if so, why was there so little activity? Why were there so few people about? Where was everybody? The place seemed almost deserted. This was his first experience driving from the gate to the hanger where he was in training. And from what he could see from the bus windows, the place seemed almost devoid of people. At other times, when he had arrived by air, he had been immediately ushered by armed guards into a room off Base Operations. From there he had been taken to a hanger, the location of which was unknown to him.

As they neared the flight line he could see only a few parked aircraft. Except for two Boeing-built training planes, known as AT-11's, and one Douglas C-47 transport, which was parked near another closed hanger, the flight line appeared to be deserted. As he neared Operations once again, he recognized the aircraft as being some of those used on the so-called Janet flights.

He had been instructed in Washington to ask no questions about anything he might see while at Groom. Everything going on there was on a need to know basis. If it was not part of your work, you neither inquired about it nor were you expected to show an interest.

Each unit in training was kept separate from the dozen or so others. When a new aircraft was towed out of a hanger onto the tarmac, the flight line became restricted. It was cordoned off, and all personnel were made to re-enter their area of assignment. You had to stay where you were until the all clear was sounded. Eckert thought this was a bit much. But nevertheless, like all the others, he never said so.

And so it happened about three days into his third month of schooling, he had stepped outside during a ten-minute smoking break. His unit was supposed to stay together for ease in account-ability. But after two months, things were beginning to get somewhat lax. Eckert had left his companions and gone outside by himself. When the siren blew to signal all personnel to return indoors away from the flight line, he was slow to respond. Before roll call could be taken by Security, the hanger next door opened and the ugliest airplane he had ever seen was rolled outside and chalked.

Guards surrounded this ungainly monster, seeming to be all wings, like a large single-engine jet-powered glider. It was of, course, the pride of test pilot Tony LeVier and the Skunk Works. It was the early prototype of a U-2 high altitude reconnaissance aircraft. And the finished airplane would, years later, have a far-reaching role to play in the Cold War. And Lt. Donald Eckert, in a brazen disregard for procedure, had committed the ultimate security breach. He had seen it close-up. It was not a passing glance, either, which might have been excused with a verbal reprimand. But he had stared at it–stared much as he might have at a beautiful, naked woman stepping from the shower. And he had been caught. He had been seen gazing by armed guards who had been given the discretion of using force under such circumstances.

They would apprehend him, treating him as an enemy agent until it was proven otherwise. He was unceremoniously thrown to the ground, handcuffed, and marched off for interrogation. He would remain under close arrest throughout the remainder of the week, until the civilian head of the Military Section of Operations of the CIA arrived from Washington. He was then taken to a room in the operations building, where he was given a formal briefing on the aircraft he had seen. Following all of this, he was made to sign a formal affidavit. This was done with his supervisor looking on. He too was asked to sign the same affidavit, wherein he acknowledged that Eckert had been briefed. Having been warned of the consequences of even revealing the name of the aircraft, they were both added to the list of those knowing of its existence; and then Eckert was released.

CHAPTER 10...MOROCCO, 1954

The small convoy moved up from Safi, going north toward Casablanca. It consisted of two jeeps and two carryalls. The carryall's carried supplies, equipment, and two young Arab interpreters, while the officers and men rode in the jeeps. The lead jeep flew a pennant on a long staff. It was attached to the front of the machine for no particular reason, other than that General George Patton's Desert Rats, who prowled the area to the North of here during the War, did so. One of the officers, of which there were two, affected the dress, and to a somewhat lesser degree, the mannerisms of one of the heroes of the Great War. The hero's name was Lawrence, who rode around on a camel rather than in a motor vehicle.

About twenty miles this side of Casablanca, the small column slowed and then turned left down an improved road to an American air base. The base was actually French, but it was French in name only. The French had years ago subdued the Arabs and had occupied the country as part of what they believed was their rightful colonial possession. Now the Americans, wanting the base for global operations in the ongoing Cold War against the Russians, were forced to pay rent to their ally of long standing.

The road to the base was a spectacularly scenic quarter-mile drive. It passed through fields of the most beautiful wild poppies to be seen anywhere in the world. In fact, most of the fields in Morocco that were not under cultivation, were adorned with wild poppies this time of year. The colors were bright red and orange, with a sprinkling of purple, unreal in their beauty, resembling a Vincent Van Gogh painting.

The officer in the lead jeep presented his credentials to the astonished American guard, who took him for an Arab. This did not surprise the young officer. In fact he was somewhat flattered that he would do so.

He was tanned from long hours in the desert sun. And because he wore a turban and a lightweight *de jalaba* over his uniform, he was almost indistinguishable from the two Arabs riding in the back of one of the carryalls.

He wore the Arab dress for several reasons: First, because it was practical and kept the sand and dust off his clothes. And second because it had been given to him by a Berber sheikh, and he was just plain proud of the fact. But the real reason might have been because he just wanted to show off a little. He wanted to make an entrance as he drove through the base. He had done this before, and he liked the way everybody stopped and looked at him. He liked particularly the way some of the women looked at him. And nobody had told him not too, so he kept on doing it.

He dismounted after being passed through the guard post. He climbed into the back of the jeep, while one of the enlisted men moved to the front. Then he stood up, holding onto the war-time machine gun mount, the weapon being carried in a storage box inside one of the trucks. He had insisted on carrying it when first he read his orders over a year ago. As the jeep started forward again, he reminded one senior officer who saw him of a Legionnaire returning in triumph to Rome from a successful campaign. The officer said nothing; he just watched in amusement and smiled.

There was one woman in particular he was eager to impress. She was the daughter of a Hungarian countess and worked as the base librarian. She lived in Casablanca and commuted from the city to the base. How she managed to find herself in this part of the world is a long story. But suffice to say, she was one of millions of displaced persons who were homeless after the War.

Her father had been the Hungarian Ambassador to the Italian court, before he became *persona non grata*. This happened soon after the Italians killed Mussolini, their former dictator. And Hungary, being still allied with Germany when this happened, became the enemy of Italy over night. She and her mother and father were unable to make it back to Hungary. They had to take refuge with the French Vichy government in Casablanca, who was sympathetic to the Axis cause. And because they were now stateless, they had no place else to go.

He directed his driver to circle the base, making sure he did not by-pass the library. This was always his first stop on returning to his home base. One of the airmen alighted from the back of the jeep and shouldered a box of books from one of the carryalls. If the lieutenant needed an excuse for visiting the library the first thing, it was to return the overdue books. But returning the books at that particular time was not the primary reason he stopped.

There was no question about it, the soon-to-be Captain Donald Eckert was a commanding presence. He did resemble, somewhat, the late great Lawrence, the fact of which was not wasted on the well-educated countess in waiting.

They were not exactly boyfriend and girlfriend, although he dated her whenever he came back to civilization. Even though they only saw each other after periods of long absence, she was hoping their relationship might develop into something more permanent. She was hoping that, at some point, he would ask her to marry. This would settle all of her problems. In particular, it would guarantee a passport and a visa to someplace else. And it would enable her to provide a better home for her mother and father than the two adjoining hotel rooms where the three of them were living.

In short, it would solve all of her immediate problems, and it would go a long way toward the fulfillment of her long-range goals. But just how far her plan had really progressed, she did not know.

Neither did Lt. Eckert know. He certainly had no idea of the role she had mapped out for him. She was to him an agreeable dinner companion, and that was about all. And she did have many interesting Hungarian friends with whom they both associated. In fact, there was an enclave of young Hungarian intellectuals who were living in Casablanca. They were all well educated and, like her, they had all been schooled in Europe's finest schools. He liked them; he liked them all. They were a welcome relief from his more or less mundane associates who accompanied him on his sorties into the wilderness.

He watched the airman set the books down on her desk as they both entered the metal Butler building, which served as the base library. She rose from her desk to meet him with a smile on her face. They kissed on both cheeks in the European manner, more of a gesture of friendship than anything else. But to the Americans looking on, it was more than that. To those who were unsophisticated and new in the country, a kiss is a kiss regardless of how it is accomplished. And as it would turn out, several enlisted men and one officer, who were standing in line to check out books, would later testify that the two of them appeared to be more than just acquaintances.

His date for the evening secured, the lieutenant had the driver lead the convoy over to his quarters. There, the entire contingent dismounted while his duffle bag was unloaded and his footlocker was being carried into one of the Dallas huts. Then a brief, informal formation was held, whereupon, the lieutenant formalized certain instructions his men had been given hours before. They were told they could do just about anything they wanted to do, as long as the vehicles were serviced and supplies were re-provisioned.

Eckert was not a difficult officer to work for. At times, some of the senior sergeants thought he might be too easy, too lax with the men. It was as though they were out there to do a job that could just as easily have been done by a civilian contract team. He fraternized with his men, much like his affectation Laurence was reported to have done in the old days. But the way Eckert saw it, there was no other way. It was difficult being military when you ate and slept with the troops in such close proximity. What was the use, anyway? Everybody knew his job and did it without much interference from him. But all that aside, the enlisted men commented to each another about how he did not seem to be an officer at all, and that he was in actuality more like a civilian in uniform.

Eckert did not make friends with any of the junior officers on the base. To be sure, he was cordial enough to those with whom he shared quarters. But he never joined in much of the friendly good-natured banter, prevalent among those officers who had been together for many months. He acted more like a stranger, which he was. And for the most part, they accepted him without caring much where he came from or what he had been doing.

But one second lieutenant in particular was more interested than the others. He asked him one evening what it was he was actually working at out there for weeks on end. Eckert told him his group was surveying sites for the installation of a new improved radar system. This system would afford better command and control of approaching aircraft, he said.

But this young officer was more curious than anyone he had talked to yet. He wanted to know why it was necessary to provide this kind of control for such a few airplanes. After all, he told Eckert, Nouasseur was going to be a depot and only a few airplanes would ever land there at one time. Regardless of what Eckert said or how he said it, he began to dig himself into a hole. It became apparent that he was becoming confused and that his explanations were not making too much sense.

When he realized the lieutenant did not believe him, Eckert asked him to take a walk. The lieutenant thanked him for the invitation telling Eckert he was not interested right then. Eckert insisted.

Out of earshot of anyone in the barracks area, Eckert told the junior officer he did not want to be asked any more questions. He told him he would not affirm or deny anything else. In fact, he said, he was not to mention this conversation again to anyone. Eckert reminded him that he was receiving a direct order from a superior in the line of duty. Then he asked him if he was aware of what it meant.

The lieutenant was dumfounded to say the least. When he expressed his feelings on the matter, Eckert told him in military jargon to "knock it off."

This was the last real conversation the two had over the next year. When Eckert came back again, this particular lieutenant gave him a wide berth. He would not talk to him unless spoken to. And then he would reply curtly in clipped sentences. But the entire episode only served to whet the younger officer's appetite for information. He never told another living soul about what he suspected Eckert was actually doing, but he kept a diary from which he quoted to refresh his memory at the pre-trial Courts-Martial of Donald H. Eckert.

Eckert had slept late, relying on his capable sergeant to see to things. He had some laundry to look after and then he took another shower. He had one the night before, but now he was looking forward to standing in another and getting clean all over again. The dust and the sand of several weeks were ingrained in his pores, and he was doubtful it would ever come out. Once in a while, they were able to set up their portable facility. But it meant heating the water over an open fire. And if he took a shower, everyone else was entitled to take one. It was not his way to decree otherwise. But all this showering took time, and time was more often than not in short supply. So they settled for a bath in a stream, or a tub when they came to a town of any size.

It was too early for lunch, and breakfast had been over for hours; but he never worried about getting something to eat. He knew the mess sergeant, who knew he had been out in the wilderness for weeks. And he knew he had been living primitively for a long time. When he showed up in the kitchen, the sergeant would cook him anything he wanted. So, following a large breakfast of steak and eggs, he wandered over to the three Dallas huts that housed Base Headquarters. Funny how the American Air Force lived. How primitive it really was would not be believed by the lowliest of Tureg or Berber chieftains. They simply would not be able to comprehend a general officer from the most powerful military force in the world living in a shack. But nevertheless he did, and he worked in one as well. And just a few miles away in the city was one of the world's truly luxurious hotels.

The runways and maintenance facilities were the two things uppermost in the general's mind, and not living quarters. His base installations were second to none. But whether he or his troops would ever see a decent place to live was anybody's guess.

Eckert entered the double hut that served as the general's office. He asked the clerk if he might see the general for a moment. When he was ushered in, he walked up to his desk and saluted, whereupon the general motioned him to take a seat. He saw Eckert so infrequently he could not remember for a moment why the lieutenant was there.

Eckert reminded him, and then the general remembered who he was. He remembered that Eckert commanded, if that is the word, a rag-tag group who reported to another commander. It came to him then that this was a courtesy visit and that Eckert was not one of his officers.

They exchanged pleasantries. The general asked if he was getting everything he needed. After all, he was required to give him priority treatment for anything he might require. These were his orders, which originated somewhere within the Pentagon and had not come down from his own headquarters.

The amenities completed, Eckert stood up and saluted. The short meeting was over. But after he left, the general sat back in his large leather chair, perhaps the only visible sign his accommodations were very much better than his lowest ranking private, and he began to think about this officer who reported to him at regular but infrequent intervals.

The last time he was there, the general had his personnel file pulled. He read that Eckert was a regular officer, but had not graduated from West Point. Strange, he thought, but then maybe not so strange. He had been advised only a few days before about one of his younger lieutenants who had just been integrated into the regular component. He could not remember meeting him, but he was told he worked in his aircraft maintenance organization. This meant he now had a total of six regular officers on his base, including himself. The other thirty or so were reserves. They had been called to activity duty from civilian life for the purpose of building and manning his base. There were also a half dozen active-reservists who had stayed in the service after the recent War.

He thought he might have all his regulars over for lunch one afternoon. But no sooner did he think it than he forgot about it. But the ratio of six to thirty-six was an improvement. Not like the old days, he thought, before the War. Then, the route to a career as a permanent officer, to his recollection, was usually through the Academy at West Point.

The exit to the outside was through another Dallas hut. It also served as the office of one, Frank Rowe. Frank had recently been an obscure and low ranking civil servant. When this job was created, Frank volunteered. The job called for an advancement on the civil service ladder and a considerable raise in pay. How he was able to secure this assignment with such low seniority would later become a subject for debate within the offices of the FBI and the CIA.

He was sent to Morocco at the general's request. The general wanted a facilities specialist, someone who could plan and lay out the depot buildings and someone who could work with the contractor's engineers to make the whole thing happen. But above all, he wanted someone who could speak for him, someone who could convince his superiors and the occasional politician on a sightseeing junket, that he was doing a good job. He wanted to be able to show them at a glance how things were purring right along.

The way Rowe went about it was really quite ingenious. At least it was impressive enough to bring a smile to the general's face whenever Rowe took center stage to explain what was going on.

He had a large table constructed. On this table he placed a number of model buildings. The display also had miniature roads and other facilities. How much was the result of his knowledge and effort, and how much was accomplished by the contractors, was unknown. But Frank Rowe gave everybody on base the impression he was the chief planner and that he had the ultimate say in these matters. He seemed to have limitless energy and boundless enthusiasm for his job. This alone served to convince the general that he was indispensable to the project.

The final approval for each step of construction was the responsibility of the Army Corps of Engineers, and not Frank Rowe. Their headquarters was in Wiesbaden, Germany. The general authorized Frank to travel on military airplanes whenever he said he needed to take off for Germany to do his *coordination*, as he called it. He hired a professional model builder in Germany, and he convinced his boss that he had to go there frequently to take care of business. The general did not care how often he went or how many hours a day he spent with his table–just as long as he was available to entertain and enlighten the dignitaries who came by gathering facts, the general did not care what he did with his time. But with little supervision, Rowe began going to Germany at least once a month and staying for days at a time. And he had been doing this long before he met Don Eckert.

It happened by chance that they met at the bar of the officers club one evening. They had seen each other before, and they had talked for a minute when Eckert had come from the general's office and passed by his display table. However, it was a rare occasion when they were both on the base at the same time. When they were, being more or less strangers to everybody else, they bonded together for conversation and an occasional game of chess. During one of their chess matches, Frank asked Don what he actually did. He received the usual reply. And Rowe asked no further questions at the time. He was satisfied with the answer, which made perfect sense to him.

To anyone who was interested, it would seem the now newly minted Capt. Eckert had an active social life. He was seldom in his quarters during the brief periods he was on base. Sometimes he was at the club playing chess with Frank Rowe, and sometimes he was in the city with the countess. Seldom was he with any of his teammates or lying around reading. Everyone thought he got enough of that when he was in the field.

As time wore on and he and Rowe became better acquainted, they began to talk about their professional lives. Frank told Eckert what Eckert already knew: Frank was spending a great deal of time coming and going between his work in Morocco and coordinating with the real planners in Germany.

"Your queen is in danger," Frank reminded him. Their games were always friendly. But even the more serious players, those who played for rather large stakes, would advise their opponents when their queen was in danger of being taken. No one wanted to steal the main piece on the board just because his opponent was not paying close attention. The satisfaction was in the engineering of a situation whereby the opponent was forced to move a major piece to protect his king from being mated. Then when he did, he left the queen vulnerable and the queen was lost.

Eckert noticed the lieutenant, the one he had had a serious talk with several months before. He was playing across the small room that served as the club bar. "Do you know the lieutenant, the one over there?" he asked Rowe.

"Yeah, why?" Frank wanted to know.

"I have forgotten his name," he said.

"If you're thinking about asking him for a game, make sure it's for fun. He's not all that good, but he is probably the best player around here. He will play newcomers if he can't find anybody with money. But when it comes to money, he'll play most anybody. I've heard he will play for some rather large stakes. I heard him say once that chess was like life; knowing this gives you an edge, he says. You can tell, according to him, how a player will play just by knowing something about his personality. If he doesn't think things out before he speaks, he says his game can be quite predictable. And if he is not much of a thinker, it will show up on the board. I realize I haven't said anything that's not obvious. But it does give you some idea of what I'm talking about. I don't know whether or not there is anything in what he says. But I do know he seldom loses, and he makes living expenses sitting right over there a couple of nights a week."

Eckert started thinking about Rowe in terms of what he had just heard. Rowe was anything but fastidious. In fact, he was rather sloppy, but then he was not in the service and he was not required to dress according to any code. He did work for the general, however, and he did meet other civilians, so you would expect him to at least shine his shoes once in a while. But maybe you could not fault him for that; the place was dusty in the summer and muddy in the winter.

What else do I know about him? Eckert wondered. Well, he was quick to reach conclusions. And at times he was somewhat reckless with facts. He wondered if his willingness to gamble with one of his hastily thought out gambits, rather than stick to one of the classics, had anything to do with this. And he wondered if it worked the other way around. Was his recklessness on the board indicitive of a personality that was willing to take chances? Eckert thought it over, and then decided he was not interested enough in Rowe to find out. Later he would change his mind.

On his next trip back Frank Rowe brought up the subject of

what Eckert was spending his time doing. They were playing chess again, and Frank seemed to be waiting for a time when Don was concentrating the hardest. The question broke his train of thought. Eckert's mind left the game for a moment, and his danger sensors seemed to kick in. And he began to feel uneasy. It was a perfectly legitimate question, one the captain was asked quite frequently. But the fact that Frank had asked him the same question once before was causing his blood pressure to rise. And if the lieutenant's theory about there being a relationship between the way a person played chess and his or her personality, then Don Eckert knew there was nothing at all wrong with Frank's memory.

Two nights later, he was sitting with the countess to be. He had started calling her Countess. They were dining in the Chez Maison, a medium priced beachfront restaurant in Casablanca.

Her name was Edit, Hungarian for Edith. He had tried calling her Edith, but she had let him know early on that Edith was unfamiliar to her and that she preferred Edit. But he never seemed to get the pronunciation quite right, so he settled for Countess. She liked that; in fact she was a little flattered.

She was heir to a royal title and a fortune through the great Esterhazy princes. She had explained to him once about the grandeur of their family estates, and how they rivaled those of the Hapsburgs, who were once the rulers of her country. She elaborated at length about how her relatives had used their wealth in the promotion of science and the fine arts. She told him of their relationship with musical genius, men such as Hayden and others. She spoke about these things, not with a sense of pride or bravado, but as a matter of fact. She wanted him to know she was from the highest levels of European aristocracy, intimating that if he ever become serious he would be marrying far above his station.

She had gone on to tell him that much of her life was like the movie *Gone with the Wind*. It had, indeed, blown away with the defeat of Germany and the Austrian-Hungarian Empire. It had all existed once, but that was before the Axis defeat and the Soviet take-over. Now, the Communists had dismantled most of what was the old Hungary, she said. And they had confiscated all of her family's holdings. Gone were the old ways, the manor house, and the family's estates. Gone were the formal balls and the cultured society, which now lived on only as a memory.

Still, she liked to reminisce about the old days. And she often fantasized about it all being restored someday, her title and her estates, all to their former grandeur. She spent long hours talking about the old days in the old Hungary with her friends. And lately, she had opened up to Eckert, who seemed to be interested in the stories she had to tell. But after she had talked for a while, she would always ask him to tell her about himself. She acted as though she was most interested in life in the United States. Most of the European women he had met were interested in this subject. But Edit was more interested than were any of the few French women he had met. And the questions she asked him always seemed to center around the same subject: What did he study in school? What was school like? What were his long-range goals and what was he doing now?

What was he doing now started innocently enough again over dinner. And then she wanted to know what the interior of Morocco was really like. She wanted to know about Berber country. She wanted to know about his relationships with the Berber people. Had he been to the Atlas Mountains to the east, and how far into them was he roaming? She especially wanted to know about the area to the east of Nouasseur. And then she sprang it on him—she wanted to know about *Boulhaut*.

They were making casual conversation, boy and girl talk mostly, when she became very serious. She leaned across the table, and for the second time since he had known her, she began to quiz him about the specifics of his job. It would not have affected him the way it did if it had not come on the heels of his being asked the same questions just days before by Frank Rowe. He wondered what he could tell her that was not classified, something that would satisfy her curiosity, something innocent. The last thing Eckert wanted was for somebody, anybody, to come away with the impression that he was doing a job that was out of the ordinary.

Later in the evening, she asked him again what he was doing. She asked him in such a way that it appeared she was interested in his career. After all, they were both single, and it did not surprise him that she might be curious about his prospects as a husband. It happened to him all the time. As soon as he appeared to be interested in a young woman, she seemed to be more interested in his career potential than she was in him. He thought it was just natural for women to do this. He could hardly blame them. They did, after all, have their own future to think about. Maybe only a fool would want to waste a lot of their time on a man with no potential. And Edit, Countess in waiting of Esterhazy, was no fool. And she definitely was not one to waste her time doing anything foolish.

She had thought about it a lot over the past few weeks and she had all but decided to sever their relationship, such as it was. He was not a foolish man, as seen through her eyes. But she summed him up as one who was not committed to marriage. But then, neither was she for the same reasons most people were. What she was committed to was marriage for the purpose of changing her direction in life. After all, she was from a culture that looked on marriage differently. Love was seldom an option with her class. They married to cement family relations and to meld great fortunes and estates.

Eckert had concluded early on that she had no realistic hope of ever recovering any part of her vast lost fortune. But every once in a while, she spoke as though her recent past never happened; there had been no War and she was still heir to the Esterhazy title. It was as though she was living in a fantasy present–she was not living in the real world. He tried to put himself in her place. What must it be like to have had everything, then to have lost it all through no fault of your own? He supposed he would act the same way–not wanting to give up, not wanting to put the past behind him. He supposed he would cling to the last vestige of hope as she was doing, reluctant to let go and face the future as it really was. And for her, the future had to lie in the securing of an American for a husband. He had been thinking about this lately, and he suspected it might be her ultimate goal.

He was correct. This was on her mind, and had been since they first met. But he was mistaken if he thought he had her figured out. He had no inkling of what she really had in mind. She knew what he was thinking and she knew he was wrong, dead wrong. But the problem had been for her to unburden herself to him, to tell him the *family secret*. She was afraid if she started she would have to go all the way. And if she had misjudged him, he might turn on her and send her to prison for a long time. But worse than that, she would have told him the secret–and then she would have lost everything.

With him as her sponsor, she would be eager to seek her fortune in the United States. But if he thought that, she knew he would be wrong again. But if it were him, that is exactly what he would do. Regardless of what awaited her in a new country, her life would be an improvement over what it was at this moment. That is how he had it figured anyway.

But she had no plans to go to America with him or with any-body else. She intended to get married all right, but not to become an American as he suspected. She intended to stay in Europe. She needed a husband in order to secure a legitimate passport. But that is all marriage meant to her. After all, she was the thorough-bred, not him. She had the blood lines of kings and rulers of the conquering Magyars and the Khans, as well as the seed of the Esterhazy and the seed of the Hohenzollern. It was not she that needed him, it was the other way around.

What was the breeding of this man when compared to her. Who was he, this man who sat across the table from her? Who was this rustic from the back woods of rural America? What, after all, was America? They, with their paltry few hundred years of civilization. What had they accomplished toward the refine-ment of civilization? What were any of them, when compared to the Hapsburgs and the other crowned heads of Europe and England?

She was working herself into a state of agitation. She was under a great deal of stress, thinking about what she should do. She was feeling ill. She recognized an embarrassing moment was about to happen. She was about to have a panic attack. Her breed-ing and refinement, if nothing else, remained. And it would not allow her to be put into a position where she might be responsible for causing a scene if she told him she did not want to see him again. But worse yet, if she told him everything on her mind, and then he rejected her proposal of marriage, what then would she do?

But if she broke it off tonight , right now...She had a plan—and it was far more complicated than anything having to do with the usual rites of courtship and marriage. But things were begin-ning to move too fast for her. First, she had seen him as the ideal mate and partner. And then she went through several months of doubting whether he was up to the task. Could he handle the secret?

And then she wondered what his reaction would be when she told him she knew what he was really doing in Morocco. He would certainly want to know how she knew. How would it work out for her when she told him how she knew? Would he tell the American authorities? What would happen then? What if she fell into the hands of the French? Could she trust him with the family secret? The secret was the thing–and always had been.

Her mind was racing ninety miles an hour now. She realized she needed to slow down; she needed time to think.

Her solution to her immediate problem was to relax. She needed some air. She needed to go for a walk. She asked him if he wanted to take a walk on the beach. That was it, a walk on the beach while she considered her next step. Should she tell him, and then propose marriage, or should she just wait and see if a marriage proposal from him might be in the offing? But marriage had to be part of her long-range plans. She could wait, but not forever. And she couldn't afford to spend more months waiting, then have it all come to naught. And by the way things had been progressing, she was all but convinced it would never happen if it was left up to him. But if she did the proposing and then told him the secret, she realized theirs might be a loveless marriage. Still, countless of her ancestors had married just this way, and most of them had eventually fallen in love.

And that is where it happened. Instead of severing their relationship as a lost cause, Edit turned on her feminine charm. And under the bright moonlight of an exotic Moroccan night, Eckert succumbed to her advances, and he told her all she wanted to know about Boulhaut. And now he knew he had a tiger by the tail and could not let go. He realized for the first time that she was a Soviet agent–when it was too late. But he could not report her, because if he did, he would be reporting himself. And Edit Esterhazy knew she had him, and she knew he would do anything for her, including marrying her. But more importantly, now she could tell him one of the great secrets of modern times. And he was going to become part of it, and what she had been planning since the War ended, whether he liked it or not.

CHAPTER 11...FRANKFURT GERMANY, 1953

He walked down the staircase past the painters who were working on the Basselerhoff. It was one of two prominent hotels in Frankfurt, the other being the Kaiserhoff across the street, which had sustained minimal bomb damage. The American conquering Army had occupied both of them for the use of their transient personnel.

Outside, a quarter block away, buildings were still in shambles as far as the eye could see. German workman had constructed small railroads to haul out the rubble and debris from the interior of the ruined buildings. Frank Rowe thought the scene was reminiscent of First World War movies he had seen of shelled towns in France. Interesting, he thought to himself, as he walked along the cleared sidewalk, how five hundred pound bombs reduced stone and cement to rubble, just as artillery shells did. No difference at all, except in this case the ruined city was German and not French.

At the corner, he watched the workmen for a few minutes and then turned north and walked across the street. The shops were full of goods. Windows of small businesses were teeming with varieties of chocolate, meats, and groceries. Where a few short years before there had been a famine on the land, now thanks to the largess of their former enemies, the Germans were prospering as they never had in history.

Two blocks further down, he turned left again and walked past one of the city's more popular *ratschellers* or *ratcellers*, as the G.I.'s preferred. One side of the nightclub, separated by a recently constructed wall, was patronized by the Germans and the other side by Americans. Occasionally, one of the more venturesome of the Americans, or a stranger like himself, would inadvertently wander into the German side. It was against the law to fraternize. A year before, the manager would have been required to call the military police. But now these indiscretions were usually overlooked. Part way down the next block, Frank stopped and looked into a camera shop window. He thought for a minute about going in and buying one of the new Lica cameras on display. Famous for their optical lenses before the War, the Germans were working hard to regain their pre-eminence in the field. Back in Morocco, occasionally someone would ask him to buy them one of these prestigious cameras. When he agreed and when he was just interested in looking around, this was the shop where he always stopped–not because it was cheaper, but because he was known, and because the location afforded him an unobstructed view of the main gate of the Russian Embassy.

CHAPTER 12...FEDALLA, MOROCCO, 1953

Fedalla, a sleepy little suburb of Casablanca, will someday be referred to as a bedroom community, if the Arabs ever became part of the twentieth century, and if they ever have a need for motor freeways and homes outside the city. But for now and the immediate future, the Medina and the White City, a large Arab modern enclave inside the city of Casablanca, built by the Americans after the War and given to the Arab people, houses the Arab population. It is crowded, but it has always been this way.

When General Patton's approached Casablanca, the French Vichy government placed hundreds of Arab women and children aboard a merchant ship in an effort to save them from Patton's landing forces. The problem was the Vichy government. They had been warned that the French Navy, including merchant shipping, must remain in Vichy controlled harbors on penalty of being sunk. The French, in a ridiculous and ill-conceived plan of defiance, sent the merchantman in harm's way and the American Navy shelled it, with a staggering loss of life. When the facts became known, the Americans and not the French shouldered the blame. Not knowing what to do, the Americans built the White

City and gave it to the Arabs as a gesture of reconciliation.

Fedalla is famous for two things: its magnificent beach and, the fact that Patton chose it for his main North African landing site. The beach stretches for miles, gently sloping a couple of hundred yards to the water's edge. The ocean is like a giant lake, without breakers. This is why the General chose this particular beach to disembark most of his armor for his upcoming campaign against the Germans in the north. This was the main purpose of Torch in the first place. It was not to liberate Casablanca, as the Vichy government supposed.

The beach suffered minimum damage from the landing and was soon returned to its pristine state by the gentle tides. Now, it was a place for walking and swimming in the moonlight, occupied only by an occasional American couple and, once in a while, a playful herd of Arab boys who used it as their playground.

Edit and Eckert had the beach to themselves the next night, the one following his admission that he knew where Boulhaut was.

She had invited him to a beach picnic, but he was reluctant to meet with her again, at least so soon. But then he was out on a limb, vulnerable. She had outmaneuvered him. She had put him in a position where he had lost his queen. And he was in danger of being mated.

She knew this, and she knew he had only agreed to go out with her again for one reason: he had to find out how much trouble he was in, and only she could tell him.

She packed a basket of what she thought was regular American food: fried chicken, some sandwiches, catsup, and a bottle of wine. She wanted it to appear as though it was another meeting between lovers for a romantic moonlight walk along the beach. But Eckert believed she wanted something more. He believed she had set the hook in him, and now she was going to reel him in. He believed she was going to blackmail him for more information.

After they had eaten, instead of going swimming on the deserted beach, as they had the night before, she lay face-down on the blanket. She waited, saying nothing. And then, turning on her side, supported by her elbow, she asked him if she could talk seriously about something very important.

He had been watching her–waiting. He knew it was why she had asked him here in the first place. He expected she wanted to discuss blackmail terms. Maybe not money, of which he had very little. But about him giving her more information, information she could sell to the Soviets. Instead, she asked him how well he knew Frank Rowe. Before he could answer, she said, "I know you know him, but I also know you know nothing about him, or me either for that matter." Then she changed the subject abruptly before he could answer.

"What do you know about Freemasonry?" she asked, as if the question was a perfectly normal, everyday topic of conversation.

"I mean, are you by chance a Mason?"

"No. Why on earth do you ask?"

"I have my reasons," she answered, with a hint of mystery in her voice.

"Do you know anything about them?"

Under the circumstances, he knew she was not making idle chatter. And certainly the question was not designed to enhance any romantic interlude. She had turned deadly serious; she had something on her mind–something he supposed was not going to be to his liking. He just hoped–whatever it was–it was going to make things a little easier rather than more difficult for him. His career was in her hands. And maybe she could arrange a long jail sentence to boot, if she saw it that way. She was in the driver's seat, and he had placed her there because of his foolishness. He had no one to blame but himself. He was feeling depressed and a little afraid of what was going to happen next. She was in a position to blackmail him, and he felt helpless. *What would he do if she did?*

His pulse began to race as he thought about her last question and what she was leading up to. "I know Masons purport to be a religious order," he said, by way of answering her question. "That is, they teach universal truths, which I understand were collected and passed on to certain craftsmen in the working guilds of the Middle Ages. These truths, whatever they are, might be considered to be religious in nature. I know they believe in a god, but whose god, I'm not sure."

"What about the Knights Templar?" She asked. "What do you know about them?"

What in the world could she be after? "Well I suspect there might be a connection. I know the Templar Knights were great builders of castles and fortifications, and that they brought back many Arab building techniques from the Crusades. I know they are thought to have financed many of the cathedrals of the Middle Ages. Some think the Templars were behind the Masonic craftsmanship evidenced by the cathedrals of the period. What Masons believe though, I don't know.

"I really know little or nothing more about the Templars. I did cross paths with them in a required English literature class in school. Spencer's *Fairy Queen* is an allegory, pitting the church against the oppressed peoples of the times. The hero is a Red Cross Knight who rides around righting wrongs. One of the wrongs he rights is a dragon he slays. This dragon represents the church, according to Spencer, and the knight errant is a Templar. That was my professor's interpretation, at any rate."

"You're right," she said, "but the church was not always the enemy of the Templars. In fact, the Order proliferated during the Crusades because of the support and encouragement of one particular pope. The Order of the Templars became rich, even as the individual members had taken a vow of poverty. It was wealth and the power of the Order that made all of Europe extremely wary of them. Individually, they were unlike anybody else. They were different, and that alone made them suspect. They swore other oaths making them feared by the Mohammedans in the Holy Land, more so than any of the other Crusaders. They were a power to be reckoned with, on and off the battlefield."

"Edit." He refused to call her Countess. He preferred instead to stick to business until she declared whose side she was on. She was in a position to hurt him badly, and until she made her intentions known, he did not feel like playing around with her. And maybe not even then. In fact, *I wonder if she knows the danger she might be in if all of this forces me to reveal any more classified information?*

"Edit, is this leading up to your wanting more information from me. If so, I wish you would get to the point."

"I knew you were going to ask me. But no, the answer is no. I am going to ask you for something, however, which is much more important than any classified information about your military. But not until you have heard my story," she said.

"I planned to tell you a family secret. But I have been holding off, trying to make up my mind. However, last night changed everything between us. Now I am sure you are the one I want to confide in. I want to tell you all about it, and after that I want to ask you to do something, something very important, something that will affect both our lives forever. But I can see you are not going to give me your undivided attention until I convince you I'm not your enemy.

"First, you can forget what you told me about Boulhaut. I

am not going to tell anybody what happened. I was just testing you. I wanted to maneuver you into a position where I could tell you my story. What I want from you is a guarantee. If you're not interested, after you have heard what I have to say, I want your promise you'll keep it to yourself."

"What you mean is, if I tell, you'll feel free to inform on me."

"Something like that. But I hoped you wouldn't say it; it sounds so sordid when put into words. Yes, I planned it this way. To be sure, I will suffer for my actions, but you have more to lose than I have. Rest assured you will be the big loser."

"I imagine I will be," he said. "Does this secret of yours have anything to do with Frank Rowe?"

"Not exactly, but he does play an incidental role. You knew he was a soviet agent, didn't you? But then, so am I. My job is to find out what you know about Boulhaut." As she continued to talk, she was looking straight at him in the moonlight. But he was determined it was not going to be like last night. Tonight, he was not interested in how she was looking at him; he was only interested in what she was going to say next.

"My parents and I were destitute before I went to work for the Communists. All our lives we were surrounded with Europe's opulence, then overnight we were reduced to eating food the Arabs fed their dogs.

"It took most of the little I earned to pay our hotel bill. Sometimes I relied on what you call doggie bags to ensure my mother and father a decent meal. Most of the time they lived on stale bread and cheap coffee. Many nights they went hungry and so did I. There were more than a few mornings when I went to work with nothing to eat, and then had nothing the rest of the day. I smelled your mess halls, and schemed to get my hands on a little of the food you threw away. So please don't get too sanctimonious with me. I hate the Communists worse than you ever could. But I also hate starving to death. And I also know what I told them about you was not really very important..."

"Edit, let's talk some more about Rowe," he said, interrupting. "Who is he, and how come you know so much about him?"

"They gave me two specific assignments when I took the librarian's job at Nouassuer. One of them was you and the other was Frank Rowe. I would not be the least bit surprised if he is watching me watch you. That's the way things work in the MVD. Everybody's watching everybody else; but then, that's not news to you," she said, in her flawless English. He marveled at her command of the language; he thought about it whenever she spoke to him. He continually pictured himself attempting to learn Hungarian under any circumstance. She told him it was not too difficult to learn a second language if you were brought up the way she was. She had a tutor and a nanny, who were both British. She told him she spoke English from infancy and that she had attended English schools for years.

"Just so you understand whose side I'm really on, let me tell you what I know about him." She spoke in a tone Eckert suspected had almost as much meaning as her words.

She wants to convince me she is on my side as she says. She also wants me to know she is allowing herself to become vulnerable. I can turn her in and she can do the same with me. She intends to form a kind of partnership with me for some curious reason.

"I'm going to start at the beginning, if you don't mind," she said.

"Please do," he replied, having to hold back the sarcasm creeping into his voice.

"You know Frank Rowe is misleading your general," she said. "He fiddles all day with his display box, and then he tells the general he has to go to Germany to coordinate with the Corps of Engineers. Most everybody on the base knows about it, including you. He has made a job for himself. But the facilities on the base are meaningless. The Russians know this, but the general and his staff do not."

"Explain to me why not. The buildings and warehouses are essential to the building of the depot."

"The Russians don't care about any depot. What they care about is the length of the reinforced runways and the *atom bombs*."

"What atom bombs? What are you talking about?"

"The atom bombs stored on the base. They moved them in two months ago. Rowe was assigned to find out when they arrived and in what quantity. It was easy for him to do this, he was involved with the planning of the storage and maintenance facility. As soon as he did, he ran off to Germany to report and collect a briefcase full of money. He is getting rich. And of course, when I found out about it there was nothing I could do to stop him. Who could I tell without implicating myself? I was afraid that if I told you, I would give myself away. What was I going to say when you asked me how I knew? But since our conversation last night about Boulhaut, and what happened afterwards, I have put it aside. I'm no longer worried about you. I'm certain now that you won't say anything about me. How you get this information about Rowe to the right people is up to you. If I were you, I would tell them a Russian over at Boulhaut who wants to defect told me." In spite of the seriousness of the situation, she began to laugh.

"Are there MIG fighter-bombers at Boulhaut?" he asked her.

"I am not absolutely positive. But why would the Russians be so interested in atom bombs at Nouasseur if there were no MIGs at Boulhaut. There are bombs at Nouasseur; I know this for sure, and I also know Frank Rowe has told them. The best way for the Russians to render this base inoperative is to strike the facility where the bombs are kept with their airplanes. And if they have no airplanes, what do the Russians care about your bombs. You can see that Nouasseur is worthless if there are no bombs to load on your bombers when they land here. And if they fly them over fully loaded, have any of you considered how they are going to land with those heavy bombs on board?"

"Maybe they intend to sabotage the bomb facility from the ground if hostilities ever broke out. In that case they wouldn't need any airplanes at Boulhaut," he said, half-jokingly.

"Maybe, but I wouldn't count on it," she said. "I believe if I were you, I would personally find that place. I would verify there was such a base and see the MIGs for myself before I started to build a case against Frank Rowe. If you can convince your people Boulhaut is a direct threat to Nouasseur, and that the Russians know about your bombs being stored on base because he has told them, your people would surely come up with a plan to catch him coming from the Russian Embassy. That's where he goes, you know. Then you would have him for atomic secrets espionage; otherwise, you're only talking about him losing his job. At most, he will only get a slap on the wrist for revealing the status of a bunch of meaningless depot warehouses to the Communists."

"Countess, how are you going to protect yourself if I turn him in? He is certain to implicate you. Are you involved in it some way? Does he know you work for the MVD?"

"I'm pretty sure he does; they had to have told him. They told me what he was up to, did they not? If you turn him in, he will figure it was me who did it. And since I know you, he is just liable to make up a bunch of lies to get the charges dropped. Anything is possible. He might even try to convince your people the three of us are working together. Why wouldn't he try and save himself by promising to name his associates. Which one of your people wouldn't jump at a chance to uncover a cell of Communist spies–meaning the two of us?"

"Countess," he said. She smiled. He said it again. I'm back in his good graces. We really are partners. She had him in a position now to hear her story. And when she told him, she would ask him to marry her. And then he would forget about everything else. She was determined to change his life forever. The two of them would go away someplace, maybe to Switzerland or to one of the Scandinavian countries. They were going to become instant millionaires. More than millionaires; with their money, they were going to turn back the clock and rejoin a lost society. They were going to have riches beyond his wildest dreams. She would adopt her mother's title and be called Countess by everybody. They would become citizens of another country, the two of them. With him at her side, she would take her rightful place among the remnants of European aristocracy, something she had always dreamed of doing. Things were going to be as they used to be, as they were meant to be before the War. All of this was within her grasp, if she could convince him her secret was true. But first she had to confess everything. They had to start out with him trusting her.

"I have a plan," she said, "and I want you to be part of it. But I must tell you before I say anything more; I had chosen you as my accomplice, maybe partner is a better word, months ago when I first met you. But I also want you to know, I can find someone else if you're not interested. In fact, I have him picked out and the groundwork has been laid. But I want you, not him. But either way, my days here in Casablanca are numbered. The only way I can get away from the MVD is to disappear. That's one of the things I want from you. I want you to help me disappear." She looked up at him, cannily, hoping she could tell from his expression in the moonlight what he was thinking. But maybe it wasn't fair to expect anything from him. There seemed to be no emotion of any kind. He was still thinking on another level. He was thinking about the trouble he was in and how he got there. And he was thinking that maybe her expression of fondness for him had been a hoax just to get information from him so she could control him. The name *Mata Hari* came to his mind as she started talking again.

"I was asking you what you knew about the Templars. Their leaders in the latter part of the eleventh century were descendants of Merovingians. Much of what I am going to tell you about them comes from family journals and lore handed down from generations of Merovingian and Frankish Kings. From this linage came the historically important Blanchfort family who contributed a Templar Grand master some three centuries later. Pope Clement V, who helped destroy the ancient Templar Order, came from this same family. My linage is tied to Blanchfort and Austrian royalty through the Esterhazy and Hapsburg lines.

"I was taught a lot about the Merovingians and their relationship to the Templars, but not nearly as much as the males in my family were. It was as though they believed they were Templars somehow. I always thought they were. But whether they were Masons at the same time, I don't know. I suspect they might have been. I was hoping you could tell me what the connection was between the two. These relatives of mine, this society of males I'm talking about, may or may not have been Templars; but one thing I know for a certainty: they were the descendants of those who took refuge in Hungary and disavowed their oath of celibacy. However, they never swore an oath of poverty–that's for sure. They accumulated personal wealth beyond reason. And another thing, there is no record of any of my ancestors ever being brought up on charges of heresy, and all the rest of the sordid stuff that went on when Phillip the Fair and Pope Clement killed off most of them. Phillip was indebted to the Templars and had coveted their immense wealth. He charged them with heresy and confiscated their vast lands and estates throughout Europe.

"The important thing to remember is the Order had accumulated secret hoards of gold, silver, and precious stones worth several king's ransoms. And only members of this so-called brotherhood I'm talking about knew about it and where it was hidden. Philip confiscated their lands and estates, as I said, and most of their treasure. But he never came close to getting it all, because only a few of the Order's leaders knew where it was hidden. Much of it was taken to Scotland when remnants of the Templars seemed to vanish. But part of it was taken to Hungary, or so I was told.

"My father wanted a male heir, not so much to pass on his estates but to pass on certain secret revelations dating back to the Crusades. I am not saying these secrets were Templar in origin, but they may have been part of Templar history." Eckert was fast becoming confused because he knew next to nothing about the subject.

"Countess, I don't have the benefit of knowing anything about the history of these people. What do you mean secret revelations?"

"Well, some scholars maintain the Temple Knights or the Knights of Solomon's Temple was an order formed in Jerusalem early in the twelfth century. Their original purpose was to protect bands of pilgrims journeying to the Jordan River to worship. The Jordan was venerated by the early Christians in much the same way as the Ganges is by the Hindus of today. So trusted were they, because of their oaths, people began to bank with them.

"First they took vows to protect the pilgrims from bandits,

and then they began charging them for this protection. The travelers were carrying large quantities of money. So the Templars instituted a kind of protective banking system. And remember, this money the Crusader knights and the pilgrims carried had been donated, and in sufficient quantity to last them for years. The Templars took their money at the start of their journey in exchange for chits. These chits were backed by the Templar's reputation and could be exchanged for cash almost anywhere along the route. This put highwaymen and the king's men of the countries they were passing through out of business. If, in the unlikely event a hold-up did take place, the bad guys were hunted down and destroyed by these knights, who were reported to be merciless."

Edit paused for a moment. Eckert, wanting to hear more, encouraged her to go on by saying: "It seems to me that without them, the follow-on Crusade would not have taken place."

"You are exactly right," she said, "and that is part of my story. Pope Innocent, who was one of the main promoters of the Third Crusade, was happy with the work of the Templars. He exempted them from taxation and from all laws other than a few imposed by him. This enabled them to collect vast amounts of money in a very short period of time. Then too, they were heavily subsidized for years by the later popes of the church, kings, and other wealthy donors who were also sympathetic to the restoration of the Holy Land."

"Edit, were these people your progenitors?"

"I can not be certain, if you are talking about a genealogy chart. But according to my uncle, we are related to the Merovingeans, a dynasty who ruled France from the fifth to the eighth century. But this is only pertinent in so far as it explains where the Esterhazy Princes acquired their wealth in the first place. What happened to it later, and where it is now, is the secret.

"Did you ever hear of two Germans during the War by the name of Canaris and Gehlen?" She asked him, appearing to change the subject.

"Wasn't Canaris head of German Intelligence or something. He was one of the good Nazis, that is, he was a Nazi we considered good for us. We hired a lot of them right after the War–people we considered to be useful, such as scientists and men like Canaris," he replied.

"Yes, well I understand they both worked for your government after the War. General Gehlen was a member of the *Waffen SS* and had been head of the intelligence organizations on the Eastern Front, and Admiral Canaris was head of the same thing at home. They both knew my uncle and my father well. They were Nazis that's for sure, and so was my father and several of my uncles, albeit, the Hungarian varieties, if that is what you want to call them. But unlike my father, my uncles were Nazi in name only…"

Eckert interrupted: "You mean your father was a Nazi?"

"Don't be so surprised; every male over eighteen years of age was. Believe me, they are lying if they say otherwise. My uncles were part of a secret group inside the National Socialist movement, as were Canaris and Gehlen. Some of them met several times at our home when I was very young. But whatever you choose to call this group, it was much older than the Nazis. I heard the name once; they called themselves the *Thule Society*. And they were descendants of what I was told were the Templars. They preceded the Nazi Party; in fact they were the first supporters of Adolph Hitler. A few years later, the Thule's elected Hitler their leader. And he later renamed it the German Socialist Workers Party or the *NAZI*.

"My father remained loyal to Adolph Hitler and to this day he believes what Hitler was trying to do was for the betterment of Germany and the world. My uncles were loyal for a while. But they became disillusioned, and they plotted with Canaris and others to assassinate Hitler. There were several assassination attempts made on Hitler's life soon after he chose to invade Russia, and after the so-called final solution to the Jewish problem became a reality. This was before the well-publicized failed plot at Wolf's Lair on the Eastern Front.

"The first failed attempt, like the last one, resulted in hundreds of officers being executed with hardly any trial. My uncles all died. But my father, who was in Italy, came under the protection of Mussolini and was spared. Then too, it was not much of a stretch in logic to believe what he told investigators–that he had attached himself to Hitler's star from the beginning. And an overthrow of Hitler's government would have left him in the same situation we are in now. What was to be gained? So he survived, but as I say, most of the close males in my family did not."

Edit paused for a moment and then began again with her story: "Before the Invasion of Russia, when the fortunes of Germany were on the rise, I was invited to stay one summer at one of our estates, the home of my favorite uncle. One day he took me and my male cousin aside and told us a story. He told us about our family history, mentioning in passing the Templars and how several of the early founders were once quartered in Solomon's Temple. He told us these knights were there for several reasons, the most important was to search for the Biblical Ark of the Covenant. But another was to discover treasures hidden there by Solomon; they believed they were hidden in underground labyrinths. I don't remember if any of this had to do with the beginnings of the Templar wealth, but it might have; he seemed to think so...."

"Countess, where is all of this now? Is this what you want me to do?–help you find it? Where is it, in some Templar castle someplace?" Eckert knew he should not have been so flippant, but he was having a hard time believing her story. He knew she was not lying to him. At this point, she did not need to; she was in a position to get almost anything she wanted from him. No, she believed she was telling him a true story as understood by her uncle. But to Eckert it was only an interesting family myth. And in a family as large as hers, and as old, there must have been dozens of such stories, none of them true–all of them fairy tales.

His words and his demeanor were not lost on her. She knew he was thinking ahead, and that he was not convinced. That was all right with her; he soon would be, just as soon as she showed him some evidence. And evidence she had in abundance.

"My uncle showed us two boxes," she went on to say. "They appeared to be two small jewelry cases, the kind you put on top of a dresser. They were both locked.

"He told us in strict confidence why he didn't expect to survive the War. He was the only one possessing the knowledge–this knowledge has been a family secret passed down through generations. It is money, wealth beyond measure, hidden away to protect it from governments, kings, and popes."

She paused again and then continued: "My uncle said this family wealth had recently been converted into diamonds. He said diamonds were as good as gold, smaller, and of course easier to handle. He said, like gold, they would keep pace with the inflation he expected to come immediately after the War. He told us we were to be partners. Each of us possessed half of the information required to retrieve them from two large safety deposit boxes in a Swiss bank. I had the numbers of the accounts, and my cousin was given the passwords. He instructed us to each hide our individual boxes and then to write and tell the other where they could be found. That way, if either of us were killed in the violence he expected to descend on all of Europe, the other was to retrieve the diamonds and then use them to establish another banking dynasty. He said he expected the one he was head of now would eventually fail, along with the fortunes of Adolph Hitler.

"When uncle was executed as an accomplice in the first assassination attempt, the Esterhazy bank and attendant fortune was confiscated. But of course not the diamonds."

"Of course not," Eckert replied. "What do you want from me, Countess? Why don't you just go get the other box?"

"Easily enough said, but not so easy for me to do. My cousin's box is still hidden on our old estate north of Budapest, and he did not survive the War, And as the daughter of an unrepentant Nazi officer, I am still *persona non grata* anywhere in Europe or America."

"What do you mean unrepentant?"

"Just a term. But whether he is repentant or not, my father is listed as a war criminal. He was a member of the Hungarian inner circle who took their orders from Hitler. And even if I had a passport, I would be picked up. He was charged with the heinous crime of helping to plan a concentration camp in Hungary for the extermination of Jews. I should point out, we left for his assignment in Italy before it was finished, so he really had no part in the actual killings. But he was charged with it just the same. And I'm certain the authorities are waiting for me to leave. Everybody knows where we are: the British, the Soviets, and most of all you Americans. I sincerely believe they would have forgotten about our family after all this time if a Jewish extermination camp had not been involved. But the Jewish organizations in your country will not let them."

"But they want him, not you."

"That was true in the beginning. But it was before I was wanted for harboring a Hungarian officer who had been convicted of war crimes in absentia at the Nuremberg Trials."

"Edit, tell me how you were able to get a clearance to work for us with all this hanging over your head."

"I came under the protection of Admiral Canaris, who in turn was spirited out of Germany by your OSS during the chaos that was Germany in the last days. Much earlier, before the first attempted assassination, Canaris had been in touch with a Mr. Cordell Hull, your Secretary of State. Canaris was to take the place of Hitler as the new head of the German government, after they did away with Hitler. He was also going to establish a new German-run intelligence operation. Its purpose was to ferret out any resurrected National Socialistic movement to take back the government after the War. Remember, they were planning a last stand of all the die-hard Nazis. They intended to gather in the Bavarian Alps for a fight to the death. It never happened, because Germany had had enough by the time the War ended. I saw much of the War's aftermath; Germany and Hungary had been pulverized by your bombers."

"What happened to this admiral?"

"He lives in America now, and has since the War ended. The history books say Hitler had him hung with the other conspirators. And for sure he would have been if it had not been for your OSS. You can bet there was a lot of money changed hands, and probably many promises of amnesty for the *Waffen SS* officers who had him in their custody. But then I am just making assumptions about this."

"Is he one of those members of this secret society you told me about."

"He is indeed. But he could do just so much to help me."

"Did you ever consider he might want the diamonds?"

"No, because he doesn't know they exist. The diamonds belong to the family. While Canaris was a member of the Thule

Society, he was not an Esterhazy. He thinks my fortune was lost when Hitler confiscated our bank and our property."

"How can you be so sure what your uncle told the Gestapo about the diamonds? They would surely have tortured him to find out if he had more money than was evident. Countess, I think you're mistaken about Canaris knowing nothing about your diamonds—incidentally, how much money are they worth?"

"In the neighborhood of fifty million dollars."

"Whew! That's enough to get a lot of people and several countries interested, to say nothing of this secret society, which you say has been around since the Middle Ages. Then, too, if this information fell into the hands of the big diamond merchants, you might be in even more trouble just a thought. But do you know what I really think? I don't think Canaris had anything to do with your getting hired. You're a local hire, and you never required a security clearance. There's no one in our government who is interested in you. But that doesn't mean Canaris and his group of Templars or Thules, or whatever, are not. Anybody who knows you have access to this kind of loot lurking about is not going to forget you. And furthermore, I believe Canaris would have found out about it from the Gestapo. A sum that big can't be kept quiet forever. And another thing, Canaris headed up the intelligence division of the Gestapo. You'd better believe Himmler tortured your uncle, as I said. And nobody withstands that for long. No, your uncle would have told Himmler's people. And I will bet they told Canaris about your diamonds.

"Incidentally, what makes you think Canaris helped you?" he asked her. Eckert was unable to make the connection, and he was surprised that she had the idea settled in her mind.

"I'm pretty sure he did, my father and he were once good friends. Father told me he knew where Canaris was and that he had written to him asking for his help. He told Canaris that I was being penalized for father's actions during the War, and he wanted to know if Canaris could say something to somebody in the right place. I needed this job with you Americans really badly; we were worried that our past was going to prevent it. Now you tell me I was worrying needlessly, that your people were not going to perform a background check on me. That makes sense now. I can see where my father might have told me that just to make me feel better."

"Countess, getting back to the point. I think Canaris has kept tabs on your father. He certainly is in the right position to do so. I think he is still associated with some kind of inside German group working with our CIA. I think he might be waiting for a sign the three of you are planning to leave Morocco. When you do, he is going to be all over you like a cold sweat. He might even be aware of your association with me. He knows you need me. And I have it figured out; you want me to marry you and leave the service. And you know what else I'm thinking? This guy Canaris is still a Nazi. And like your father, he hasn't changed much. Who knows what he will use your money for if he gets his hands on it. And if I helped you with your plans, we would both be in more trouble than we ever dreamed possible."

CHAPTER 13
SOUTH OF THE RIFF HILANDS, 1954

Camped almost four hundred miles south and east of the Riff, close by the windward side of the mighty Atlas Mountains, hunkered down in the desert near the foothills, the small contingent of Americans waited out one of the major Siroccos endemic to this part of the world. The Riff Massive came to be known to Broadway theatre goers in the twenties, and to a larger audience of movie attendees in the late thirties. The medium for bringing this about was Sydney Romberg's musical production of *The Desert Song*. Stage, screen, and later television, capitalized on the romance of the area and liberally mixed it with the whimsy of fiction. Twenty six years after the movie appeared, live television would present a remake starring the popular romantic singer Nelson Eddy.

But to Don Eckert and his men, there was nothing at all romantic or Broadway-like about a wind storm with temperatures of one hundred and ten degrees Fahrenheit and climbing. The Tureg inhabitants of the Sahara have a saying: When men are trapped in sand storms of the Sirocco, even murder can be condoned. And these storms lasted sometimes for days at a time.

Eckert's men knew the Sirocco well, as did the desert tribes. The natives saw the wind as an experience in survivorship. But the gung-ho Eckert viewed it differently. Instead of hiding under the protection of a tarp and consuming endless jerry cans of drinking water, of which there was a shortage, Eckert gave the order to move out. Exactly where they were going no one knew, not even Lieutenant Raymond, his second in command.

They were in old Foreign Legion country, which was completely devoid of greenery. Five miles back they had passed a Legion fortress, dating back to the fictional *Zunderneuff* of *Beau Geste* fame. The fortress was made of pounded mud that was slowly but surely eroding away to dust. But had any of them been appraised of the unique history of the area, they would have been anything but impressed or even remotely interested; their only concern was survival. Water, or the shortage of it, was the problem. And it was not unique to them; it was shared by any other desert wanderer caught in this moisture sapping Sirocco.

The captain called for the lieutenant the team navigator. He asked him to show him on the map where they were. Then he asked him to take up a new magnetic heading, one that would place them deeper into the foothills and farther from water.

When they had traveled about three hours, he ordered the column to halt and to take cover. The wind subsided somewhat as it grew dark. But it would freshen again, if freshen is the word, in the morning. It blew all night; and at midnight the temperature was 118 degrees Fahrenheit. It was hotter than any of them had ever experienced it at midnight anywhere. One of the airmen said he had seen it hotter in Baker, California, on the road to Death Valley at high noon. But that was at noon and not at midnight. And for what it was worth, he did not think it got this hot at midnight in Death Valley or anywhere else.

This was nothing, commented one of the master sergeants. He said he had seen pictures of German tank crews during the War frying eggs on top of track protectors on Tiger Panzers in Libya. Whereupon one of the younger men asked the cook if he would attempt to duplicate the feat at lunch tomorrow. He said he wanted to take a picture of the event for his grandkids. They all had a laugh, even the captain, who had been reticent and withdrawn for the past several days.

They were in no immediate danger, providing the wind did not go on too much longer, and if their water held out. There is one thing we can be thankful for, said one of them: "We don't have any camels to worry about."

Then began a general discussion of camels and their humps, and how long and how far they could go without water. Several of them backed their opinions with supposed conversations with Bedouins they had met on the edge of the Sahara, while others had talked about the subject with Berbers south of Agadir. And another quoted one of the Blue People from further into the Sahara. This led to another all-out friendly debate about who knew the most about survival in the desert, the Blues, the Bedouins, the Turegs or the war-like Berbers. It was generally conceded that the Arabs knew little about anything. They were thought of as city dwellers and rug merchants, a term of derision among the hardy, peoples of the desert, and also to the new American Desert Rats as well.

Eckert, who had been listening to the conversation, smiled to himself. He rather suspected none of the native desert dwellers could speak English well enough to discuss much of anything. And his Arab interpreters could speak little more of their dialects than could his men. Still, with a few common words and a lot of pointing and gesturing, a rudimentary form of communication was possible. And when it came down to this, his men had become experts.

Chow that night was a canteen cup half-full of water and a K ration. This kind of prepared staple was a left-over antique from the last War. Much like Hard Tack, the supplementary food of the trenches in the First War was eaten by infantrymen on bivouac until late in the thirties.

The following morning the wind had died down, but it was still hot. The area was still under a high pressure system, causing a right rotation around the isobars. The flow was off the Sahara, with the winds still paralleling the mountains.

Master Sergeant Steven Busby had been walking outside the camp just after dawn. The dust and blowing sand had cleared somewhat, and he was eagerly searching the ground and scanning the surrounding terrain with his binoculars. His glasses were part of his desert attire. They were usually seen hanging from a strap around his neck, and he seldom took them off-much like a gunfighter and his pistol back in the Old West–or *Feldmarshall* Erich Rommel, the Desert Fox. But his main interest now was not so much the horizon as it was the ground around the bivouac area.

"Lieutenant" he called out softly, as he neared his sleeping form under a large personal tarp. His voice was just audible above the wind. He was interested in waking the officer and not the men sleeping nearby.

Lieutenant Ralph Raymond had alternated between discarding his water proof canvass cover, which protected him from the blowing sand, and leaving it off in a futile attempt at getting some relief from the devastating heat. Early in the morning, he had decided it was better to be protected from the wind and the sand then it was to try and get a little cooler. As dawn broke over the Atlas and the wind subsided a little, exhaustion overtook him and he fell into a deep sleep.

The sergeant knew this. But even under the circumstances, he did not hesitate to awaken him. "Lieutenant," he said, "I have to talk to you."

As he said it, he gently shook him. Under other circumstances, Busby would not have touched the officer unless he had been ordered to do so. But clearly this was no ordinary circumstance.

"We have to talk; it's very important." He let the officer wake up, and when he was sure he was coherent enough to understand him, he said it again.

"Wake up, sir...please. I have to talk to you now."

"What's up, Steve?" he said, as he turned over.

Raymond was an affable fellow with an even personality. He was not given to peaks of emotion. Stable was the word that best described him. And slow to anger, and maybe slow to react in a crisis might also describe his personality. The sergeant had summed him up this way months ago. And to date, he had not seen anything that might have changed his mind. He liked him, but when it was necessary to get a job done quickly or where a leader was necessary in a crisis, he much preferred somebody like the captain. But that is exactly what he had come to talk to him about. There was no captain; he had vanished.

"Come with me a moment, if you will...please." Raymond knew the sergeant was not given to histrionics of any kind. If he wanted him to get up and take a walk before the sun was fully up, then he had a good reason.

"Where to?"

"Just away from camp. I don't want the others to hear." Raymond could not imagine what was so important that they had to talk, even before he had taken a leak.

The thought occurred to him as they were walking downwind of the others, who were showing no signs of having been disturbed. What must some of the planners be thinking? He had heard some crackpot had written a paper at one of the military schools, wherein he advocated integrating the sexes. The purpose was to increase the size of the services, following a proposed discarding of the draft. What would some of them do right now if women were present? What would a woman do? As far as he was concerned, the entire world was a man's latrine. While a women…they would probably have to carry along one of those portable toilets you see on construction sites. The thought of toting around something like that on a truck brought a smile to his face. But since he was in the lead, the sergeant could not see him. He thought it was funny, and he figured Busby would think so, too. But then Busby's demeanor, when he awakened him indicated this was not the time for joking around. The Sergeant was all business, and he had no time for frivolity. Still, it was funny. Maybe, Raymond thought, he would save it for another time.

He turned his head and asked the sergeant if they had come far enough. Then he realized something out of the ordinary. The sergeant was carrying his map cases and navigational instruments.

"Lieutenant, the captain left in the middle of the night, and he has not come back."

Raymond caught the hesitation in his voice when he said left. He knew he almost said deserted. That is what he meant, anyway. He meant Eckert had left intentionally, and he was not expected to come back

"Why do you say left?" Raymond asked the question with a hint of disapproval in his voice. The other term was more to the point and more expressive. But neither of them said it, although they both knew what the other was thinking.

"Check your map case, sir. See if the extra map and compass are gone."

A quick forage through his belongings caused Raymond to

look up with a perplexed look on his face. But all he said was, "Right."

He asked the sergeant: "What do you make of it, Steve?" In reality he was asking himself. They both knew or thought they knew, but neither wanted to be the first to spell it out.

"Are you suggesting this is a repeat?" Before Busby could answer, he asked him "How far away is it?"

When away from the captain and the men, Raymond often called Busby by his first name. They had become good friends in the past few months, although neither of them would admit it. These kinds of things happened all the time between different ranks, and between officers of different ranks. Sometimes a senior would refer to a junior by his first name; but it was considered gauche for the reverse to happen. They were closer than their own kin at times; however, rules of courtesy prevailed. These customs were as old as the services themselves, and they tended to strengthen the bond among them.

"What do you think happened then. I mean, is it the same as the last time? What do the men say happened? I need to know. I know you don't want to cast any dispersion on our commanding officer. And under different circumstances, I wouldn't want to hear your answer to such a question. But now I need to know what you think. I obviously have to make a decision, and I want your opinion."

Busby sat down on a nearby boulder. He started to hem and haw before he settled down. He had a slow Western drawl, and he was not given to rushing into things before he had taken the time to think them through. This was even truer of him when he was talking to an officer. He had learned a long time ago that you better have your facts straight when briefing one of them. They were all alike in this respect. Give one of them some bad poop, and if he briefed one of his superiors and got himself into trouble, then you were in deeper yogurt than he was. It did not matter how well you knew each other, they could forget that in an instant. That is why he was hesitant to speak now.

"Sir,…I, ah…"

"I know what you're thinking, and what they're saying," Raymond interrupted him. "You all believe he was caught shacking up with Sheikh Abby's daughter, don't you?"

Abby, as they called him, was the nickname of the Caid in the Tiskrit oasis district to the southwest. He was a Berber chieftain with several hundred war-like tribesmen at his disposal. His name was Sheikh Abdul dar el Mohammad Ben Hadj. The Hadj at the end of all of this, if you ever got that far, and if you could remember it all, was held in very high regard. It meant he had gone to Mecca on a pilgrimage. And in the days of his youth, it meant walking or riding a camel. Sometimes it took more than a year to accomplish.

At times he was known among his people as el Hadj, meaning The Pilgrim. When the name was used in his presence, it pleased him. It conferred on him the respect due his exalted rank.

Eckert, who was quick to understand the meaning of the term, used it on every occasion he could find without appearing to ingratiate himself with his eminence. He used it much as he did the term general when in the presence of a general officer. Somebody, years ago, told him generals liked to be called general, and he had never forgotten the advice.

The Shiekh looked forward to Eckert's frequent visits. He was most impressed with the young officer and his quick wit. He liked to beat him at chess, even when he suspected Eckert might be giving him the advantage from time to time. This did not detract from the esteem in which he held the officer. The Shiekh saw it as a tactical move, one calculated to do Eckert some personal good. And the Shiekh admired the politician in the man. He saw him as one who was interested in getting his job done; he admired a man who was interested in getting on in the world. He liked him so much, he started thinking of him as one of his own. He had several sons Eckert's age, and he did not like any of them nearly as well. Then, too, the thousands of dollars Eckert brought him from time to time helped him along in his decision to someday make him his son.

That is what made the incident so outrageous and provoking when it did happen. Captain Donald Eckert was believed by the Sheikh, and his entire tribe, to be an infidel. The Sheikh saw this as an accident of birth, and it could be overlooked in certain circumstances. But he had also broken a taboo, one they were hesitant to talk about. He had accepted the hospitality of the Sheikh's tent, and then he had sought out and slept with his younger daughter. Not only was she young, but she was a virgin to boot. All the *fatimas* in charge of her upbringing and schooling swore to that. And el Hadj believed them. And when he was told of the violation of his daughter, and the affrontry to his hospitality, he threatened to kill Eckert on sight.

"You think he slipped away in the night and returned to Abby's camp, don't you," said Raymond.

"Sir," said Busby, " I don't know what else to think. I surely don't think they came in here in the middle of the night and swiped him and a jeep from right under our noses. Still, I wouldn't rule it out. If Abby wanted him badly enough, he just might try it. And who wants to argue that he doesn't want him awfully bad."

"I never heard a thing after three. I was awake until then. But after that I think I zonked out. How about you?" he asked Busby.

Busby answered: "I think the way the wind was howling, he could have snatched him at most any time. But you're right, early in the morning would probably have been the time it happened, if it happened at all. In a way, I would like to think that's what did happen. I don't want to believe he got the hots for her again and took off. Let me see the map. How far did you say it was to his camp?"

"About two hundred miles. Do you think he could have gone there for water?" Raymond's reply was little more than conversation, and he knew it. But he had to say something. He was unwilling to believe the captain had deliberately abandoned them after bringing them this far out of the way of a known source of water. Still, that is where they were, and that is how they got here. And there was no sense in trying to come up with a reason.

There was no excuse for his leaving, none at all, and Raymond was planning to put it in his report just that way. And the more he thought about it, the angrier he was becoming.

"The question now, Lieutenant, do we go home or do we go to Abby's place and try to find him? I don't like the idea of just going off and leaving him. There has to be a reason why he left. It doesn't make sense he would just take off."

"Take off to where, and for what purpose?" Raymond asked him.

"There are only two places he could have gone," Busby said, frowning. "He could have gone back to the base or he could have gone to Abby's. He didn't go down to the corner for a beer–that's for sure. The extra jerry cans of gas and water on the truck are all accounted for. So wherever he did go in the jeep, he has not gone any further than the cans he was carrying. He can get water at Abby's, but not gas."

"He can also get shot by one of Abby's boys, too," Raymond replied.

"Steve, I want to change the subject for a minute. That's all the time we have before the others start rousting around. Look, I have something to say to you and I want to ask you to forget it as soon as you hear it, if you know what I mean."

Busby nodded his head in the affirmative; Raymond could see him clearly now in the dim light of the blowing sand.

"For some time now," Raymond began, "I've suspected we're not out here for the sole purpose we think we are. Oh, what we're doing is for a purpose, all right; I've never doubted it for a minute. But I've thought now for a long time about there being more to it than scouting-out future radar sites. I've seen the captain reading technical manuals. You knew he keeps them in his foot locker. And they have nothing what-so-ever to do with our radar equipment. It's just a hunch, but I think it has something to do with an abandoned base to the north and east of here.

"I know the existence of a mystery base around here someplace is just a rumor," Raymond continued, "but I can't get it out of my head. If there is such a place, it has something to do with us. I have nothing factual to base this hunch on. But I have watched the captain poring over the maps and searching the horizon like he is looking for a familiar landmark. Maybe I'm reading something into this now, I don't know. I hope not."

"I've heard the rumor. What if this place is for real? Now you're running the show, where will we go?" Busby spoke in his slow drawl as he searched for some indication in Raymond's face that he might have some kind of plan.

The lieutenant looked at Busby silhouetted against the rising sun and wondered what he was really thinking. Then Raymond said: "What if what we're doing is just an excuse for being here? What if we're playing a kind of high-stakes chess game with the Russians? And what if our real purpose is not what we think, but a kind of gambit to keep the Russians guessing, while the captain observes whatever it is he is supposed to observe and then reports back what's going on out here? I think by report I mean he reports to a contact, who reports back to whomever."

Busby nodded his head, indicating he understood. Raymond went on to say: "What if Washington suspects the Russians have occupied this base, the one I'm talking about? Now, if that just happens to be the real reason we're here, it makes for another possibility. I mean, it might be another explanation for where he went. Just what if he went up there under the cover of the storm to check on something? What if he knows more than we do? What if he has inside information the Russians are here, and maybe with their MIGs, too? There's no reason why he would have told us, is there...?"

Busby stopped him to ask a question.

Raymond interrupted him: "Just a second Steve," he said, not wanting his train of thought disrupted. "What if the Russians and not Abby have him. And what if we go storming into Abby's place and spook the camp. There's going to be one big complaint just like the last time. And we're going to have the French army or the Foreign Legion on top of us—that's for sure. And no captain to show for our trouble."

Busby nodded in agreement. And then broke into a knowing smile that Raymond couldn't see in the blowing sand. But all of a sudden it struck them both as though somebody had turned a light bulb on in both of their heads at the same time.

"You know, Steve, I never did believe the nonsense about him and Abby's daughter. When was the last time, or the first time for that matter, that you heard of an American getting close to a native woman. Only in the movies. And I'll tell you something else, the captain is not noted for being a swordsman, right? The story about this Berber girl is something that's really out of the ordinary. Not only is she way off limits, but he just isn't the kind of guy to try something with her. Forget how dumb an idea it is. Dumb or not, he is just not likely to be that interested. I just know this. I have felt it in my bones from the very beginning.

"And when did he see her?" Raymond went on with his address to the one man jury.

"Have you seen her? And when the French Army interfered and got him investigated for a courts-martial, how come with all that power trying to get him in trouble, how come the whole thing was dropped? Why wasn't he at least relieved of his job? I'll tell you it looks mighty fishy to me, and it always has. No. I don't believe he ever had anything to do with her. Abby cooked it up. And I'll tell you something else–he did it to get us run out of the area."

"But why?" Busby asked him.

"Let's go back to the Russians and the base up there. If that's where he went, he had to suspect the Russians might be there or he wouldn't have gone. If they are, then they must have something to do with Abby and his accusations. I know the captain was in good with the sheikh. I know it, but I also know these guys have a history of being best friends with the one who pays them the most. Now, just suppose the Russians are operating in this area, and Eckert was sent here to spy on them and they know it. Why wouldn't they take some kind of action to get us out of here? And who better to do it for them then Abby. I know there are a lot of ifs, but what else have we got? Nothing else makes any sense," he said, with a frown on his face.

Busby looked at him rather incredulously, but after a few seconds he turned and looked at the ground, thinking. And then, finally, he lifted his head up into the blowing sand and nodded agreement.

"What are we going to do Lieutenant?"

Raymond answered: "It's roughly two hundred miles to

Abby's camp, and another seventy-five or so north to Agadir. We can get water at Abby's and fuel in Agadir. The alternative would be to head directly west over the mountains to the coast road, and then turn north to Mogador on the way north to Casablanca. But can we find a road or a trail over the mountains?"

"I've been thinking the same thing," Busby said. "And I agree with what you're thinking; we wouldn't have enough fuel to get to Mogador, even if we could reach the highway. And we both know nobody is going to sell us gas for government chits before we get there. And we don't have enough francs left among the lot of us to buy a dozen gallons. And they won't take military script this far away from a city; they have no way of cashing it in."

"All right, let's make up our minds and then get on the road. We've a long way to go, and we're going to be mighty thirsty come noontime. This is what I think we should do," Raymond said. "See if you agree."

Busby hated it when he did this. *If he is the leader then he should lead*, he thought. They had in effect agreed on a course of action. Now it was the lieutenant's place to sum it all up and issue instructions, not ask him his opinion and then start all over again. *Too bad, he has everything going for him-education, military bearing, and the rest of it. But he's not decisive. He has a hard time making up his mind. He knows what to do, he just hesitates to do it for fear he is gong to make a mistake. And that's eventually going to be his downfall.*

"Can I make a suggestion?" Busby asked him.

"Shoot."

"Let's get moving on a course toward Abby's place. Think over what you want us to do, and then tell me while we're moving. I'll drive the jeep. The two guys in the rear can't hear us if you don't want them to. When we've ironed out the kinks in your plan, I'll brief the men at the first stop"

Busby emphasized the words your plan. So far, though, he had done all the planning. And he expected most of the real thinking in the future was going to be his to do.

He was smart, as most senior non-commissioned officers were. Most of them have a way of getting officers to do pretty much what they want done. Most officers know when they are being manipulated, if they are, but they usually do not mind. That is, the smarter ones who get the job done do not mind.

Two hours later, Busby gathered his men in the protection of one of the carryalls. He knelt in the sand with a stick in his hand for a pointer. He drew a map while the others looked on, eager now to find out where they were going, but more eager to find out when they were going to get some fresh water.

"The lieutenant has our position roughly here. He won't know for sure until he can get a noon shot with his aviator's sextant. But we are pretty sure we're about eleven hours away from Tiskret and the Berber oasis."

The men looked at each other. None of them wanted to return there for a while. They had stirred up a hornet's nest the last time, and it was not too long ago, either. And they would just as soon see it calm down before they went back. However, none of them interrupted to ask a question. They looked at each other, but none of them objected. They needed water, and if Abby and his horsemen were going to give them any trouble, then it was going to be his problem. They had several cases of dynamite left over from their survey work, and the lieutenant had his side arm. Then there was the machine gun, which could be broken out and installed on the jeep mount.

Resistance by the Berbers, from strictly a military viewpoint, was fruitless; everybody knew this, and so did the Berbers. There would be no objections from them if the Americans insisted on approaching their water. Under those circumstances, they would give them all they could carry. But riding into their camp behind a machine gun was going to cause another incident. Walking in pretending to be friends might be even worse, and there might be violence if they did. But it was not going to be their problem. If it was going to cause another incident involving the French, then it was going to be a problem for the Pentagon. Right now, their immediate concern was water and hot food and some decent shelter.

"Lieutenant, come here a minute." Raymond had waited until after dark to join his men. The sheikh had insisted they camp outside his perimeter. He was not afraid of them, he just did not want to appear to be close friends any longer. Tribal hospitality dictated he invite Raymond to dinner. However, that is as far as he intended to go.

Sheikh Abby was cordial enough, but only just as far as custom required him to be. He did not want somebody reporting to somebody else about how he had grown to be friends with Raymond in the same way he had with Eckert. Raymond was not invited to inspect his prized horses or to play chess after the meal. Abby had been told by Eckert that Raymond played a fair game. But Abby did not care for a game with Raymond. So when the meal was over, with scarcely a dozen words spoken between them, Raymond excused himself with the customary belch and left the tent.

"Lieutenant, come over here out of earshot of Abby's sentry."

"What's up, Sarge?" It was apparent Busby had been waiting for him since before nightfall.

"Come over here and bring a flashlight. Over here, shine

your light about ten feet over that way. Can you see it?"

"Yeah," said Raymond. The wind had blown the top layer of sand away, and underneath was the hard imprint of a truck tire.

"What do you think?" Busby asked him. "Is it one of ours?"

"It could be our truck, but it's riding on their tires. Look at that tread. Where did you ever see an American tread with diamonds in it?" he asked.

Their trucks were unreliable, of shoddy construction and they frequently broke down. Both of them knew the Russians preferred driving American equipment, which was given to them in great quantities during the War.

"The Russians have been here, and not too long ago," said Raymond.

"Do you think we ought to pull out before sun-up? I don't want to wait for Abby to change his mind and stage another Eckert raped my daughter thing."

Busby looked at him, but did not bother to answer or to nod his head.

Raymond said: "I'm not sure I have everything figured out. I'm not so sure Abby isn't playing a move ahead of us. There's one thing we can be sure of though…"

"What's that?" Busby interrupted him to ask.

They had been standing in the moonlight talking for about ten minutes when they observed a figure standing in the shadows. He was a Berber in native dress. His face was shielded with an extension of his wound turban.

The figure moved toward them while they stood watching-spellbound. Neither of the two Americans spoke. Finally, when it became apparent he was approaching them to talk, Busby stopped him with the usual greeting. They both could see his ceremonial dagger was still in the scabbard and his hands were down at his sides.

Busby spoke in a low voice: "*le bes a' lieke.*"

The figure replied with a curt "*le bes.*"

"What do you want?" Busby asked, hoping he could speak English because neither he nor Raymond spoke enough Arabic or French to carry on much of a conversation.

"Never mind," he whispered in perfect English. "Your friend is not here. Be careful. Get out of here, now! *Immishi!*"

"Who are you?" Raymond asked."Are you CIA? Where is Boulhaut, do you know? Is there such a place?"

"There is, but you have no business there."

"Did Eckert go there?" he wanted to know."

"I said, *immishi*. You know what it means. Now get out of here before I shoot you both." With that, he turned around and moved back into the shadows of the dust-colored moon.

"Lieutenant, let's get the hell out of here and up the road to Agadir. Maybe we can get food and gas for our watches when we get there. Then let's go find the captain. What do you say, sir?"

Busby was visibly shaken by the encounter. This is something they had not bargained for. They had just met a real man. This was not a movie-type spy; both of them recognized a man on a mission, and one who had the potential for violence of the worst kind to get what he wanted.

"I'm with you," Raymond said. "What do you think about the two of us leaving straight from Agadir and going to look for that base? You send the others home and tell them to keep their mouths shut about the captain. Don't tell them where we're headed. Tell them if we're not back in two weeks to report the entire incident to the provost marshal. Tell them under no circumstances are they to say anything to anybody until then.

"I want to get him back," Raymond went on to say, "and I want to make it look as though this incident never happened. If the captain is any way involved in what I think might be going on, then nobody at Nouassuer has any business knowing. And another thing, if we let it out what we think, and it turns out to be true or nearly true, I've got a gut feeling I'm in some way going to be in big trouble."

Busby was surprised that Raymond did not ask his opinion. But he wished he had not said what he did about becoming involved. Whatever was going on, they were all involved, whether they liked it or not. If Eckert was involved in some kind of an undercover operation, unbeknownst to them, and the Air force in some way became embarrassed, then they were all in trouble for not figuring it out and telling somebody. The Inspector General, who usually investigated these kinds of things, had a peculiar habit of implicating innocent bystanders. They both knew this, but neither said anything.

But they were between a rock and a hard spot. They were torn between reporting Eckert's absence and causing an investigation into something that might be classified need to know. On the other hand, if they kept it to themselves and they screwed up, and especially if somebody got hurt, they might cause an international incident.

There was an on-shore flow of cool air moving in off the ocean at Agadir. The day was going to dawn bright, with no threat of blowing sand. Raymond commented in passing about how he was glad they had weathered still another of the horrendous Siroccos.

They had driven two miles up the beach to a secluded inlet they knew. And while it was still dark, they went for a swim. At first they wore their clothes, lathering them up as best they could and then washing them in the surf. Then they took them off and washed themselves. They were planning to change into dry clothes and hang the others from the gun mount. In the wind they dried quickly, and much of the salt was blown away. It was not a satisfactory way to wash clothes, but it would have to do. There was no time to find a proper laundry.

They had two cups of French coffee, heavily laced with chicory, and two croissants at a roadside diner and gas station. They also ordered *sanwi jambon* in lieu of eggs, which were not available, and then sat back and relaxed for a few minutes.

"Who do you think that guy was, and why did he tell us to stay away from Boulhaut? He obviously knew the captain. Do you think he is the captain's contact?" Busby was nervous, and he asked the questions of Raymond in rapid fire.

"I think Eckert could tell us if he were here and if he would" Raymond replied. He was still very agitated with the whole situation—and particularly with Eckert. He knew there was no way he was going to avoid trouble. And he knew it was going to, somehow, affect his recent application for a regular commission. And although he tried to hide his feelings from Busby, he was afraid the sergeant saw through him.

Busby had nothing really to lose, and in spite of himself, Busby was beginning to enjoy the intrigue. The whole thing had taken on a kind of adrenaline-producing air, the same way a Western movie had when he was a boy. He had grown bored with the never-ending travel—with the constant bivouacs—and the primitive living was beginning to take its toll on his otherwise, good disposition. Now, for the first time in months, things were less monotonous and more to his liking. It showed in his face. And Raymond knew he was starting to enjoy himself, and the lieutenant became more agitated at the thought.

Out of sight of any prying eyes, they stopped the jeep, and laid the maps on the hood. Raymond started to plot a course back into the mountains.

The men had been ordered by Busby to return to base, and

now they were alone.

Raymond made a couple of false starts. He could not get Eckert out of his mind and the trouble he might have caused. He started again and then stopped, uttering several strong curse words. It was obvious he intended to get something straight with his commander the next time he saw him, if ever he did. But Busby knew how he felt and what he intended to do. He also knew he would never say anything to him personally about the captain. And he was glad of that.

It did not take a genius to realize that if the Russians were at Boulhaut they would not care to have the world know. If Eckert had been sent by somebody to check to see, and if the Russians caught him, it was for sure they were not going to feed him a hot meal and turn him loose with their blessings. Both of them knew how somebody like Eckert could vanish into these wastelands without a trace. And the Russians need not do it either. The Russians need not kill him, not necessarily. The Bedouins or Turegs would do it without blinking an eye, for a price. And the Russians would jump at the chance to turn him over to them, just to acquire his jeep, if for no other reason. It would be just one more in their inventory for some officer to later sell. After all, American material left behind from the War was to be seen in towns from Tunis in the north to Timbuktu in the desert. And some desert chieftain would pay a lot of money, or he would provide a lot of favors to somebody who would arrange for him to get his hands on one.

"How do you spell this phantom base?" Busby asked.

" 'Boulhaut,' is the way, I think. To tell you the truth I don't know. It's spelled 'Bullo' if you spell it phonetically. But that's Italian and not Arabic or French. I don't know whether my way is right. And you can bet the Arabs won't recognize the name, even if they're sitting right on top of it. And of course the Russians will have their own way of spelling it and pronouncing it, too. This is worse than looking for a needle in a haystack."

He spit out the words, and cursed again, using another four-letter word common to the language of the barracks. But Raymond was a gentleman, and although he spoke Army Creole fluently, he seldom used this kind of language in the presence of enlisted men. This was just one more thing not written down in a book, but understood. Maybe among officers of his own rank he would not hesitate to use it, but never around women or senior officers, and never around enlisted personnel either.

"Do you think we ought to look for the base first or for him? How do you plan to proceed?" Busby knew what needed to be done, but he thought he would give the officer a chance to respond before he told him how things were going to be.

In a way Busby liked working for Raymond, who never imposed his will on him. It gave him a lot of latitude to operate, and it encouraged him to think. Busby liked that. And Raymond understood. He was not lazy. It was just that he understood Busby. And he would give him his head and act on his suggestions just as long as he did not screw up. He knew this was not management by the book, but he did not care. And who was to say which way was best anyway.

They left a valuable camera as a pawn for the food and several jerry cans full of gasoline. Most of it they gave to the men in the carryall. But there were still several cans left over-enough to see them to the mountains and back and then some. And they had plenty of water, enough to last them longer than two weeks. They had acquired two clay water jugs from the gas station. One of them they wrapped up against breakage; the other one they filled with water from one of the water cans They suspended it from the machine gun mount in the back so it would not break when they hit a bump. Water seeped through the pot and stayed wet on the outside. Evaporation from the moving jeep and the hot sun kept the water cool.

From the same vendor, they bought a dozen liters of paraffin. This fuel was high-grade kerosene, which they burned in their Primus stoves. The Primus was a simple unit, preferred by the Arabs. It could cook or heat water one pan at a time. It was so simple it worked reliably. And because of this, and the fact that a liter would burn almost forever, they preferred it to the one the military issued.

Raymond remarked to Busby as they prepared to move out: "I think we ought to approach Marrakech from the back side. I mean we ought to go east from here and then swing north and back again west. Here, take a look. See where the road heads out again to the north and to the east? See, here by El Kela'a Srarhna? I want to continue east about another twenty miles or so from there and then get lost out in the wilderness. I mean I want to stay out of sight for a few days. We'll rest up and look around. I want to find a shepherd kid or run into a caravan coming down out of the mountains. I want to talk to somebody who is not on the take of any Russians, if they are in the area.

"Then too, this route to the east side of Marrakech will give us a better chance of meeting traveling Arabs than will the coastal highway."

Busby listened to him with some surprise. He had obviously made a plan to locate the base if it really existed. And he had not relied on him to do any of the planning. This showed progress.

"Do you think we'll be able to communicate with any of them?"

"I think we can," Raymond said, "with a sand map and a stick. That plus our pigeon French. Oh, and don't forget the usual non-touristy phrases in Arabic, you know the ones that always brings a smile to their faces."

"Do you have anything in mind? I mean, why this location to do the reconnoitering?" Busby asked him.

"Look here," Raymond said, as he pointed to a line on the map. "See this river, the 'Quam er Ribia.' It pours into a large lake. And if I'm not mistaken, the lake is called Boollo or something that sounds like it. I heard Eckert mention it several months back, before you joined our team. Eckert is something of a fisherman, I guess. He was always talking about trout. But he said bass were just as good. Anyway, he had a pole and some tackle he carried. One of the men asked him about it one day, and he told him he might drown some worms if he found the time. The airmen asked him if there were mountain lakes where we were going, and he said the one he had in mind was fed by a fairly large river. Nobody paid any attention to him at the time. We never had any free time, and we didn't expect to have any, at least not for going off someplace fishing.

"We were camped on high ground about twenty miles from the village of el Kelia'a Srarhna a couple of months later. We tested a portable unit there. As I recall, we were about two weeks calibrating the instruments. About half-way through our stay, Eckert decided to go fishing. He found the lake he had been talking about on the map about twenty or so miles to the north west. One of our Arab boys told him it was good fishing. The boy said it was loaded with fish because the Arabs never found the leisure time to fish. I remember he told Eckert the name of the place. It also sounded something like Boulhaut.

"The mountains ranging to our south east about a hundred or so miles are shown on the map as the *Haut Atlas*." Raymond continued. "It's part of the Atlas chain. What does *haut* mean to you in French?"

"I don't know. How about classy or hot?"

"No, *chaud* is hot. I think *haut* means more like big or

popular or something. I think an area or town or a lake named Boulhaut would tend to mean an in or popular lake. A number one or large lake. That's what I think anyway."

"How about high as in high fashion or high cuisine or high mountains?" Busby commented.

"Okay, I'll go along with that," Raymond said. Then he paused for a moment and looked down at the map again before speaking.

"My point, if I have one, is simply this: Boulhaut lake might be named after a town not shown on the map where this mystery base was built by our guys. The only thing that makes me think twice about what I just said is: Why would they build an installation so far from anyplace? What are the troops going to do for recreation? It's seventy-five miles to Marrakech to the south, and somewhere around a hundred and fifty to Casablanca in the north. It doesn't make sense."

"Maybe that's why they abandoned the sucker," Busby said, with a smile.

The two of them slept most of the next day and part of the next night. They arose around midnight, ate a couple of K rations, and set out in the jeep. They had not seen anyone close by since they left the main road, so they had all but abandoned the idea of talking to somebody walking along the road or working in a field. They figured if they ran into somebody any time soon, they would probably be traveling with a caravan.

"I want to come across some Arabs who are familiar with the lake area. If we can give their kids some rations or something, we may be able to talk to them for a few minutes." Raymond said.

They had been traveling through more foothills. The land was not too productive, although they did see an occasional herd of goats. And everywhere the fields were full of wild poppies. Twice in the distance they saw Berber tents. They were large and made of black canvas. And they were big enough to walk around in. Once they saw a woman kneeling at an open fire. When she saw them, she covered her face and ran into the tent. They both knew they were not going to get any information from her. And if they trespassed on her land, the males of her family could be expected to react. The last thing they wanted was an incident of any kind. They really wanted to meet a boy who was cooperative. From experience, they knew the younger males usually spoke French, and once in a while they spoke some English.

They thought about giving the kid a ride in exchange for information. The ideal would be to find a male teen who had been around a little, give him some food, and let him drive the jeep. Once they were big buddies they would get him to tell them about anything they wanted. They had used this technique in Berber country before and it always worked. Young males were crazy about driving a jeep.

It was well after midnight. They had been wandering around for the better part of two hours and had not seen anything. They thought they may have started too late. Arabs usually travel with their produce early at night. They arrive at the market place after mid-night for an early start in the morning. They sell their goods and then spend their money on things they need in order to live. They rest up and start back the next day. They don't usually travel in daylight either way, although the team had come on a few moving caravans on lesser-traveled roads during the day. The reason for this is because they believe they can better be seen by drivers at night. They use small mules for pack animals, with camels bringing up the rear. They attach red kerosene lanterns to the saddle of the rear camel, and then tie a reflector to its tail. When you come on a caravan at night, you can see it from a long distance. And when you get closer, you can see the reflector swinging back and forth as they walk along.

Raymond said: "Let's take another look. Let's pick out a town of some size and then go find a road to stake out about ten miles from the place. The only two lakes shown on the map are over in this direction." He pointed with his flashlight to the cross-road up ahead, and a body of water some thirty miles distant.

"Another thing," he remarked to Busby, "we should pay more attention to the topography of the map. Our people aren't dumb enough to pick out a mountainous area for a jet aircraft landing field. This base has to be somewhere on a plateau or flat ground. Flat ground can usually be found near a lake. On second thought, let's go toward this lake shown here on the map and check it out. We might also find caravans watering their stock there."

Why didn't I think of that, Busby said to himself.

They stopped about ten miles from the lake and slept until about an hour before dawn. Then they drove down the road toward the lake, and when they saw moonlight reflecting off the water, they stopped again.

"Take your knife and see if you can cut us a couple of fishing poles from the cane growing along the edge," Raymond said. "I'll see if I can find some string. No need to have a hook. We'll just carry the poles on our shoulders. If we see somebody, they'll never know the difference."

A half-hour later they almost stumbled on a dozen camels and an equal number of small Arab mules. The camels were lying down, and in the center of them was a small dung chip fire, smoldering. A coffeepot of hot water for morning tea was hanging from a metal tripod.

As they approached, the camels began to bay, setting up a terrible din. A voice was heard shouting in Arabic; they stopped their racket as though they were well-trained dogs. The Americans knew they would be witnesses to an unmerciful clubbing if the animals had continued on. Natives took reasonable care of their livestock, but they were harsh with them if they did not immediately respond to commands. It was almost as if they expected them to be able to reason.

Raymond nudged Busby, and Busby, who spoke the better of the few Arab words they knew, called out in the gathering light, *"le bes a lieke, le bes schwia, le bes um'd'Allah!"* He knew the greeting was way overdone. But it's the phrase he always used, and it always got the desired results. Other than Allah, he had no idea what the individual words meant. He also believed the words were slang and not taken from the Koran. Another breach of etiquette, which labeled him American and not one in the know.

Strangers seldom used a form of the language that was not in the Koran. Americans were not expected to know this. And furthermore, Americans did not go around stalking and robbing Arabs for the paltry little they might find. Being immediately recognized as an American allayed any fear the Arabs might have had of strangers approaching them. Busby knew this, and he did not hesitate to put on what he called his American act. He did not care to be mistaken for a Frenchman by calling out in French. A Frenchman would be expected to speak in French and not Arabic, a gesture calculated to remind the Arab of who really owned his country.

Americans who made an effort to speak their language always managed to please the Arabs. Then too, the Arabs usually smiled whether they were pleased or not. They reasoned that if a service of some kind was wanted, they might make some money. And another thing that endeared the Arab to the Americans, the Americans always over-paid or over-tipped for everything.

His limited Arab vocabulary now expended, Busby was prepared to switch to his limited French. Limited yes, but serviceable, after a fashion. Serviceable among the Arabs and Berbers, perhaps, but less so among the French themselves. The French prefer not to encourage conversation unless the speaker is proficient in their language. They are not usually interested in talking to visiting Americans, who, when left to their own devices, are noted for the fracturing of languages. The Americans left their mark on the German language after the War, and the French are not interested in the same thing happening to their proud Gaelic heritage. At one time, it was the language of diplomacy, and the one universally recognized as the world's common language. Now it has been replaced by English, the language of commerce and science. The French are jealous, and quite often they do not hesitate to show their displeasure by preferring not to speak to Americans when addressed in French. This makes them seem unfriendly, which many are not.

"Do you speak English?" Busby yelled to no one in particular. There was a long pause and then Busby called out again: *"Bon jour, Sil vous plait. Y-a-t-il quelqu'un ici qui parle anglais?"*

Someone answered: *"Je parle Francais un peu."*

" Je suis Americain," said Busby, in his thick accent.

As if the Arabs couldn't tell, thought Raymond. "Ask him where we are. Ask him what this lake is called in French?"

"Quel endroit est-ce?"

"Bullo" was the answer. And then some rapid French that neither of them understood.

"Parle lentment, sil vous plait." Busby asked him to speak slower.

Raymond was starting to breathe faster as he heard a word that sounded like Boulhaut. Busby looked at the lieutenant, who nodded his head in the affirmative. It was just getting light enough for him to see the expression on his face, which Busby interpreted to mean ask him the golden question.

"A quelle distance se trouve le Russi aerodrome? sil vous plait. Est-ce que cette route mene a?"

Raymond approved of his approach. He was not asking them as though he did not know there was such a place. He was acting as though he knew, but was confused as to where the base was and where the Russians were.

"A quelle cote c'est trouve?" Busby asked.

The Arab motioned to the road they had just came to the lake on, and then motioned it was on the other side of the lake. And then he pointed towards the rising sun and told them it was about ten kilometers in that direction.

Both of them thanked the group, which had now gathered around the Arab speaker. And since they had all the information they needed, they both smiled as Busby now evoked the blessings of Allah on the company. They turned and waved goodbye, leaving the Arabs with perplexed looks on their faces.

Here were two odd Americans appearing out of nowhere, apparently to go fishing, and then they walked off looking for some obscure Russians. The Arabs fully expected to be asked where the best fishing was to be found. They were ready to answer that it was good anyplace on the lake. All they had to do was wave their hand, meaning you could catch fish anyplace. Of course, this also meant if you had the time. But then, Americans always seemed to have an abundance of leisure time.

The Arab party started to discuss this as they began to busy themselves about the camp.

The Americans were an enigma to the Arabs. The Arabs saw them as being like spoiled little children in many ways. Still, their technology spoke worlds about them, little of which the Arabs understood. When the subject came up about this apparent paradox, which it did many times in their casual conversations, some one often said that only Allah understood these Americans.

Then one of the younger ones remarked about how one of his friends had seen an American airplane once with as many as ten engines. Six of them had propellers and four of them were *reaction*, he said. They all began to laugh at the perceived exaggeration, as if anything that large could actually fly. Raymond and Busby could hear them in the distance.

Busby told Raymond as they walked away: "The bastards think we're retarded, just because we'll pay the first price asked for a stupid rug. They don't even think we have sense enough to count our change correctly."

He had been told this by an Arab once, and he figured those they had just left thought the same thing. It was not only the Arabs, but the French who shared the same opinion, too, he told Raymond.

Raymond agreed with him completely.

An hour later found them approximately five miles to the east of the lake. They had mutually decided the best way to cross the river that fed the lake was to travel up river past the muddy delta.

The jeep had four-wheel-drive, and could go most anywhere without getting stuck. But Raymond told Busby he did not want to chance it; getting marooned out here was the last thing he wanted to happen. Then too, they could see there was a well-worn trail, maybe centuries old, that led along the river. Raymond was looking for a place to cross, one without a steep bank and with shallow water.

So far they had not seen such a place. They stopped to talk it over. They agreed if they found one, it would in all likelihood be a caravan crossing. And maybe, just maybe, if Eckert came this way he might have used it, too. Perhaps some Russians might have, if there were any in the neighborhood.

Another hour had taken them to the place used by the locals to cross the river. It was not the best, but it looked as though it might be the only place. Raymond showed Busby where the gradient lines on the chart were getting closer. It meant, he told him, the terrain was getting steeper and the river could be expected to get faster. If they did not try here they might not get another chance, he said.

They climbed out of the jeep, and they both began to look for tire tracks. They found none among the hundreds of hoof prints embedded in the mud.

The water was shallow enough that the engine exhaust was free of the water. The sturdy little jeep was built for combat in conditions just like this, and they had no trouble crossing. Neither of them even got his feet wet.

At noon they pulled over under a tree and ate two K rations apiece.

"Have you noticed, Lieutenant, how we've been climbing but also the ground is beginning to level out. Is it possible the river did this centuries ago?"

"Not only possible, but it's the only answer for where this valley came from. It had to be eroded by the river ages ago. Feel the soil. This was once a flood plain. I'll bet even now they get some flooding. That river is out of its banks in the spring, I would bet anything on it. What it means to us is that this valley is wide here, and for a long way up ahead."

They both looked at each other as if to say, if I was surveying the area for a place to build a decent runway, this is where I would look.

"I suggest we get up in the high country above the valley," Busby told the lieutenant. "If we don't, we might run smack into the runway or even into some Russians."

Busby continued: "We're spies as far as they're concerned.

We have no business being here, and we are in a military vehicle and in American uniforms. We're in plain sight right now, and I don't like it. I can see why Captain Eckert might have picked the sand storm as a good time to visit this place, if he was really looking for something here.

"I sure want to believe it anyway," Busby went on while the lieutenant listened. "It means he didn't leave us because he was getting fed up with the sand. He had a reason. But then maybe we're assuming too many things without knowing much about anything."

"I guess I agree with you," Raymond replied. "I think he was looking for the runway. I think he wanted to know how many airplanes were here, and their type. I'm almost positive he was reporting to somebody who was really interested–and for reasons neither of us can guess. I think somebody has been using us as guinea pigs. I mean we're out here primarily just so Eckert can keep his eyes on things.

"That guy back there at Abby's camp was no Berber," Raymond went on to say. "Oh, his mother and father were, but I bet he was CIA. And I'll bet you anything he is a graduate of one of those CIA eastern universities, just like Eckert. You knew that, didn't you? You knew Eckert came from and eastern school." He stopped for a minute, waiting for Busby to think over what he had just said. When there was no reply, he started again.

"And another thing, while we're on the subject. That Berber knew what he was talking about and warned us to stay away from here. Why do you think he was so insistent about us getting out of Abby's place? Abby is mad at Eckert, not you and me. And why did he use the word *'immishi?'* I'm not Arab, but it even makes me angry."

"It's an attention getter all right. I never saw an Arab who wasn't really insulted when he heard the word," Busby volunteered.

"What does it mean, anyway?"

"Scram, literally," Busby replied.

"Why would he warn us to stay away from here if Eckert was in danger. Unless Eckert was in some kind of jeopardy and we couldn't do anything about it?" Raymond asked. They both looked at each other. And then Busby spoke. And even before he said what he was thinking, Raymond nodded his head in the affirmative.

"Let's get out of here, Steve, I don't give a damn if there are no airplanes. There's a base all right, and Eckert has known it all along. And there are Russians here, too. The way the Arabs at the lake reacted when you mentioned Russi gave it away; they obviously were not trying to hide the fact. And did you notice the way they were quick to acknowledge the Russian's location when they thought we were in the know? That alone ought to tell us something."

"What are we going to do then, Lieutenant?"

"I'm through looking for him. The closer we get, the easier it is to spot us. And we're in a foreign country, and we don't want to get shot or end up missing in Lubyanka prison. He has been on his own and he still is.

"Let's get out of here right now," Raymond said again, as he started to walk toward the jeep. "Let's head for home, down the north side of the lake and west to the highway going north toward Casablanca. I want to get to the Provost Marshall or maybe the general. I want to find out what's going on before somebody drops a net over us."

They traveled that afternoon and most of the night, stopping only for brief periods and for two or three hours of sleep. The next afternoon, they pulled into the gate at Nouasseur. They were detained by the guard, who was seen to place a call on a field telephone.

"Lieutenant, I have orders to request you wait here for the officer of the day. What for I have no idea," he told Raymond. "And Sergeant, I have orders to place you under arrest."

Busby looked at Raymond with a pained expression. And with a gesture of his hands that said, Why me?

Raymond answered him: "Don't worry, Steve, they want me, too. He just doesn't have the authority to arrest me. That's why he is holding me for the O.D. or the Provost or both."

"Lieutenant, this is an Article 32 interrogation. In case you are not fully aware of what that is, it is part of a pre-trial investigation, which could ultimately end in court-martial charges being preferred against you." The officer who was speaking sat across the desk from him. Raymond recognized him as the base Judge Advocate.

Raymond said to himself: Something is really wrong here. Even if they suspect Busby and I are in someway connected to Eckert's activities, they are proceeding way too fast.

"Captain Eckert has been placed under arrest and has been flown to Wiesbaden, Germany."

"May I ask why?" Raymond asked.

"You may not."

"What am I being charged with?"

"Nothing. I said you were being investigated."

"What then am I being investigated for?" Raymond asked. The look he gave the major bordered on insubordination. The major said nothing but his demeanor indicated he was not playing a game and would not tolerate this kind of an attitude. He was normally a nice guy. Raymond knew him to be personable and carefree.

He was a recalled reservist who was a partner in a Cincinnati law firm. He was losing out on a large salary every day he was away, and he was not happy. His general conduct was very unmilitary, and he did not care. In fact, you might say he had the most unmilitary bearing of any officer on the base. But it was obvious to Raymond something big had made him change. And this change was what had the usually unflappable Raymond worried.

"Sir," he said, "will you tell me what this is all about? What am I being investigated for?"

"That I can do," he replied. "You are being investigated for suspicion of espionage."

"Espionage?" He let out a sigh, and then quickly recovered. And then the usually slow to react Lieutenant Raymond gathered his wits about him. And he vowed not to answer another question.

He admittedly knew little about the Fifth Amendment to the Constitution. But there was one thing he did know: he did not have to speak even when he was ordered to do so. Even if they gave him some kind of immunity from prosecution. He knew he and Busby were innocent of any wrongdoing of any kind. He told the major he refused to answer any further questions on the grounds it might tend to incriminate him.

The major sat with a pained expression on his face. All he had wanted was some quick answers to a few questions. But the formal investigation for espionage had been instigated at the highest level, against his recommendation. And now one of the government's key witnesses against a suspected espionage ring refused to talk because he had attempted to scare him, and Raymond was obviously not going to be cajoled into cooperating.

"Major, can I ask you one thing? I'm curious. Does this have to do with aircraft located on some secret Russian base east of here?"

"Why do you ask me that? Lieutenant, you would do us all a favor if you answered just two questions. What do you know about a Hungarian woman who is the girl friend of your commander and a civilian employee by the name of Frank Rowe? What, if anything, do you know about their alleged activities to steal atomic secrets?"

"Atomic secrets? I thought this was all about airplanes at Boulhaut," he replied.

CHAPTER 14

RAFFLES HOTEL, SINGAPORE, 1985

It was my third trip to Singapore, and my third visit to the hotel known as the Grand Old Dame of the orient. Somerset Maugham once called her the legendary symbol for all the fables of the Exotic East. And she is still acknowledged as being more legend than hotel.

She had undergone a recent refurbishment, allowing her to regain her former persona as one of the truly luxurious hotels in the world. She now stands, once again, as a jewel in the crown of a city noted for extravagance and first-class accommodations. She has been reinstated to the days when royalty, writers, and wealthy celebrities once held sway. A few of the bentwood tables and rattan chairs, once her trademark, still can be seen on the veranda as a reminder of yesteryear. But the white linen tropical suits, once worn by the famous and near famous, still remain in abundance, to give the place a certain inimitable style and cachet.

With twenty-four-hour valet service, gourmet meals, and some nineteen restaurant/bars to choose from, I'm looking forward to my next two weeks stay. And I must tell you that my reservation was costing somebody almost as much money per night as my digs was costing me a month. It costs so much that I feel guilty about going to sleep.

Speaking of sleep, the last telephone call I received came about the same time as the first two, that is to say, in the early morning hours when you hate to be awakened the most. Why Herb insists on doing this I don't know. And why he has this penchant for whispering on the other end of the line, when he knows no one else is around to hear him, is more than I can say. I shouldn't complain though. I'm being paid, and paid well.

One thing you can say about him, he's not tight with his money. But then it may be somebody else's money. The further along I get into this novel of ours, the more I suspect there are others involved, people who are as interested in seeing it published as he is.

I suspect some of them might be disgruntled ex-agents, guys like Roy Collins, for example, who got the boot just a few years before he was set to retire. No laughing matter when you're passed over and kicked out of a firm, any firm, when you're past your prime and you're subject to losing a fairly large pension. Some paltry severance pay thing isn't much compensation. I can personally attest to that.

And all you can think of when they hand you the papers or whatever is revenge. Most guys go passively down the road kicking the proverbial horse chips, talking to themselves. Then they sit on their porches and stew and lick their wounds. But Roy Collins was no ordinary guy. I guess you might say it's why he was working for the Company in the first place.

I can't help wondering if his widow isn't going to get a cut of the royalties for Roy's part of the story. If she is, then Herb will see to it she is well taken care of. But she just might end up on the short end of the stick again, sitting on the hot seat like the rest of us, wishing Roy had never been part of whatever it is we're doing. If so, this hot seat may not be the first time for her, but it most definitely is for me. I'm sure it won't be for Herb, who if his demeanor is any indicator, has spent the last thirty years of his life running around dodging somebody or other.

And something else comes to mind–this whole expose thing might have started because of Roy. I understand he had been away from the Company for some time. And then almost as an afterthought, he had been brought back.

Some Ivy League dude came to him bearing an olive branch with a tale about returning for one last operation, and of course the usual carrot dangling on a stick. In this case, the carrot was the reinstatement of his lost pension in exchange for his promise not to write a book You know, every time somebody gets mad at somebody in the CIA they threaten to write a book and destroy the rest of them. Well, according to Herb, Roy was not given to idle threats. Anyway, he bit at the carrot. And then like the others down the street, several years ago, somebody shot the hell out of him.

I took a cab from the Changi Airport. Twenty minutes later we turned into Beach Road and headed up the short tree-lined drive to the main hotel entrance. Exclusive, close to the business district, but far enough away that it might as well have been located on the moon.

All around was green, verdant green and exotic plants found only in a tropical rain forest. Green everywhere. Green so thick it reminds you of key lime Jell-O shimmering in a mold. And the smell of humus to take your breath away. Hot humid heat that strikes like a Turkish bath when you open the door, and then slowly wets your underclothes with a soft dampness. Heat and humidity that make your senses crave liquid refreshment, and cool ceiling fans working behind filtered air-conditioning. But for the moment, it's all a thrill to an adventurer like myself who has never experienced the Asian tropics before or stayed in a place so rich in history.

My first appointment with Herb was for late morning the next day. Our routine went something like this: He would read what I had written and then critique it the following day. He would make sure I understood what it was he was trying to say by elaborating on his story. We might start to discuss something, and then he would stop to answer a lot of my questions. When that was taken care of, he would say, "Now let me tell you what really happened." And then he would start all over again with a story having a completely different twist.

He called these twists gambits. He says the CIA has several gambits, which are part of each covert operation.

First off, by law, Congress must approve of all covert activity laid on by the National Security Council for whatever reason. When I asked him who Congress was, he never got around to answering me, because he didn't know. Was it the combined membership voting or was it the formality of getting the approval of one member on some committee? I think it is the latter. What kind of secrecy would we be able to maintain if more than a couple of these blessed public servants of ours knew what was going on? I ask you.

I don't play chess, although I'm thinking of learning how, so I don't know what a gambit is exactly.

Herb explained it by saying: "Chris, old buddy, a gambit is an opening move and then the counter by your opponent and then your reply."

The object of the game, he tells me, is to block your opponent's king from moving. You do this by removing his men guarding his king by what might be understood as devious means. When you entice him with an opening move into taking one of your pieces so that you can take one of his, and by doing so gain an advantage in position then you have executed a gambit. Some gambits are classical moves named after the masters who first used them. Others are moves of your own. Suffice it to say there are many opening moves or gambits possible.

But in the case of CIA operations, there are supposed to be fixed moves with planned outcomes, that is, gambits designed to take advantage of your opponent's weaknesses.

He says there are usually three major diversions or gambits in any operation, two of which are misleads. He says the first one is a cover story released for the benefit of the general population, press, and Congress. The second is for the sole benefit of your opponent's intelligence organization, deemed to be smarter than the first group. Then there is the third, which is the real reason for the operation. It's always top-secret, he says, with a need to know. And, hopefully, it will never be discovered by either of the first two groups.

Some agents have seen a number of these gambits over a lifetime of service. And some of them, of necessity, might have bordered on the illegal. The threat of a disgruntled agent revealing such a project to the press or through a book, with certain of his own embellishments masquerading as truth, is something that constantly plagues the leadership of intelligence agencies. At least it bothers those of free nations; the others simply don't care whether it's illegal or not. And not only does it bother the heads of the CIA, but the same applies for the military as well. And every once in a while one of these undercover exercises comes along that involves two or more governments and their combined military forces. "Think a minute," he said, "anybody who knows anything about the wars of the last several generations can come up with any number of good examples."

I thought about it for a while and could think of only the one that made the news. It caused an international uproar at the time. It was the U-2 incident when the Russians shot down Francis Gary Powers. Powers was an Air Force pilot who temporarily left the service to work for the CIA. He was flying over Russia from a CIA base manned by our Air Force at Incerlick, Turkey. They were supposed to be engaged in such worthwhile activity as sampling the atmosphere to determine if Russia or somebody else was illegally exploding atom bombs in the air. There were other things they were supposed to be doing, as well. But they were actually mapping Russia. It seems Russian maps were not very accurate. They had to be more accurate for the targeting of intercontinental-ballistic missiles, which had not yet come into the inventory.

Herb told me that most successful covert operations meet with the overwhelming approval of the public, if they become known. One that did, according to him, took place during the height of the Cold War, and is analogous to a gambit in chess:

He told me that in 1961, "This nation was close to becoming engaged in a thermo-nuclear war with the Soviet Union. We came closer to nuclear war than, perhaps, at any time in history, including the Cuban Missile Crisis of 1963," he said.

"During the 1963 exercise in brinkmanship, the Soviets did not want to risk an all-out war with America at a time when they were decidedly at a disadvantage, so they backed away.

"But in 1961 things were much different," he said, "then, the new B-52 bomber, which was this nations primary weapon of deterrence, was in trouble. Our ICBM program was in its infancy. The few Atlas booster rockets in the Strategic Air Command's inventory were fraught with engineering difficulties and were being hard pressed to stay combat ready. The medium-range

B-47 bomber was all but phased out; those that were still operational required access to bases in England and Morocco to carry out their missions. And these bases were vulnerable to sabotage and destruction from a Soviet first strike.

"Submarines, at the time, had no strategic capability and were not part of our deterrent plan. Likewise, aircraft launched from naval carriers did not have the range required to penetrate into the heartland of the Russians.

"It became increasingly evident we were vulnerable to attack, because the Strategic Air Command's War Plan, which called for massive nuclear response to a first strike by the Soviet Union, was not completely workable for lack of military hardware.

"The problem," Herb said, "was major structural defects in our new long-range B-52 bombers, fleet-wide."

How Herb knew this he never would say, but he knew.

He went on to tell me: "The wings and key fuselage attach points were beginning to show evidence of stress fracturing, requiring major rework to avoid a catastrophe. A few aircraft at a time from each bomb wing were immediately grounded for an extensive factory retrofit. This was in addition to those already on the ground on standby alert."

He went on to explain to me: "A study was undertaken to determine the turnaround time for the remaining aircraft being used for minimal aircrew training. In the event of a Soviet attack, they had to be recovered, refueled, and the necessary maintenance performed to make them airworthy. And then they had to be uploaded with two-megaton hydrogen bombs. The results of the study showed the first of these bombers could not be readied for takeoff in less then thirteen hours. The last one could not be readied in less than twenty-one; those involved in *Sky Speed* or factory modification at one of several bases would not be available in less then forty-eight hours. By this time the war would have essentially been over."

Herb paused for a minute to let the seriousness of the situation sink in, and then he began again: "Clearly, something had to be done lest the Soviet Union discover our weakness and be enticed to attack, believing they would suffer acceptable damage from our minimal response.

"A classified operation, code named *Down Field* was conceived. It was followed by *Brass Rail*, and then with the advent of the Cuban Missile Crisis, the modified plan became known as *Chrome Dome*. It called for around-the-clock flights toward the Soviet Union, with the maximum number of aircraft available in the air at any given time."

He had been talking as though he himself had made the study. But I knew he had been speaking from a report he must have read. When he began again, I rather suspected his remarks were supposition rather than factual, although what he said next made a lot of sense to me.

"The early phases of the operation would not have been possible if they had been dependant on approval of the White House and Congress, who at the time did not have a feel for the urgency of the situation. Then too, if our allies had been consulted, a country such as France, with its large Communist population, was expected to reject any such proposal. And time was of the essence.

"The first move of the gambit was to manufacture a fall-back position, necessary if the participants were discovered. When one of our bombers crashed in Spanish waters, the program became known to then President Eisenhower and to the American people. The cover story explained that these flights, with nuclear bombs aboard, were actually practice missions in the event the program became policy. But the Soviets had been led to believe quite differently. They believed it was an effort on our part to keep part of our aircraft airborne at all times to avoid sabotage on the ground or destruction from their first strike. The real purpose, however, was to be in position to immediately retaliate if first attacked. Some of our bombers previously used for aircrew training were airborne, and unless recalled, they would have continued on to their assigned targets in the Soviet Union. Neither the people, press, Congress, or the White House was aware this was happening."

What he said next was not new to me. I remember it well, as did most people who were old enough at the time: "In 1963, the Soviets attempted to install nuclear-tipped short-range missiles in Cuba, some sixty miles from the United States. They were stopped cold by President Kennedy's warning. They hurriedly removed their missiles from Cuban soil, and those at sea turned around and went home without further fanfare. And this is important," he said, pausing again: "None of the aforementioned bystanders, not the public nor the press, or the Congress, chose to criticize the Strategic Air Command or the CIA for skirting civilian authority with their pre-empting operation."

I remember the rest of it happening just the way Herb went on to tell me it did. He said: "President Kennedy's order to cease and desist was not seen by the Soviet Union as an idle threat, because by this time the President and the Soviets both knew we had airborne bombers flying around the clock toward targets in the Soviet Union. Airborne Alert was a successful gambit. It was a reality that gave America a tremendous advantage in the end game. And by winning the end game, we avoided a nuclear war. We guaranteed the continuation of the peace, the curtailing of the Soviet Union's military meddling in world affairs, and it set the stage for the ultimate defeat and eventual dismantling of what President Ronald Reagan would later call The Evil Empire."

We had been talking about a couple of disgruntled agents before he started explaining to me about two of the many covert operations involving the CIA and the Air Force that I have been writing about.

Speaking of disgruntled agents, I asked Herb if he thought we ought to quote some of these expose books they wrote to make a point. He had told me about several, which are available in any library. He looked at me with that enigmatic smile of his before he replied. Then he said, "Any reader can check out one for himself if he really wants to know." I took that to mean he didn't care one way or the other whether our readers believed him.

"Do they damage the CIA, these books?" I ask him.

"They do indeed," he replied, "and sometimes they cost friendly agents their lives. But this is the price we pay, I suppose, for being a free nation trying our best to compete with totalitarian governments. We are handicapped and we always have been."

We were still sitting in the so called Writers Bar. Where it gets its name probably comes from the fact that Somerset Maugham used to hang out here. And so did a lot of others, albeit not nearly as successful. Just as Hemingway had his favorite spot in Madrid, Barcelona, and in Key West, I suspect Maugham did much of his note work setting right here where we are. But who knows.

"Herb," I said, "if you don't mind, I would like to go back over the part where you were in Germany and getting ready to shoot Heisenberg."

"You misunderstand," he said, quickly, looking at me over the top of a soft drink with some sort of fruit hugging the lip of the glass. "I think you misunderstand. I wasn't going to shoot him at that point. I had all but gotten over the idea. Even before our private meeting, I was pretty sure he didn't know how to sustain a nuclear reaction, which is the first step toward building a bomb. No, I didn't see the need for it. However, my friend Lindquist from MI-6 sure did.

"You know, I found out later Lindquist was with British Intelligence, just as I had suspected all along. He turned out to be a chore; but then no one knows how they're going to react under similar circumstances. He had seen hundreds of innocent people killed in England during the Blitz and he was angry. And when he found himself together with a bunch of enemy strangers who were plotting more destruction of everything he held dear, it was more than he could bear. I eventually settled him down. It wasn't easy, but I finally managed."

"Just for the sake of argument," I said, "what difference would it have made, as far as your assignment was concerned, if you would have let him toss a grenade into the lecture room and then the both of you had taken off?"

"Plenty," he replied, his countenance changing, almost approaching a frown. And then without pausing to search his memory, which you might expect would be somewhat dimmed by time, he continued on, hurriedly. "Heisenberg claimed after the War that the reason they were unable to build a fissionable atomic pile with natural uranium was not because they didn't know how, but because he, Heisenberg, had torpedoed the project. Recall, he came on strong with Bohr in Denmark about how Germany, under his guidance, was ahead of the Allies. But the truth was, as things changed in Germany, he changed. After the War he bandied it around about how he could have made a bomb in the early years, if he had really wanted to. He says he was misunderstood. He tells everybody he was always a loyal Jew; he says he was holding back. And all the time, he says, he was really just acting out a part for Heinrich Himmler's benefit. Of course, there is nobody who believed him, especially Niels Bohr. And few do today. But the point is, he had Himmler convinced he knew what he was doing and that he was always on the verge of a breakthrough. In the meantime, he was wasting money and assets that could have been better used elsewhere."

"You mentioned a plan," I said. "You told Lindquist you had a plan. You said you were going to take advantage of the situation and ultimately ensure that Germany never succeeded with her atomic efforts. What was that all about, anyhow?"

He looked at me for a moment, and then he replied, "It occurred to me as I was listening to Heisenberg that he never understood how to compute the *K factor*. He knew it was necessary, all right, but he never could figure it out. And then I realized his ego was so big he couldn't conceive of any Americans doing it either. That's when I knew I had him."

"Do you care to elaborate?"

"Sure, I'll be glad to, but in order for it to make much sense, I have to briefly go back over what happened at Chicago. Recall, they constructed an atomic pile in an abandoned squash-racket court. This pile resembled a kind of large beehive with straight sides part-way up and then rounded off at the top. It was made of blocks of graphite, alternating with uranium oxide embedded into some more blocks of graphite. They had to use an oxide because they had no pure uranium. They were afraid the impurities in the uranium they had would absorb the neutrons and stop the reaction before it got started. However, they had installed several rods of cadmium to slow the reaction down once it did get started. But the key to the whole thing was this so called K factor.

"Fermi, with the help of some others, including my friend Walter Zinn, had accomplished what Heisenberg and his people couldn't do, regardless of what he said later. I know. I was there and I talked to him about it. And I knew he didn't know how to calculate a working value of K. He simply did not understand what I was showing him or talking about …"

"What are you talking about?" I interrupted to ask him. I

was trying to get him to tell me. I had sheets of notes, good background. But I still didn't understand the main reason why Heisenberg couldn't build a bomb.

"I'm talking about the value Enrico Fermi described as unity. Or the K factor." Herb said.

"When we were at Princeton, Zinn clued me in on one of the nations most closely guarded secrets. He said the pile must have unity in order to work."

I sat in the cool bar listening to Herb, and now I was watching the wheels turn in his head as his memory banks recalled verbatim what Zinn had spent countless hours teaching him. He was concentrating, trying to get it simple enough that I could understand.

"Chris," he finally said, "Fermi's term, unity, means that the pile when completed must have a reproduction factor of K, which is greater than 1. It can't be too large or too small. If it's too small it won't work, and if it's too large it may release neutrons too fast, and the reaction will not be sustained. It's far more complicated, but that's pretty much what I mean, in layman's terms. If Heisenberg had been able to solve the problem of controlling the neutrons, above all had he been able to determine the secret of obtaining a working value of K, they might have been on their way.

"Zinn and I had discussed this for one full day. We went over the math formulas until they were pouring out my ears. And I might also add here, Heisenberg never understood any of them when I showed him. His knowledge never scratched the surface of the problem."

Then he answered the next question before I could ask it: "Oh, I got myself criticized for talking to him about formulas," he paused as he took another sip from his drink.

"I couldn't resist," he said. "Like Lindquist, I became a little militant. You had to have been there to experience the arrogance of Heisenberg and his entire entourage. And there was a genuine need on my part to shut them up. I just wished the others who were spilling over with adoration for him that day could have seen his face when he realized he was not even on the same page as Fermi and the others back in Chicago."

"Did you really give him the formulas?" I asked him, dreading his reply. For if he did, if he had aided him in any way to determine the exact size of a pile, given the fissionable materials in use, it might go a long way in explaining why he suddenly vanished from society years ago. They, meaning the Company, may have concluded he talked too much. Old Herb might have lost his credibility. They might have figured: if he gave something that critical to Heisenberg then, what had he compromised lately?

"I got in trouble over it–big trouble." That was his answer, when I asked him what action they took when they found out what he had done. I pressed him for more information.

He said: "I mean I didn't really give Heisenberg anything he could work with. But I had a hard time convincing Donovan and some of the others of this. They didn't want me fooling around with the subject at all; it was too highly classified. But when I explained why I did it, and what good it was going to do for our side, they forgave me. However, in some cases not completely. I think I garnered a reputation for being a maverick. They liked the subterfuge I used against Heisenberg, but they wanted to be the ones to call the shots. I guess I was working too far outside to suit them, because, obviously I was to learn later, they never really did forgive me."

Then he stopped for a minute and watched some visitors coming into the bar. After they sat down, he turned to me, his concentration returning:

"Do you remember the science fiction movie, *The Day the*

Earth Stood Still, with Michael Rennie and Sam Jaffe?" I thought about it for a minute and then nodded my head in the affirmative. But it had been a long time and I was not sure how much I remembered.

"Rennie's character was from another planet," Herb said, as he began to set the scene in the popular movie. "He had just landed on Earth. He made it a point to look up Earth's most brilliant scientist, played by Sam Jaffe. He went to Sam's home. Sam was not there so he went into his study through a large open window and made himself at home. He saw a blackboard full of complicated equations, which he recognized as having to do with rocket propulsion in space. He took a piece of chalk and made certain corrections, which he knew Sam would recognize as being done by somebody not living on Earth. The space man didn't have to tell Sam everything he knew to get his attention. All he wanted was for Sam to understand the superiority of his science."

I was becoming caught up in the story again and eagerly awaiting the point he was going to make. I knew there would be one. I guess I realized for the first time what an interesting conversationalist he was. Many of his hosts knew, but I was experiencing it for the first time.

Herb continued: "The people living on other planets in our solar system were not interested in our local wars, as long as we were using conventional weapons. But now that we had developed atomic weapons it was a whole new ball game, as far as they were concerned. He told Sam to either find a way to get rid of them or we were all going to be destroyed.

"Well, the dialogue between me and Heisenberg was not unlike that scene in the movie," he said.

"I never told Heisenberg enough to do him any good," he continued. "But in the same way the alien from space showed the Earth scientist, I showed Heisenberg on his blackboard enough to convince him we had solved the K problem, and I convinced him we were well on our way to making a bomb.

"And I also told him, unless Germany surrendered before we had a bomb, they too were going to be destroyed.

"He asked me if I had any idea how big a bomb would have to be to work. He told me he was not exactly a neophyte in these matters. Then he reminded me that Germany was the first to fission an atom; and soon thereafter, they started thinking about the feasibility of building a super bomb. He said they knew more than we did about how big the delivery machine would have to be.

"I told him I knew all right. He smiled at me, as he told me he didn't think so. He says, 'Contemplating an airplane of that size is ridiculous—too silly to consider' is the way he put it. Then he asks me if we intended to get this new bomb of ours into Germany on a train."

This was all new information coming from Herb. I suspected he had kept quiet about a lot of his conversation with Heisenberg because of his diminished position in the Company. I have no other way to explain it, other than to say that even then he might have been planning to write a book in order to destroy them all. I couldn't help chuckling to myself at my own quip, but I said nothing about it to Herb.

"I remember watching Heisenberg crawl back into his smug shell," Herb went on to say, "the one I had seen in the lecture hall that morning. When Heisenberg jokingly asked me, with a smirk on his face, if we were not going to use a train did we plan on 'hooking several bombers together to haul it over.' Again, I did another thing I was roundly criticized for: I told him we already had such an airplane. He almost fainted dead away when I convinced him we did have an airplane, which we intended to test very soon. Then I told him it was much bigger than the B-17

Flying Fortress he was most familiar with, and we expected it to be able to do the job quite adequately. I also asked him: 'Why, if we couldn't build an atomic bomb, were we building such a huge airplane?'

"Fear was written all over him now. Here was a scientist who could visualize the power of such a bomb. And he had seen first-hand examples of American and British airpower and the destruction it was capable of creating with conventional bombs. The expression on his face reminded me of a man who might be staring at the *Four Horseman of the Apocalypse* riding across the German sky. He stared at me, his lower lip quivering, while he was thinking of something to say.

"Then I hit him with a left hook," Herb continued, smiling. "It was a sharp punch, which brought him quickly back from his reverie. I told him if he didn't sabotage their heavy water experiments, he personally was going to be destroyed right now. I told him MI-6 would have no trouble finding a way to let Himmler discover for himself how important this K factor really was. Then I asked him what Himmler's reaction would be when he came to realize how little Heisenberg knew about the subject. Then I asked him what his Nazi protector was going to do when he realized that Germany had no practical program to produce a bomb. I told him that when Himmler fully realized Germany was going to lose this war, he was going to blame him." Herb, still talking about his conversation with Heisenberg, went on to say: "MI-6 will prove to Himmler you're a loser, and they will show him why you're not the man to be running Germany's atomic energy program. Then I laughed when I asked Heisenberg how he was going to enjoy living in a concentration camp for the rest of his extremely short life span."

"What did he say to that?" I asked, with a smile on my face. We were both enjoying his story immensely. The visitors who had walked in a minute ago were smiling too, the way you do when you don't understand why others in the same room are having a good time. But they're not bothering you, and they're happy, and it makes you happy. But I could not help wondering what they would have thought if they had had any idea what we were really going on about.

"I got a little wound up, I guess. I had the great Nazi sympathizer against the ropes and I started to lay it on," he said.

"I told Heisenberg that in addition to all of this, he had better see to it that we got away safely. If he didn't, and if he lost his head and the Gestapo became involved, before I was through I would tell them everything. And then I bragged. I told him something to the effect that Himmler would know all about what he didn't know by supper-time. I also couldn't resist telling him I would see to it that the first bomb dropped was on his home town. This last thing was all pretty much bravado and Heisenberg knew it, but he was rapidly coming to understand my point."

Then Herb got a playful look on his face as he remembered a game he played as a boy. "It's what we kids used to call a peeing contest," he said. "Heisenberg and I were like two little kids engaged in a peeing contest. That's exactly what our conversation had degenerated into, a peeing contest. We were like two boys trying to see who could pee the farthest. And like the peeing contest, my remarks to him meant absolutely nothing of any consequence. But it was a relief to release all my pent-up emotions, to sound off like a juvenile. Our battle of wits was something akin to this child's contest. But to me, it was exactly the same as a ball game. It's important to win, just because it feels better than losing."

I asked Herb a couple more quick questions: "Do you think you had anything to do with the fact they never had a viable program? I understand after the War, our Atomic Energy Commission looked at it very closely and then proclaimed they hadn't gotten very far. They said the German effort had been vastly over-rated. Do you think it was because of Heisenberg? Do you think he saw the light? Do you think he heard the flutter of angel wings after you talked to him? Do you think he was instrumental in slowing things down considerably?"

"I'm sure of it," he replied, "but again, there were certain people in high places in the Company who didn't see a clear relationship between my talks with him and what became evident after the War. And since they believed I had over-stepped my bounds, they had made up their collective minds to leave me out of the picture. They ignored me completely when it came time for the accolades to be passed around. They never gave me the least bit of credit for the ultimate outcome. And that's why to this day, Niels Bohr and his colleagues blame Heisenberg's scientific inadequacies exclusively for Germany's atomic failure."

The next two days were spent sorting my notes and rewriting parts of what I had already written to agree with the recent things he told me. At one point, I wanted to check with him about something he had said. I couldn't find him. He was not staying in the hotel. The concierge had somebody call around town–no luck. He wasn't anywhere to be found. But somehow that doesn't surprise me; that's just the way he is. And who's to say he doesn't have good reason for all this secrecy and role playing.

Our next meeting is scheduled for the middle of the week. At the rate we're going, this will take forever. And I suspect there's a lot more to come.

I've had this gnawing feeling in my stomach for some time now that he is holding back something really big. I figure he's waiting for just the right moment to spring it on me, whatever it is. It may be, if he tells me now, he thinks I'll take off. It may well be he intends to get me accustomed to the good life. And then I won't be able to give it up, no matter how big the can of worms might be that he wants to open. Maybe my life is going to be in danger, too. After all, those guys who got shot across town a while back were for real. I checked on that business early on. The newspapers around here were full of it for weeks.

But I must say, since my good fortune in meeting Herb, my financial position in the San Francisco community has risen steadily. Risen quite rapidly, in fact, so much so that I have moved to another community. Yes, things have been looking up for me. And I'm not eager to return to the flophouse I called home or to the life I was leading. And right now, I'm looking at the world through rose-colored glasses.

I was talking about Herb and some of his rather peculiar behavior: Is it paranoia I am observing or does he have a real reason for the way he acts sometimes? And of course, if the cause is real, when is it going to spill over onto me? Am I going to sac- rifice my freedom for a life like his? Even if I'm able to live as a millionaire, is it going to be worth it? Is the fact that I have lived so long as a near pauper going to cloud my judgment? Did he choose me because I was down and out, and he believed I could be seduced with all this clean living? Is this what I really want, money and what it will buy? Is this why I'm at this beautiful hotel instead of some cheap rooming house across town where I belong? I don't know. I don't have the answers. But there's no Santa Claus; this much I do know. Life has made me a pessimist, and I'm afraid this bubble of good fortune is going to burst at any minute. And something else, that small feeling I have that things are not exactly as they should be, lives in my stomach just below the surface, and it tends to cast a shadow on this whole episode. And I'm sure if I let it, it will end up ruining the whole experience

Herb missed our next appointment by two days. I kept checking in the bar, but no Herb. At one point I thought he had abandoned the project and left me hanging out to dry with a whopping big hotel bill. Another time I thought the bad guys had gotten him.

When I did see him, he offered no explanation. He just comes and goes as it suits him. His hosts have long known about this boorish behavior of his, and they evidently have been conditioned to put up with it. But I don't care for it very much, and I'm thinking I might say something to him. But on the other hand; what do I care, really. I have nothing better to do than to write this book. And I would rather waste time here than in San Francisco. However, there is another thing I've thought about-not a lot, but I've thought about it. And it is starting to bother me a little. What if his comings and goings at odd times is part of a plan? We all know many fugitives move around a lot. They purposely do it so as not to appear predictable. Maybe they teach you this in spy school? But I long ago concluded that Herb never went past the first grade in spy school.

"Talk to me about Don Eckert," I said to him. "There are a lot of gaping holes in what I was able to glean from the notes in the dossier you gave me." He had shown up, asking the concierge to find me and have me meet him at the same place. All of a sudden he was ready to go again without the slightest intention of apologizing for keeping me waiting.

"Okay. I guess the best way is for you to hold your questions. I think I can cover most of what you're looking for," Herb said.

"Before you start," I said, "I have to ask you. Did you know Eckert before Morocco? Where did you first meet him? What was the relationship between the two of you? How do you know so much about him?"

"Yes I knew him for a long time, but not before he came back from there. He was always quite closed-mouthed about what he had been doing, either in the Air Force or the Company. But having said this, there were odd times when we were together, when he answered specific questions. He was just hesitant to volunteer much without being coaxed is all. Most of what I do know about him comes from the details of a Company report given to me by Roy Collins. After Roy became disenchanted with the Agency, about the time he was let go, he looked me up. He knew I had an ax to grind, too, and he thought I would be the best one to hold copies of all his papers. He had access to Eckert's file. In fact, he was his contact in Morocco.

"Collins managed to microfilm a lot of things, including Eckert's file. No big mystery; I simply gave you a printed copy. But there's a lot left out, I admit. What I'm going to tell you now is not contained in any report. I got it from Collins and Eckert personally."

Herb began to lower his voice as though he was passing on a secret. I would not have been surprised had he looked around to see if anyone was listening. "Do you remember the Berber Eckert and Busby met at the Tiskrit oasis, the one who told them to get out of the sheikh's camp? Well, he was another of Collins' contacts. He was keeping tabs on Eckert and reporting back to Collins. And he knew the Russians had Eckert, and the operation had been compromised."

I interrupted him to say: "I didn't know the Russians had Eckert–that's news to me."

"Yes, well, Raymond and Busby suspected there was some kind of a deal made over Eckert. They more than half-way suspected the Russians had caught him, and it turned out to be true. It was confirmed by Collins years later. He told me that Raymond and Busby had passed on their suspicions to the Air Force investigators. Eckert had arrived back at the base before they did, and they couldn't figure out how he did it without additional fuel. I guess he figured he was going to swipe some from the Russians. But Raymond and Busby figured the Russians gave it to him to get rid of him; of course this was after they had gotten everything they wanted from him.

"Remember, the CIA knew he had not passed on any atomic secrets to the Russians. I mean secrets about bombs stored on base at Nouassuer; he didn't know anything about that. Atomic secrets were just a dodge for the Air Force to hold him after they caught Rowe. He had gone to Boulhaut and got himself caught. And in doing so, he ruined all the CIA's plans; plus he lost the super-classified technology that had been placed in his care. That's why the Agency was so angry with him. Eckert was able to get this information to Collins, who alerted the Agency. They, in turn, cobbled together a plan to get him out of the clutches of the Air Force and save him from a courts-martial. Remember, I wrote in my notes about how the CIA didn't particularly care what happened to him because they were plenty mad. But they didn't want a trial, which would end up revealing their presence in Morocco and what they were doing there. I believe it was around that time the wheels were put into motion to get rid of Eckert. As it turned out, getting rid of him meant permanently. But not immediately, not just hauling off and shooting him. That might be the way of the MVD, but that's not the refined way of the Company. That's not the way of the suit-and-tie set. They could always use him in a constructive way. So they marked him for future use and kept him around as though all was understood and forgiven. But what they really had in mind was to use him as a pawn in the third gambit you are writing about. But I'll tell you more about it–all in good time."

"Where to start with Eckert?" he asked himself out loud.

"How about starting with Boulhaut or whatever it's called," I said.

"All right, as good a place as any," he replied.

He started to talk again, and I settled back with my notebook and pencil poised for a long, interesting story. I was getting myself prepared to go down a very crooked road with a lot of twists and turns, and I was sure Herb was not going to disappoint me.

"You know," he said, "the CIA had determined that the USSR was not going to stop their expansion unless we countered with some of our own. If it continued on unchecked, as it had in Germany, Cuba, North Korea, and elsewhere, we were going to be in grave danger of losing our freedom some-day. That's why we ringed them with air bases. Then too, we knew they couldn't do anything about it.

"Boulhaut was the fourth base planned for Morocco. It was planned for use as a fighter base to protect our bombers at the three other bases from attack while they were on the ground. But it became evident before it was completed that Congress was not going along with the master plan. They didn't think it was necessary and it was too expensive. Then, too, the Air Force didn't put up too much of a squawk when it was cancelled.

"I think it was being pushed by the CIA more than anyone else. But the thing of it was, they didn't see how we were going to be able to just walk off and forget it. As it turned out, the Russians did not hesitate to occupy it when we left, and our French allies did not run them off either. In fact, I know France was getting money from the Russians. But nobody on our side raised any objections. It was all a big embarrassment to us. And coming on the heels of a long, drawn-out cost scandal over Nouasseur, they chose to forget about it, and the quicker the better..."

"Was that the beginning of the secrecy thing, about Boulhaut base I mean?" I interrupted again.

"Yes, that's right," he replied, "the CIA did not want Congress or the Air Force investigating that base. They didn't care for anybody meddling in what they saw as their affairs. Oh, another thing, the huge cost over-run at Nouassuer was because of the runways. They were reinforced concrete to a depth of several yards. That's what I read in one article in the Reader's Digest, anyway. It seems excessive, but maybe not when you consider the size of the bombers and the weight of the bombs they planned to carry.

"The construction company hired for the job was Morrison Knudsen, one of the best and most reputable firms they could find. But the runways had to be re-built several times. We had to buy material from the French, who were gouging us at every turn. Then too, as it turned out, the French cement was not up to required specifications and they had to be done over. You see, neither the contractor nor the French were aware of the static load per square inch on the aircraft's wheels. So neither of them was that diligent in construction. And when Congress and the press wanted to know why so much cement was necessary in the first place, they were told it was for the huge ten engine global bomber known as the B-36. This was not true; it was just another cover story. The real reason was for the jet bombers, the B-47 and the B-52, with higher wheel loading, which were also going to be loaded with heavy atom bombs. Both of these aircraft were still in the testing phase. As soon as they became available in a few short years, they were going to be using those bases.

"The B-36 was a lousy aircraft, hard to maintain. It had a long turn-around time. You flew it once, and then you had to spend hundreds of man-hours and days before it could fly again. Not the most desirable attribute of a combat aircraft.

"The answer to this problem was to phase out the B-36 as soon as the B-47 was ready. In the meantime, they did rotate some B-36's into Nouasseur to show the flag and to help convince the Russians their expansion days were about over. But it was a mislead; we wanted them to believe the B-36 was going to occupy Nouassuer for a long time to come. We didn't want them to know too much about our long-range plans for the new airplanes."

Herb paused for a minute in his monologue to see if I was taking it all in, and then he proceeded: "In the meantime, the Russians moved aircraft into Boulhaut. How many and what kinds, how they were organized, and whether they could sustain a maximum maintenance effort with the necessary supply of parts, where their supply lines were, etc., and a whole host of questions needed to be answered in order to assess the threat. That's where Eckert came in.

"His activities with the radar sites I told you about were for real. But much of it was busy work. It was a reason to keep him in the area. While appearing to work for the Air Force, he was actually working for the CIA. He was also there to keep tabs on the valuable sabotage equipment he had planted. And to keep Roy Collins up-to-date concerning those things I just told you about."

I held up my hand to get him to pause a minute. I was falling behind again and wanted to catch every word, all of which was most important to the story. "What sabotage equipment?" I asked.

He paused for a few seconds and then started again: "The CIA knew the Russians knew about Eckert and what he was doing. It was expected the Russians would make him their business. The Russians figured Eckert was periodically spying on their daily activities. And since they had no mission there, unless a full-scale war broke out, they didn't care that much about what he did or how much he knew. What he had done though was mine the base. And that was the real reason he was there."

"I have to stop you again Herb and ask a question. What do you mean by mining. Isn't that what they used to do in World War 1 in the trenches? Isn't that what they used to do in the olden days? Didn't they dig under the other guy's trenches from out in no-mans-land and then plant dynamite under him to blow him up?"

"Exactly," he said. "That is exactly what he did. Only instead of dynamite, he hid a small nuclear device. It was a kind of dooms-day machine. It contained a complicated but almost fool-proof triggering mechanism. It was advanced state-of-the-art and highly classified. It was designed to sense the kind of activity associated with an enemy attack. This thing he had hidden was not as explosive–that is, it was not the same as those we think of when we think of an atom bomb. It blew up all right, but not that much. What it did do was mostly scatter radioactive isotopes to a degree that rendered the base uninhabitable or anybody on it incapable of doing much more of anything. That's what he had been doing out at Groom Lake, learning how to assemble and calibrate this device."

"I don't understand how this device could determine when an attack was eminent." I asked, confused.

"I'll tell you what I do know about it," he said. "Roy Collins, my source for all of this, didn't know an awful lot either. But what he did know, he told me when I asked him the same question.

"You have to understand something, Mayo, old buddy," Herb said. "BOB's, meaning bombs stored on base, as opposed to those flown in, have to be checked out and fused. You can't do it in the air in a fighter/bomber like the airplanes the Russians had at Boulhaut. At certain points in the procedure on the ground, the bomb case is opened for a few minutes, and the core of the reactor to be is exposed. At this time, there is an emission of low-grade radioactivity, which can be picked up by these super-sensors of ours. They used new solar-powered nicad batteries to power the sensors, which were calibrated according to an algorithm scale. The problem was, they had to be periodically inspected and recalibrated if necessary.

"The Russians were known to have stored tube or gun type bombs at Boulhaut, similar to the one dropped at Hiroshima. They were cheaper, smaller, and simpler than the spherical implosion types we now use. They are constructed in a way that requires the insertion of a nuclear bullet in the barrel. When the bomb is triggered, the bullet is shot into a hole in the fissionable material at the other end. This causes the material to reach critical mass and the bomb explodes. These strategically placed sensors picked up radio activity when this insertion or fusing process was carried out.

"Now, I ask you," and here he paused for dramatic effect, "why would they be arming and fusing their bombs, if they were not planning to attack us? That's the premise, at any rate. And once the Russians began this fusing, the sensors Eckert had hidden triggered the atomic device he also had hidden there. Our would-be attackers then instantly become special kinds of neutrons running around out there in space. A new element, perhaps, for the Periodic Table."

With that last irreverent remark, Herb smiled a kind of gallows humor smile at the irony of the thing. But what he was really smiling at was the fact that an explosion, if one had ever occurred, would have appeared to be an accident. The CIA would later have given out a story to the world press about how the Russians had occupied our base illegally for the purpose of starting a war. And unfortunately, one of their inferiorly constructed bombs had blown up, and they had been *hoisted on their own petard.*

But the big thing was, as he explained it to me, with Boulhaut destroyed there could be no first strike by Russia. Our base at Nouassuer would have remained intact, along with the atom bombs stored there, awaiting the arrival of our jet bombers from America. They would have been uploaded and flown into the heart of Russia as the War Plan called for. "You see," he said, "Nouassuer was the key to the whole thing. The Russians would never have attacked us until they knew for sure their fighter/bombers had destroyed the atom bombs at Nouassuer."

At this point he did stop, which allowed me to catch up with my notes again. He ordered us some iced melon from the bar while I perused my poor penmanship. It was times like this I wished I had taken shorthand classes in high school. But would you believe it: in those days it was thought of as being kind of sissy if a boy took classes stereotypically seen as being in the sole domain of would-be female secretaries.

"Herb," I said, "you have left something out. It all sounds believable but there is a lot more to it, isn't there?" He smiled that all-knowing smile of his, the one he reserved for the slower mind, and nodded yes. But it was equally obvious he was not going to tell me about it, not yet anyway.

He continued again: "Eckert had earlier been brought up on court-martial charges for causing the big furor down at Sheikh Abby's oasis. They charged him with statutory rape of Abby's daughter. This too was a gambit to get everybody looking the other way.

"The Russians knew about Eckert; he had been seen before at Boulhaut. So they hired the Berbers to get rid of him. Shiekh Abby set up the brouhaha, even going so far as to alert the French Army in the area. When the scene was ready to be played out, they chased Eckert and his team out of camp and up into the foothills.

"These fierce looking Berber warriors rode pell-mell, whooping and hollering behind Eckert's convoy. They were shouting and waving their antique muskets, their greatest performance to date. You must understand, they were skilled at putting on similar displays of daring-do for the public. But come to find out, they weren't good for doing much else.

"But Eckert and his men were not aware of this; they never witnessed one of their staged productions. They were scared silly. That's just what Abby wanted. Understand, Abby liked Eckert. He didn't want to hurt him just scare him out of the area or cause an incident and have the French kick him out. But what Abby didn't want was exactly what happened, and it ended up causing all the trouble."

I was listening intently to his story. I had forgotten my notes and had set them aside momentarily as a waiter approached Rosenthal and asked him if he could bring us a cup of coffee. Herb looked up at him and smiled as he brushed him away, but I could tell he was slightly miffed at being interrupted. He looked at me and my notes and then nodded, by way of telling me he would wait until I had caught up. After a few minutes he started again:

"Abby thought Eckert and his men would see through the sham. The deflowering of a daughter, and the resulting chase of the would-be bride-groom out of camp and into the hills by the father, was a time-honored scenario played out thousands of times for thousands of years in third world countries. But Eckert knew nothing about this Mideastern custom, and they took off like scalded dogs. He thought he was going to be caught and skinned–for what, he wasn't sure.

"Now, when the tribesmen got too close, and they lined up for one of their ceremonial charges line-abreast, Eckert ordered his .30 cal. machine gun unlimbered, mounted, locked, and loaded. And then, to the great surprise of the tribesman, he fired a hail of half a belt over their heads. He followed this up by throwing half a dozen sticks of the dynamite they had been using for core mapping among the horses. The upshot of the whole thing must have resembled a Max Sennett comedy. A half dozen riders were thrown, while the rest panicked and high-tailed it for home."

When I stopped laughing at what must have been a very funny scene, Herb started again: "Abby was embarrassed, and the Russians refused to pay him for getting rid of Eckert unless he got the French Army involved and made the scandal official. So that's why Eckert was brought up on rape charges to get rid of him. But that too was a sham. Some attorney from the CIA showed up. He gave the judge advocate pictures of the so-called Berber princess. The poor girl had contracted smallpox years earlier and was as ugly as sin. And so everybody had a big laugh at Eckert's expense. Then to get along with the French, who had to appease the Berbers and the Russians, who were not officially there, the Air Force dropped the charges and the CIA whisked him out of Morocco at the insistence of the French government.

"But now here's the thing that got him in real Dutch–none of the rest meant anything, it was all for the benefit of the press and anybody else interested. Eckert was in serious trouble all right, because he had gotten caught checking up on the device he had planted, and as a result, he had lost our latest technology.

"He had gone there under cover of the storm. He had tried to get to it before; but even though Russian security was lax, he hadn't been able to get close enough to his package to make sure everything was okay. But he figured this time he couldn't miss, what with the poor visibility and all. However, daylight caught him. The dust kicked up by the Sirocco had settled down somewhat, and he was seen.

"The Russians were elated at finding the nuclear device, which probably resulted in a commendation for their commanding officer. And then there was this new sensor technology, which had also fallen into the Russian commander's hands, gratis. Now, the Russians didn't want Eckert. But they didn't want him snooping around any further. Remember, they weren't supposed to be there. Well, they refused to pay Abby unless he reported the daughter incident to the French, who brokered a deal between the CIA and the Russians to keep him away. Eckert was out of the stew; but like me, he was never trusted again or given another important assignment. Oh, I guess it was expedient to let him keep his jeep; otherwise they would have had to drive him to the highway so he could hitch-hike home." This last remark brought a smile to Herb's face, as though he was enjoying an inside joke.

I changed the subject. I asked him what happened to Edit Esterhazy and Frank Rowe, and whether Roy Collins knew anything about what happened to them. He said he did, as he rummaged through his briefcase. He came up with yet another dossier, which caused me to spend two hours later that night reading reports, along with Herb and Roy's comments about the two of them.

It appears Edit and Rowe didn't know each other. That is, in the beginning they didn't. And their reasons for becoming Russian spies were quite different also. Edit wanted some financial security for her mother and father. They were living in a hotel, which was taking most of her wages. Her pay scale had not been set by the Americans, but by the French. The Arabs were paid the least, less per day then the cost of a European meal. Next came the Jews, who fared a little better. Then the Europeans, and the most went to the French.

She had been working at some obscure job in the city when a friend told her the Americans were going to hire a few secretaries and a librarian. She put in her application, along with a resume of her scholastic accomplishments. She had no trouble getting the librarian position.

A few short weeks after she started, she was contacted by a Russian agent. He made no promises, but said he would be willing to pay her a fairly large sum of money if she could manage to cultivate the acquaintance of one Lieutenant Donald Eckert.

Later, she told Eckert she didn't pay too much attention to the Russian agent until he, Eckert, came into her library. He came in with one of his sergeants to check out a box of books. She struck up a conversation with him, and he asked her to go to dinner that night. After the second date, she contacted the Russian agent and went on the payroll. They agreed to pay her a small salary and large bonuses for specific information they wanted. The first assignment she was given was to find out what Eckert was really doing in the area around Boulhaut base.

When her plan to marry Eckert fell through, that is, after he was transferred and no one seemed to know exactly what had happened to him, she took up with a roving free spirit from Sweden. This individual owned a fairly large sailboat, and one day he came into Casablanca harbor and set his anchor. How she came to know him was not contained in Herb's notes.

The two of them fell in love and were later married in a civil ceremony. The young captain was on a round-the-world trip. He planned to sail around Africa, crossing the Atlantic, and then doubling the horn. But after their marriage, he cancelled his plans and went back to Sweden with Edit. He was the son of an industrialist. He promised to use his father's influence to get her parents a visa to live in Sweden. The neutral Swedes were not that interested in the wartime affairs of her father, anyway.

In the meantime, Eckert caused a file to be opened on Edit without telling Collins about the night the two of them had spent on the beach. She was watched for about three years and then dropped for lack of evidence of involvement in any further espionage activity. Eckert was most interested in whether she was going to stay in the intelligence business. Obviously, if she did, she was at some point going to pose a threat to him, maybe even blackmail. But he never saw her again, and the file became inactive after five years.

Now, Frank Rowe was another matter altogether; he was caught with a briefcase full of cash coming from the embassy in Frankfurt. He had been enjoying himself immensely, playing the role of *agent provocateur*.

He had finagled his present job at Nouassuer, which at best was temporary, and he knew he was going to have to revert back to a much lower pay scale in a couple of years. He wanted to make hay while the sun shined. He was charged with the flat-out selling of nuclear secrets and turned over to the FBI for prosecution.

His attorney plea bargained what was seen as a sure conviction. His defense was that he never had access to anything worthwhile, so what was there to worry about. The U.S. attorney then asked why the Russians were paying him rather large sums of money for useless information.

The next day, I asked Herb, "why exactly were they paying him the big bucks?"

He replied: "The Russians wanted Rowe to help Edit discover why Eckert was messing around in the area around Boulhaut, all right; but they were more interested in atom bombs at Nouassuer. They wanted to know where, what type, and how many. That's where the atomic secrets thing came in."

He continued to tell me without my asking: "They had Rowe dead to rights about selling out our bombs-on-base secrets. However, they changed their minds about going to trial and went along with a plea when, to save his neck, Rowe raised the specter of one Donald Eckert. Rowe said he had valuable information, which he would be willing to trade for a guarantee of a much-reduced sentence. He said his information concerned Boulhaut base. He told the authorities he was a good friend of Eckert's, and that he really had been after information from Eckert about his activities at Boulhaut. This business of going to Germany all the time to coordinate the Nouasseur layout was a ruse to visit his case worker. He said he seldom talked to the Russians about the installations at Nouassuer, because they could have cared less. He told them that what Eckert had been doing at Boulhaut, was what he was being paid for. He obviously didn't want to admit to the bombs-on-base thing, so he used Eckert and Boulhaut as his alibi for having been paid so much by the Russians. And here again, the CIA knew Rowe was lying and they stepped in to protect one of their own, Eckert.

"A full-blown trial was avoided after a lengthy investigation involving base personnel, including testimony from the chess playing officer who had been keeping notes on Eckert. Eckert's testimony against Rowe was not required, and the CIA presence in Morocco was left secretive and virtually unknown to the general public and the Congress. And it remains so to this day…"

I interrupted again to make a comment. I said: "I see. It remains hidden until now is what you mean."

He just smiled again. And then it dawned on me. This was old hat history. The CIA was not going to get too bent out of shape over something happening this far back in the past. What they were excited about was far bigger, and whatever it was it had just happened. And those in charge right now were the ones who were going to get hung out to dry. And therein, lies the rub. That's what this book was really going to be about, not some stroll down memory lane. It was some new gut-busting caper. It had gotten Eckert and Collins killed and had put Herb's life in danger. Now it had placed me in harm's way, for all I knew.

Herb more or less disregarded the interruption and carried on as though I had said nothing.

"What the CIA learned from Frank Rowe about Eckert's activities was not nearly as important as what they learned he didn't know," Herb said. "As it turned out, they had figured Rowe to be much more important than he really was. But when he wanted to talk about Eckert, they thought Rowe was going to implicate Eckert in his scheme to compromise our nuclear secrets. They believed there was a ring of serious Russian agents operating in the area, which did not include Eckert. When they discovered it was all very low-level stuff, they were glad to accept the plea to get him out of their hair. Everybody came off happy, including Frank Rowe, who was facing a ten-to-twenty slam-dunk sentence. He ended up with five to ten in Leavenworth and was kicked out of civil service."

"You mean everybody came off in good shape except Eckert"

"Yeah, that's what I mean. And Roy Collins too, don't forget about Roy." This last remark of his was made with a kind of catch in his voice as he remembered his two friends and what had happened to them. And it caused me to think again about what I was doing. And to tell you the truth, I went around for the next week or so in kind of a dark funk.

CHAPTER 15
DRESDEN, EAST GERMANY, 1972

The two of them sat on a park bench. All around was evidence of the devastating Allied bombing campaign laid on during the waning months of the War. Bombers from the 15th Air Force at Foggia, Italy, had pounded the city without letup for weeks. However, where Western Germany had long ago been polished of scars, as a result of the infusion of billions of dollars of American taxpayers money, East Germany, under Russian occupation, had not fared nearly so well.

Neither said anything; both were staring at some ducks paddling on a pond. One of them was privy to some important intelligence information, however, he was taking his time before saying anything to the other.

In the distance could be seen huge mounds of rubble, covered over with dirt to look more natural. In fact, everywhere they looked they could see evidence of the War's aftermath. It appeared as though some giant glacial hand, had spawned huge erratics and terminal moraines, rupturing the once pristine landscape as it passed over. Heaps of broken bricks from destroyed buildings had lain about for years. Then slowly, some of them had been salvaged, cleaned, and re-used. But instead of becoming part of beautiful new buildings again, as they had in the Western part of the country, they had been re-laid by amateur workman. The major population of once skilled craftsmen had been chewed up in the meat-grinder that was the Eastern Front. A proud nation, once known for its skilled labor, had of necessity settled for mediocrity and shabby construction as the norm, all of which contributed to the general squalor of the area. A few feet under the soil were huge mounds of hard-scrabble masonry that had not yet been trucked off to a dump somewhere, and might never be during the lifetime of the two visitors. The reason was that the government of East Germany did not have the money–the citizens already being taxed to the point of near revolt–and the fact that there was so much of it and no place left to put it.

Alexi Voroshilov was the first to speak: "How long has it been now, tavarish?" He asked.

Roy Collins took forever to answer: "I have been gone. I haven't been around for a while." He knew he didn't have to explain. He knew his old friend knew. Voroshilov knew everything. As MVD Division Director for International Operations, Alexi knew everything there was to know. They may not be the best builders in the world, these Russians and East Germans, but they do not lack for skill when it comes to undercover intelligence work.

Collins knew this was not a social meeting between two old adversaries now turned friends; but he did not have a clue as to what they were meeting about. He had been given instructions to contact an Alexi Voroshilov in Dresden. There was no explanation proffered, no suggestion about how to go about finding him. All of which made Collins suspect his superiors were well aware he knew Voroshilov; and they knew he did not have to be told where he was. That they did know was of grave concern to him. It meant, at last, they were aware of his association with Alexi. And another thought occurred to him out of the blue, as he stared at the dismal scene around him; maybe they had known all along and it had been the reason for his recent dismissal. He started to ask his friend if he knew and then stopped in mid-sentence, eliciting a curious look from his friend.

They were both worn out, not by years, but by life itself. They both had seen too much. Both had participated in too many covert, stress-inducing assignments, the aftermath from which had left them depressed for months. Then when they began to recover, new assignments had been laid on—one after the other. There had been no let up, no time for mental recovery, until they had become saturated, and both had lost their idealism and zeal for the chase.

In their youth, they had been close opposites. At one time they actually fired their weapons at each other. But over the years they had come to know one another well, first by name and reputation, then by sight, and then by direct association. And each regarded the other as a worthy adversary. They liked each other, each had made it a point to keep in touch, if not physically, certainly through reports and file updates, which were readily available to them both. Now the idealism of politics and eagerness for the promotions of their youth were an almost forgotten thing of the past.

It was about ten years ago when they both recognized a kind of malaise, a laziness that was slowly engulfing them. Both saw it coming about the same time. It was then they started passing secrets to each other. Both knew the intelligence information they shared *quid pro quo* was obsolete and inconsequential; but their superiors did not know. And that is how they both justified their positions, without doing too much damage to their countries.

"Alex, what's all the secrecy about. Is it the Russian in you or is it a habit left over from the old days?" Voroshilov had been glancing around as though he had been taking in the scenery.

"Why do you have to ruin the moment with talk of business. Why can't you watch the sunset and the ducks and talk of old times. Is it the American in you that always has to be doing something."

The two old friends continually chided each other about one thing or another, and they had done so for years. They had this symbiotic relationship that, if known, would have gotten Alexi shot outright. And maybe something bad would have happened to Roy, but it would have been longer in coming and much subtler.

"If you insist on discussing business," Alexi looked over at his friend and said, "let me ask you what happened to your friend, the Air Force captain by the name of Don Eckert?"

"Why do you bring him up after all these years?" Roy asked.

The Russian looked at Roy again with a genuine look of surprise on his face and then said, "I don't really believe you know do you?"

"Know what?"

"Know why you are here."

"Why should I," Roy remarked. "All I was told is to come here and find you. I don't have the slightest idea what's going on. Incidentally, what did you ever do with the gadget you swiped off Eckert in Morocco?"

Alexi smiled and lit a cigarette, holding it between his thumb and first finger with his palm facing inward. "I must ask you old friend if you can give me some decent tobacco before you leave. Oh, the little bomb you so graciously gave us. We didn't do anything with it. We figured it was more prudent to leave it alone than to start making them. We didn't have a real need, and no plans in the future to use one. You of all people know it is a guerilla weapon. And you know we are not in the habit of using these kinds of things on anybody, leastwise our friends. You are one of our friends, are you not? Can you picture me blowing you up with such a thing?"

Roy gave him kind of a funny smile as if to say who is kidding whom, but he said nothing.

"Then too," Alexi continued, "if we had some in our inventory there would be more than a good possibility somebody would steal one and use it against us. That might be one of the reasons. That, and the fact our money could be better spent on larger devices, you know what I mean?

"So what happened to the kid?" Alexi asked again.

Roy replied, by way of answering his question: "I never heard. I lost track. You know I kind of liked him, although I always thought he was a bit eccentric, if somebody his age with no money can be considered eccentric."

"I'm glad you liked him," Alexi said, as he arose and walked over to the rail where he could better watch the ducks. "I can't sit still for hours like I used to. I have some kind of arthritis in my back and I have to walk around. Do you want to go for a walk?"

Roy never said anything, but he knew it was an old habit that was hard to break. Voroshilov was still old line MVD, and he got antsy when he sat around for very long. He always suspected somebody was watching him.

"I started to say I am glad you liked him because you are going to be working with him again. Him and that other eccentric, you know the one Donovan liked so well, the brain they call Rosenthal." He removed a small notebook from his inside jacket pocket and then said: Herbert Rosenthal. You people all have funny names, and I find them hard to remember and almost impossible to pronounce at times."

Roy knew Alexi, and he knew he sometimes added a lot of words to a conversation, which was no more than filler. Sometimes he did it to get his memory in gear, and sometimes he did it to put his listener on the defensive by keeping him waiting while he got to the point. Collins sensed he was doing it now. But maybe this time he had something disagreeable to say and he was reluctant to spit it out.

A few minutes later, Alexi's demeanor changed. Collins thought he might have purged his mind of the need for more small talk and was about to tell him what he wanted to hear.

"A big operation is in the offing, old friend," he said, as he looked behind him and then at the ducks, as if they were props in some elaborate scheme to overhear what he had to say.

"We Russians are in charge. At least we are in charge of the planning; your charter for PP Operations will not allow it. But you can assist a foreign nation if your National Security Advisor to your President deems it to be in the best interest of your country. Well believe me, this one is in the best interest of both our countries. But isn't it wonderful; for the first time since the War, we are all working together in a common cause."

Voroshilov never failed to amaze Collins. Alexi knew everything, right down to the organizational slang of the Agency, such as PP Operations–meaning Psychological and Paramilitary.

He paused again before going on with what Collins believed was more small talk. "You know, the very first time I ever saw an American was at Paltavo. You brought in a squadron of your bombers, accompanied by some of the most amazing and most beautiful fighter airplanes I had ever seen. I was able to see your technology up close, and I became a closet American admirer on the spot. And to tell you the truth, I have been one ever since. If you ever say anything about it, I will deny it, let me tell you.

"We helped you shuttle your airplanes against German targets, some of them right here in Dresden, before they flew back to their home bases. It felt good then, and it feels good now working with you Americans again."

Roy's mind was wandering, but it became focused when he heard the phrase "working with you again." Roy knew he had been sent to meet Alexi for something. And since the Russians were going to be the planners, Alexi could be expected to know more about the details than did anybody else. Roy was about to find out the importance of what they were going to be doing. And now he realized he was expected to bring the overall plan back to brief his people.

Voroshilov had risen steadily in the MVD and he, Roy, knew he never became personally involved in any minor operation. That in itself told him there was something big coming up.

"Alex, what do you know about this?"

"All in good time, my boy. But first some refreshment for old time's sake." With that, he removed a small bottle of vodka and two glasses from the satchel he had been carrying.

"You know, in my country it is considered boring to get to the point of a business transaction too quickly. You Americans, with all your wealth, do not enjoy life like we Russians."

Roy waited before asking him any further questions. He knew it would be useless to discuss anything more until they had consumed several glasses of vodka. He knew from experience that this was his way of putting you at ease to lessen the shock of what he was going to tell you next.

"All right, Alex, tell me what you have been doing lately. If you insist, pour me a glass and then tell me your life's story. I know you are going to eventually, if the bottle holds out."

Alex smiled at him and then said, "I am going to make a

Russian of you yet."

"This much I do know about you," Roy said, as he reached for some vodka and a slice of dark rather disgusting looking bread and cheese he was being offered. He knew this was a Russian custom, a symbolic gesture more than anything else. This was Alex's way of saying he was his friend. Roy took the bread and cheese reluctantly, but he knew he would consume every crumb before they were through talking.

"You were recruited from the Army into the People's Commissariat for Internal affairs or the NKVD," Roy began, "I also know you were taught a kind of pigeon English by American G.I.'s at Paltavo when you were quite young. And that you later studied English in a military school before your several tours in the United States."

"Yes, I did work in New York, and I did learn the rudiments of your language while I was still in Russia–and strangely enough, from your own soldiers. You see, in those days there were not many of us Russians who could speak English, so once I could make myself understood, I was a likely candidate for our Intelligence Service."

They had sat down on another bench, this one out of sight of the ducks. Alex stopped eating in order to light another cigarette. He coughed a few times as the strong acrid smoke irritated his throat.

"Those things are going to kill you, Alex. One of our universities has just completed a study that proves they are bad for your health."

"What a waste of time and money. Everybody knows that, so what is new? Why don't they make a study on how to quit; then they would be doing something useful." The subject of education in the two countries was an endless good natured debate between the two men since first they started talking about things other than supposed intelligence secrets.

"Do you recall during the War how we helped you," Alexi said, "and we would have helped you even more had there not been a man so close to your President Roosevelt. This man, this J. Edgar Hoover, was paranoid about we Communists. He always thought we were trying to subvert your government and make it into a carbon copy of our own. This Hoover of yours might actually have cost a number of Americans their lives, because he was reluctant to seek our assistance earlier in the War."

"I was almost too young to remember personally," Collins said, "but you have to admit, Alex, in those days during the Great Depression, your country was behind certain labor organizations that were interested in establishing your own brand of collective bargaining unions. Ours is a free country, and we would not have thought too much about it if it hadn't been for your ideology. You must admit, when Stalin and Lenin both stated your goal as a nation was the overthrow of our government, Hoover did appear to get a little paranoid, as you say. At any rate, he certainly was reluctant to do business with you under any circumstances. And our president felt the same way for a long time. And maybe at the time they were justified. Anyway, let's not talk politics.

"Does this story of yours about our joint venture during the last War have anything to do with what you're planning now?" Collins asked him.

"It does, but only so far as it refreshes your memory about how things used to be," Alexi answered. "Because in spite of this so called Cold War our countries have been fighting, forever, we once cooperated to our mutual advantage. And if we drop our individual prejudices we can do it again. During the Great Patriotic War, when we were being overrun by Germans, our two countries banded together for mutual assistance. Besides those bombing ventures, we were most successful at some other things as well. But unfortunately, that is the last time we have ever cooperated in much of anything else."

"Refresh my memory," Roy said.

"Well, Colonel Donovan, head of your fledgling OSS, in spite of your FBI director, got limited approval from your president to contact us. We were never able to quite understand how you could ship thousands of tons of much needed War material into our port at Murmansk to help us, yet you still saw Communists behind every tree."

Alexi saw an opportunity to teach Collins something about the War in Russia. One of the things that galled him most was the lack of knowledge and interest shown by the average American. The Russian was unable to countenance what he believed was a blasé attitude toward the twenty-six million deaths the Soviets suffered at the hands of the Germans.

"Your Donovan had the foresight to realize as the War came to a close that your airmen who had been shot down over France and Germany were in grave danger. There were two large prison camps, one up by the Polish border and the other right here in Eastern Germany. He realized the closer our Armies got to those camps, the greater the danger. He foresaw a time when the German guards would cut and run, leaving the prisoners in the midst of the general population to fend for themselves. These civilians had been harshly dealt with by your bombers, and he expected them to seek revenge. Then too, they did not want your people to find their way back home to do it again. Donovan believed the German people were going to kill them at the first opportunity, and he asked your President Roosevelt for permission to contact our NKVD to ask for our assistance.

"His plan was to have our commandos raid these prison camps before the German guards abandoned them. Once we acquired the prisoners, we were to transport them into the interior of Russia, where you could send in airplanes to fly them out. We used our base at Paltavo to do this. Before the War ended, hundreds of your personnel on our soil were working to save these airmen. And another reason for the base at Paltavo, as I have said, was to shuttle your bombers back and forth to German targets. It was a real ambitious and farsighted plan, promoted in spite of much narrow-minded opposition on your side. But it worked. And now we are faced with the same problem. We have a common enemy. And we also have shortsighted men on both sides who do not realize this fact."

Voroshilov paused for a minute waiting for the inevitable question as to who the enemy was.

"The common enemy tavarisch is China," he said. "She is Communist all right, but she is just as much our enemy as she is yours. It may not be apparent to you now, but she is. Believe me. And do not bother to ask me how we know. Just trust me on this, we know."

"Alex, old friend, when are you going to get to the point. Are you suggesting we are going to attack China, you and I?"

"Not exactly, but you are not too far off the mark. You are not far off at all," Voroshilov replied, as he began to explain what was going to happen.

CHAPTER 16...LANGLEY, VIRGINIA, 1972

A blue, chauffeured Buick with U.S. Air Force markings left an upper-class neighborhood on the north side of McLean, Virginia. It wound its way through morning traffic, turning off Montvale Way onto Ball Road and then right again for the short drive to the building housing the Central Intelligence Agency. There was no senior Air Force officer in the back seat, as might be expected. But there was a civilian, a Carl McDermott, who headed up the Military Operations Division.

They entered the gate via a circuitous route. They seldom took a direct path; always it was different, and always it was selected at random. And always it was chosen by the passenger and not the driver.

Having discharged his passenger at the front entrance reserved for department heads and their assistants, the driver proceeded toward Newport News.

Inside the foyer, McDermott crossed the tile floor, avoiding stepping on a large organizational seal, which was some sixteen feet in diameter. As he walked toward the elevators, he looked up from force of habit at the almost full-sized mural of an officer in the uniform of a major general. This proud, imposing figure was an excellent likeness of William Donovan, the wartime founder of the OSS and the first director of the CIA. The painting had been placed in its present position as a tribute to Donovan, who had served honorably and well in the First World War and who had sacrificed much for his country in the second. It was also a constant reminder that he had been the embodiment of what the CIA was supposed to stand for.

McDermott moved like a man with a purpose toward a waiting elevator. His eyes now refocused on the floor, he glanced neither to the right nor to the left, lost in thought. A man with a genial personality on the surface, he was thought to be bubbling like a caldron deep in the bowels of his psyche. And more than one of his colleagues had quietly voiced the opinion that one day he might boil over when least expected.

He did not bother to ask his secretary for a rundown on any meetings scheduled. He had called ahead. He wanted to see certain people, mostly the heads of branches who had already heard the name of the project known as The Russian Plan. And he wanted them assembled and ready to go upon his arrival.

He walked into a private conference room off his office and took a seat at the head of the table. He looked up and nodded to those assembled and mentally took a role call. Pity the poor straggler who chose to come to work late this morning, one of his aides thought to himself.

Something big is about to happen, Ralph Levy whispered to one of his more trusted friends before McDermott was seated. And now he was sure of it; he could see his supervisor's engine running particularly hard, as though it was in the wrong gear.

McDermott glanced down the table over his half glasses at the assembly and then paused before saying anything. It was quite clear he was having second thoughts about who should be in attendance. Two weeks before, when he had received a quick run-down on something the Director referred to as the Russian Plan, he had personally chosen those present. Now, after hearing a detailed briefing by Roy Collins, late last night at his home, he had changed his mind. This was too sensitive. He would designate it need to know, which meant not all of them were going to be privy to any part of it. Those who remained seated refrained from watching the others leave. To be asked to leave under these circumstances was to be recognized as one who was not on the highest rungs of the totem. That is, they were probably not on the inside track for advancement.

This was one of those programs calling for an insertion into a foreign country without their permission. And it carried the highest operational designator, because it would result in extreme embarrassment if it were ever compromised. Not even Roy Collins had been asked to attend. He was not the head of a branch; but that was not the real reason. It was because he had long been on the outs with McDermott and the Director himself.

When things had settled back down and McDermott had his ducks in a row, he called the meeting to order. Pencils and paper, which had been placed on the table, was now being picked up by his secretary. His first announcement was an advisory that no notes would be taken and that the operation they were going to be discussing had the highest of priorities.

He began by telling them they were going to be involved in a covert operation by the now coded name of *Operation Gobi Desert*. He followed with a statement that his office was in receipt of orders from the National Security Council, which had secured the necessary go-ahead authority from Congress and the White House some weeks before. He said he had only been given the basics of the plan at that time and none of the details nor the expected outcome, because they had not been known. Hopefully,

in cases like this, he said, if all went well neither the few par-
ticipating congressmen nor anybody outside the Company would
ever know what happened. But this case was much different than
any other McDermott had ever staffed. And eventually all concerned would come to know about it in the minutest detail.

Contrary to popular belief, the CIA does not institute covert
activity on its own. This is the job of the President's National
Security Advisor. Once begun, however, they were at liberty to
do most anything they thought was justifiable, if it was in the best
interests of the nation. And they were the judges of what exactly
those best interests were.

The National Security Act of 1947 had effectively cut off
Congress's monitoring function. However, President Eisenhower
foresaw a problem with this early on and had taken steps to seek
a remedy. He had established his own committee to oversee the
Agency. But with his passing, the situation had regressed back to
the way it was before. And now they justified their position with
a reasonable argument: the more Congress got into the act the
more the danger for compromise.

The Second World War had shown the Congress to have
been full of indiscreet politicians. And when some of them had
been plied with hard liquor, which was often the case, they
became loose cannons. And the more there were of these good
citizens who had a direct hand in things, the more room there
was for compromise and attendant loss of life. This situation had
made it difficult to coordinate plans with Great Britain. During
the War, the British were afraid their highest secrets were going
to be compromised by one of our more mouthy politicians. And
when it happened, it could very well place their own undercover
agents in danger. To avoid this eventuality, certain procedures had
been established between Roosevelt and Churchill that bypassed
Congress. And in later years, the CIA had come to believe that

coordination with this branch of government must be kept to a trusted few members.

"This operation is PP," McDermott exclaimed. "However, we shall dispense with the psychological aspect. It will be para-military, a slash and burn, in and out. The Russians are responsible for the planning; however, we'll have to secure our own exit plan and follow up, because I don't trust them to look out for us.

"Ralph," he said, as he looked again over his half-glasses at Levy, his chief planner for operations. "We must have a fall-back position, and a general briefing with a dance-off for those who are outside, but who feel they have a need to know. I'm speaking of Budget and some of the others.

"Our cover concerns a need for an interdiction of four people, one of them is Russian. And incidentally, this is some kind of benchmark. We've never, not in most of our memories anyway, participated with the Russians in any kind of activity.

"Basically," McDermott began again...the sound of the filler word always rubbed Ralph Levy the wrong way. He did not like McDermott very much, considering him to be below his intellectual level. Frankly, Levy, a graduate of an Ivy League school, and his boss, who was from a Midwestern university, did not always agree on everything. The proper use of the king's English was one of those things.

Levy had been given the unenviable task of rewriting all of his inter-departmental talking papers. They were always liberally scattered with filler words and hackneyed phrases. Levy's objections to their use were often cause for disagreement, although in the end McDermott usually acquiesced. But it took much of Levy's time, and he had come to resent McDermott's lack of education. He figured it was all well and good to be an attorney or whatever, but he saw the English language as a subject that should have been mastered before progressing on to something else.

McDermott was his superior because of his intelligence and his proven management skills. When he was hired away from one of Washington's prestigious law firms, it was assumed his ability at written communication had been well established. But Levy and McDermott's secretary were aware of his shortcomings. And Levy knew that one of his more important jobs was to make sure his boss was not found wanting. Levy was the supervisor of a branch, and he found this sort of thing demeaning. And he resented McDermott taking his time with something he considered to be outside his job description. When he suggested the job be taken over by one of the bright new people, he had been told he was doing a good job. The truth was, McDermott did not trust just anybody with what he considered to be as important as anything else coming from Levy's office.

"We are going into China with four people to establish a beach-head." Whenever possible, McDermott chose to couch his phraseology in military terms. Some of his colleagues chose sports terminology, however, he never particularly liked sports, and he had been in the Army. He had never been in combat, but considered it a minor oversight on the part of history.

"This operation will be conducted in two phases," he continued, "the first is the beach-head, the second is the actual seek out and destroy.

"The destroy part is going to take the most effort from a staff stand-point. And it's here we'll encounter the highest probability for a screw-up. Being compromised on the enemy's soil will put us all in a world of hurt. So I warn you at the outset, we had better get it right the first time. There will be no second chance."

Levy admired McDermott for his ability to express himself in platitudes and Company jargon. He thought to himself: *this briefing is going to supply me with comment about his inadequacies for some time to come.* As underlings, subservient to a powerful man, privately ridiculing him was the only way in which he and his colleague sitting next to him could maintain some kind of personal identity.

"As far as finding the target is concerned," McDermott continued, "the Russians have done it for us. It's a large fission reactor power plant experimenting with deuterium water using natural uranium. What is of the gravest concern to the highest heads of both our governments, and perhaps those of England and the United Nations as well as all of Europe, if they knew about it, is the fact it's a breeder and China's chief supplier of U-235. But the UN and the Europeans are not going to know about it because they will talk it to death, and in the end the *gooks* will still go right on making weapons grade plutonium. And you better believe it, sooner than later, if they are allowed to continue, they are going to have the bomb."

McDermott paused for the briefest of seconds to let his constituents absorb the ramifications of what he had just said. Before any of them could raise their hands to ask questions, he pushed on.

"Right. We are going to blow this baby, with minimal help from the Russkies, I expect." No sooner had he said it than he wished he could have retracted both statements. He was constantly forgetting that some members of his own staff had been recruited from the MVD. And some of them were Chinese with impeccable credentials. They did not deserve to be the object of his racial slurs. And he knew after he had said it that they were going to find out. And as far as the Russians were concerned, they were serving with distinction, too. Their loyalty had never been in dispute. They were working for this country but considered themselves to be Russians; they thought of themselves as working for the liberation of mother Russia from a repressive dictatorship.

Looking down the table again, his gaze settled back on Levy. "Ralph, I want you to pay particular attention to plausible denial when you put together our exit plan. The Russians are responsible for the overall. But rest assured they're going to have another one in their hip pocket, and it's going to put the blame squarely on us if anything goes wrong. This means we're going to have to swipe a copy of the real plan if we can, and then formulate one of our own accordingly. That's where the plausible denial comes in. If something screws up, we want to be able to say they were responsible–deny we ever had anything to do with anything, and make it plausible. Blame the Russians–are we clear on this. And I caution you all. What you have heard here will remain here. There will be no exceptions. Understood?" What he meant was there will be no water cooler talk with anyone not at the table.

Levy sat smarting in his chair. McDermott always did it this way, maybe without thinking. But it appeared to all present that he, Levy, did not know his job. His superior seemed to be always stating the obvious at his expense. Where McDermott saw it as a supervisor's responsibility to cover all the bases, Levy saw it as over-the-shoulder supervision. In fact, he thought it went a step further; he thought McDermott was showing off a little at his expense.

"Get hold of Roy Collins and see if he can get Voroshilov to get us a copy of their real plan ahead of time. I don't want any surprises. He owes us several favors. If this doesn't work, tell Collins to lean on him a little. Tell him I want a copy, even if he has to buy it. Voroshilov is coming up for retirement and can use the nest egg, although I'll put in with you if he doesn't already have several of those stashed away in a Swiss bank. And I'd give plenty to know how much is in that slush fund of his."

Levy had been thinking, his mind now going a mile a minute. He knew from experience his boss was going to ask him how long it was going to take him to put together a rough draft of something he referred to as his talking paper, something to poop him up, as he was fond of saying.

McDermott would be expected to answer any and all questions put to him by a layer or two of insulation between him and the Director. And being the smart operator he was, he knew the question-and-answer sessions could start any time. Based on his experience, McDermott knew he would be called on to recite as early as the first thing in the morning. And the only way to survive in this politically oriented bureaucracy was to always be prepared. Levy knew this, and it meant he and several of his people would be expected to work most of the night. And then do it all over again when they found out from Voroshilov what the Russians really had up their sleeves.

The question came a few minutes later. Not exactly a question, but rather a statement. He knew McDermott expected him to work from now until it was finished. He was not surprised when he said, "Can you have it ready by morning?"

"Yes sir," was his reply. The way Levy said it had an edge. McDermott missed it, but the others in the room, who were frequently in the same spot, did not. It should not be too bad, it could have been on the week-end, and then we would be expected to work straight through to Monday Morning. He did not mind that much. But he had to work his people overtime. He was not trying to win any popularity contests, but he hated to be constantly on the receiving end of what he saw as McDermott's insensitivity toward his people and his lack of foresight and planning. It was as though he did not care.

"Alex, you owe me one," Collins said, "maybe more than one, how about it?"

They were drinking coffee at a sidewalk café in Paris, on

the West Bank of the Seine. It was their second meeting on this subject and they had been discussing the Plan. Not the one the Russian was going to give him now, but the one the Russians were reluctant to talk about, the one they intended to keep to themselves. Collins had just been handed an Operations Plan, which was in English. What he really wanted was the one McDermott had sent him there to get from Voroshilov.

A quick look at the one he had just been given told him the format was much like the one used by the U.S. military. He asked Alex why that was. He asked him if they had appropriated the format or whether he thought it was original. Alex smiled and shrugged his shoulders when told it came from one of the schools at the Air University.

"You invite hundreds of student officers from third world nations, and you teach them military science. What do you expect?" was his answer.

"I know this one is for show; you explained it all to me in Dresden," Collins said, as he leafed through the pages. "What I'm more interested in, though, is the one in Moscow–the one that lays out what is really going to happen."

Alexi smiled again, saying, "How much *fluce* do you have?" The exaggerated motions and the inflection of his voice when he said *fluce* was a poor imitation of an Arab rug dealer. It was pure camp, which told Collins his friend had a lighter side, one he had never seen before.

"Seriously," Alexi said, "I would rather you give me a little something for my hope chest than to trade favors. This way I will still be indebted to you. You would not want to go away knowing we were even. You would never have an excuse for coming back if we did."

"How long is it going to take to arrange?"

"Maybe three weeks."

"Too long," Collins replied.

"What do you suggest then?" Alexi shrugged.

"How much of it do you remember, and how much are you willing to take for the verbal now to be followed up with a written?"

"You know the going rate is fifty thousand American. Get caught and it is normally twenty years in Lubyanka. But this one will get me shot." Collins looked at him for a few seconds. His smile of a few moments ago was gone. Here was reality. No one in Russia jokes when they speak of Lubyanka. Shot maybe, but not Lubyanka.

"How much of it do you remember?"

"All of it, almost verbatim. Trust me."

"Good enough."

"Fifty thousand?"

'Right, we have a deal."

"That McDermott wienie will not renege, then?"

"He might if he gets a chance. But I'll not give him a chance. I'll get him to commit to the price before I give him anything. I'll make sure he agrees in front of some of his people, maybe Ralph Levy. He's a good head, and he would be more than overjoyed to blow the whistle on him. That way he could arrange a transfer without prejudice. Yes, he would be the one to witness the promise."

Alexi smiled a complimentary smile–a well done from one professional to another.

The thing about most Russians, Collins observed, they like to interject slang into a conversation with an American whenever they can. They figure the one who can speak with the most slang speaks the better English. Where they learn it though, Collins had no idea. Maybe from the shoe-shine kids in the larger cities? And maybe the movies?

"You tell him if he refuses to pay me he is going to get himself castrated some dark night. And you tell him I said so *tavarish*, I kid you not." Collins had heard him use that expression more than a few times in their general conversations. He thought maybe Jack Paar, the old *Tonight Show* host, was currently the rage on television in Moscow. He figured about fifteen years late was about right.

"Do you object if I record what you're going to tell me?"

Alexi shrugged his shoulders and gestured with his hands as if to say he did not care.

Collins removed a small state-of-the-art recorder from his inside jacket pocket. Alexi asked for permission to examine it; then he said, looking first at the recorder and then glancing up at Collins, "My, oh my, what have we here, Dick Tracy or Flash Gordon?"

A few seconds later, Alexi's facial expressions had changed completely. Now he was all business again. "I understand, old friend, you are going to be one of those to go in. If so, let me tell you right here and now to watch out. Keep your wits about you at all times. There is something about this one that does not ring true. I do not know exactly what it is, but I do know there are some deals that are going to be made. Even the plan I am going to tell you about right now has twists and turns. And it might be superceded by yet another one. I cannot tell you about the others because I do not know. And the worst part, it is so sensitive they are purposely by-passing me. I have nothing to go on, just a feeling. Have you considered that McDermott might have your friend, Ralph Levy, working on yet another one right now, one you know nothing about? It is a fine business we two have chosen for ourselves, *tavarish*. And there is something else that has occurred to me. Every major player in this operation is on the outs looking in. Every single one is under some cloud or other, including myself.

"Yes, my people have suspected us for some time," Voroshilov said, "I have a sneaking suspicion they are using me for this one job, and then it is the Seine or the Volga for me some dark night."

"What are you going to do?"

"I am going to take the money you give me and run."

"Where to?

Someplace cheap, and someplace where they have no ice and snow."

"You told me about a Russian girl. You know, the one you said came from China or Tibet–the one I didn't want to tag along for obvious reasons. Is she under a cloud like the rest of us?"

"She is, indeed, Voroshilov said, "That is what I am trying to tell you. It may be coincidence that she is, if you believe in such things, or it may be because I am Russian and always *tre suspici*. But I tell you, I do not like it."

Collins looked at him with a concerned expression: "Do you think this is all a ploy to get rid of us after we blow the power plant? Do you think they got their heads together, my people and yours, and decided to use us just this once more? Do you think it is really possible they called me back to do this job, and then they planned to do me, after I threatened to write a book?"

Collins complexion changed. Alexi could see he was visibly shaken as the whole nasty plot began to unfold before his eyes. Collins was sharp. Usually he was quick on the uptake when looking for misleads, but this one had temporarily gone over his head. "And that bastard McDermott! Is there anything he is not capable of doing?" He was looking at Alexi when he said it, but he was really talking to himself.

"Suppose you start from the beginning and don't leave anything out. I want it straight." Collins told him.

"All right, here it is, quick and dirty. This is what I know for sure: You, Eckert, Rosenthal, and a Russian girl are going to meet in a building in Singapore. There you are going to plan the mission. Actually, it is all planned for you. What you are going to be doing is familiarizing yourselves with what is going to happen. You are going to be dropped by parachute near the Tibetan border with your equipment. You will become like Tibetan nomads, and live with a tribe for several weeks before you do anything at all. Then, as the tribe wanders closer to your target, the nuclear power plant, you are going to sortie by horseback as far as you can. You are supposed to be on a simple reconnaissance mission to determine the best way to blow the plant and to see the lay of the land for yourselves. You will leave after another few weeks and make your way by horse to the mountains. There you will change back into some European clothes, where you will pose as mountain climbers. You will stay there for about a week, acting like you are going to climb something, and then you will change your minds and leave."

"So what am I paying you all the money for? What you are telling me you have told me before. And there is something else that comes to mind."

"What?" he asked

"You may just have euchred yourself out of fifty thousand dollars."

"It would appear so; but as you say, I haven't really told you anything else you don't know. There is nothing in this written plan you have in your hand that is new, and as you say, nothing I just told you comes as a surprise. But what I am going to tell you next will frost your eyeballs. When I have told you what is really going to happen you will agree I have earned my money. Besides paying me, there is something else I want."

"What is that?"

"You can give me some more of your cigarettes and the tape recorder."

Collins smiled at him and then handed over a carton of cigarettes from his duffle bag. He knew Alexi was a chain smoker who would do about anything for an American cigarette.

"Here, take these. I wish there were more. But you can save them for special occasions to remember me by."

"I will, and thank you. I say, do you have an extra cartridge for the machine?" Collins nodded as he removed the used one and put it inside his jacket pocket. He loaded the recorder as Alex watched him, and then he handed it to him.

"Okay *tavarisch*, what is in the written plan I just gave you is for the benefit of your boss. He knows you are going to read it before you get back. But what you should really be concerned with is what else I am going to tell you. It is for you alone. And of course for Eckert and Rosenthal as well. But not before you are in place.

"Now pay attention: the woman is not to know that you know anything about this new stuff. This is most important. Do you understand me? If she finds out you know, she will kill you all and make her way out by herself. Our people and yours, too, cannot afford to take a chance on anybody knowing what is actually going to happen.

"Well, the real skinny, my friend, it ain't going to happen the way they want you to think it is."

Under other circumstances, Collins thought it would be funny to listen to Voroshilov practice his slang. He realized he had been watching some old Humphrey Bogart movies recently, and that is who he was this week. Next week it would be James Cagney or somebody else. But right now he was not amused. He was scared, real scared, and his friend was not helping him much.

"How is it going to happen then?" Collins asked.

"Well, as you know, the first trip in is for practice, and to get your explosives and other equipment into place. If all goes well, then you go back in a few weeks to finish the job. That is what everybody, including the Europeans, will be told.

"But here is what is really going down: You are not going to blow anything. That would make it look like sabotage. Sabotage is a political thing and is not going to get much press coverage compared to an accident. And the real plan has always been for you to make it happen so it looks like an accident.

"You, my friend, think you are going to blow it up. But the Russian woman is going to make it melt down. All the way down. She is going to make it look like the worst nuclear accident in the history of nuclear fission. And the reason for the accident scenario is to bring worldwide attention to China and her illegal activities. And you are going to put the fear of God into the rest of the third world who are experimenting with nuclear power plants for the sole purpose of making plutonium bombs. I mean Pakistan and India and Korea and all the rest. You, tavarish, are going to be part of an operation that is going to change nuclear policy on a worldwide scale for the next thirty or forty years.

"And you may not be able to escape with your lives, unless you have your own exit plan. Because the one I am telling you about now calls for you all to be consumed in the radioactive cloud, just as thousands living in Tibet and Mongolia will be. That is what it is all about. One great big disaster that focuses on the problem to get the attention of the free world, and to get a final overall policy having some teeth in it.

"And here is the thing. It is going to be so big, both of our countries and England will ally against the fence sitters, like France and Germany. We will impose our will on them to make the world conform, through military action if necessary.

"The written plan, the one in your hand, calls for you to blow the plant hoping to get China out of the nuclear business; it is the one you are going to take back. But McDermott and Levy are in on the know. They have conspired with our people to come up with a new one, the one involving a melt-down, which I have just explained to you. And for the real scoop, which gives you a chance to save your lives, you owe me fifty K. How does that grab you? How do you like them apples?"

"Oh! And what about her?" Roy asked.

"Do not worry. She will be taken care of in due course, I kid you not. Did I tell you to leave her alone? Well that may be another reason you do not want to get too close to her; do you understand?"

Collins nodded his head and Alexi continued: "If you really understand, then pay close attention to what comes next."

Collins nodded his head again.

"This is what is actually going to happen then. As I said, you are going to carry in a sizeable amount of explosives. The written plan is to blow the plant to reduce the nuclear fallout as much as possible. But the Chinese are going to know it is sabotage and blame the Tibetans. But what is actually going to happen, as I have said, the woman is going to cause a melt-down and scatter a much larger radioactive cloud, which will blow toward Tibet and the desert tribes in the area. We Russians will appear on the scene as if by magic. We will give out the story that we detected it first and rushed to the aid of the nomads, who of course are some of our own people. So we will maintain we have a right to be there without the Chinese government's permission. We will give the world press the story and the pictures before the Chinese can get on the scene with a cover story. We will convince the press it is an accident and not sabotage. Sabotage will get much less world reaction than will an accident. An accident, caused by people who are viewed as technically inadequate to handle nuclear power, will raise the hue and cry from one end of the earth to the other. And hopefully, the United Nations will then pass a resolution getting all third world nations out of the nuclear power plant business. Then, with your help and the help of Britain, we will force the UN to act to prevent them from getting back in again."

Before Collins could interrupt to ask a question, Alexi continued: "The woman is the key player. She is going to set the charges inside. You and the other two are there just to see she gets close to the place. She is supposed to set the charges to blow the reactor. But now get a load of this. She is not going to blow the reactor. She is going to put the charges on the intake cooling valves–not enough to destroy them, either, but enough to jam them so the computer cannot regulate the water surrounding the reactor."

Collins was flabbergasted. At first he was in denial. Nobody would risk the lives of thousands of innocent people just to make a point. But then he asked himself, What would it take to wake-up the world to the real nuclear problem i.e. illicit power plants in the hands of screw-ball dictators like Saddam Hussain and Quadaffi and the rest of them. Does the end justify the means? Yes, it does. It is not only justifiable, the way they see it, but it is plausible. It is more than plausible it is just the thing they would think up between the two of them–NSC and the MVD.

"As I was saying," Alexi continued with his explanation of what was going to happen, "when the computer becomes unable to regulate the water protecting the reactor, technicians will by-pass it and try manually to shunt in a secondary emergency supply. Once that happens, the klaxons will sound off automatically. When they go off, you will be witness to a Chinese fire drill."

He stopped momentarily as he started to laugh. Then Collins started to laugh at the saying, as the picture became reality in their minds. Alexi had no idea where it came from. He had picked it up someplace, and because it was so expressive, he had remembered it.

"Do you know where it originated?" he asked Collins.

"Yes, in San Francisco in the late1800's.

"How is that?"

"Well, the area known as the Barbary Coast was full of wooden tenements. They teemed with Chinese Cooley laborers, sometimes as many as ten men to a room. There were, of course, no electric lights yet. But there were gas lamps. Occasionally, one would get knocked off the wall in one of the many scuffles that broke out. And sometimes a kerosene lamp on a table would get knocked over inadvertently, setting fire to a tinderbox structure. When the alarm went off, the hapless Chinese, who were deathly afraid of fire, ran around stumbling over each other. They poured out the windows and over the roofs trying to get to the ground. The ensuing melee was often worse than the fire itself. But the confusion of people running around can easily be visualized, what with all the shouting and passing out of false information about where the fire was located. It all added to the confusion, and it became known as a Chinese fire drill."

Alexi, who had no soft spot in his heart for the Chinese, had started to laugh. The longer Collins talked, the more vivid the scene in San Francisco became to him and the louder he laughed. The laughter became contagious; the two of them released built-up tension as they laughed uproariously at the imaginary scene and the reality of the scene that was going to take place in the Gobi.

"As I was saying, before we had our little laugh," Voroshilov paused again as he wiped a tear from his eye. "The valve charge is not going off at once, of course. It may be delayed as much as twenty four hours. But the point is this, and I kid you not, she is not going to be around when it does go off, and you are."

"Now let me tell you again about the details of what is really going to happen. Keep it under your hat–my, what a quaint expression. Keep it there, under your hat, until you are alone in the Gobi; then brief the other two."

CHAPTER 17...TIBETAN PLATEAU, 1972

The four of them were sitting beside a dwindling campfire, which was located on the vast Tibetan range north and west of the Himalayas. This area, where upwards of two million nomads still live, is one of the most rugged rangelands in the world. The altitude and general harshness of the area continues to keep the Chinese, and particularly the Tibetan farmer, out of the region.

The nomads raise horses of the small pony variety, as well as yaks, sheep, and goats. Cattle do not fare too well because of the severity of the climate and because of the altitude in the high alpine grazing areas. The yak is said to be the most important animal on the Steppes. It supplies the nomad with food, transportation, fuel for cooking and heating of the tents, and most importantly, their long hair is woven and braided for dozens of different uses.

Women and girls weave the long hair into ropes and wearing apparel, as well as long, wide braided bands, which they use to cover the framework of their tents. A typical tent consists of several long, flexible poles bent and tied at the bottom with yak hair rope. The framework is then overlapped with wide bands of woven and braided yak hair. They are constructed so as to keep the rain and the wind out and to keep the inside relatively warm during the extreme temperatures found in the high valleys at night, even in the summer. When the tribe decides to move, which is often, they simply roll up the yak hair bands, tie the poles to a yak, and they are ready to travel to the next grazing area.

Their movements are organized so as to best preserve the grass between large meadows, to protect the fragile ecosystem, and to take advantage of pastures located in different areas at different seasons.

They have learned over the centuries to mix their livestock as a way to protect their livelihood in event of severe frost, unpredictable droughts, and snow storms. A typical herd might consist of a mixture of sheep, goats, yaks, and horses, all grazing side by side.

Most nomads have a tribal home base, which is usually their traditional wintering area. In the spring they venture out in a wide circle, returning to their home in the fall. On the annual trek they live in yak hair tents, while some of them abandon their tents for more traditional houses in the winter. Some living in Nepal and India have combined herding with the planting of crops. However, they still move their herds to the high grazing areas but grow grains in the lower valleys.

The four adventurers had been parachuted into the upper western-most part of the Tibetan province. To the north and east lay the flat lands of the Gobi, where their instructions said they would find the new Chinese power plant.

There was nothing to do after the sun went down, so they usually went to bed to keep warm. Their hosts had provided them with a yak hair tent, one of some fifty located near the foothills of the plateau. They had yak hair blankets as well as sheepskins. And they slept on both sheepskin and yak hair rugs for pallets. They had found it to be fairly comfortable, if somewhat crowded for the four of them.

The Russian girl had been brought along, and now that Collins knew all of the details of the operation, he was surprised at himself for objecting to her in the first place.

She had proven invaluable. As advertised, she spoke Tibetan as well as her native Russian and English. In fact, he did not see how they would have been able to come this far without her. In most parts of the world, somebody spoke a little English. But in this primitive back-water no one did.

When they first met, Rosenthal had attempted to communicate with her in the language of the Sanskrit. He knew Tibetan was not supposed to be related to Hindu or the languages of Nepal. But he also knew their script was the same as Sanskrit, the ancient language of India, and he had been looking forward to spending some time with her to see if he could discover what, if anything, they might have in common. He knew from his studies that ancient Buddhist and Brahman manuscripts had been taken from India and translated into Tibetan. Herb believed that in the process some Sanskrit may have found its way into the language.

They had been listening to Herb and the woman conversing in English, with Herb taking notes. When it became too dark for him to see, he stopped. The woman, who was bored, and who looked upon Rosenthal as being a truly odd duck, had eventually ignored him and had gone into the tent to sleep.

But Rosenthal was not through talking for the night, and he began directing his remarks to the other two. He had been holding court on the ancient Tibetan language for the past hour, telling them about how he intended to make a study of the language his hosts spoke and its relationship to the Aryan language of the Indus Valley.

He had been explaining to them about the origins of Sanskrit and its effect on modern civilization. This led him into an explanation of the origins of the Aryan language, and how Adolph Hitler had made a quantum leap from the so-called Sanskrit/Aryan language root to the actual genetic derivation of the ancient Germanic tribes.

"That whole business of having superior Aryan blood, as opposed to Semitic, was just so much bull," he told them. "The fact the so-called Aryans of the Indus may have spoken a form of Sanskrit at the time the Semites in the Fertile Crescent were speaking a form of Hebrew had nothing to do with the origins of the Germanic tribes.

"The Aryans migrated from the North Country to the area in and around Pakistan, eventually becoming the largest segment of the population in the Indus. They were supposed to have come from the mythical Thule. And, according to Hitler, they brought with them all the blood lines of a superior Nordic race. Over the centuries they were supposed to have dispersed into Greece and Rome and finally, according to him, they became the roots of the ancient Germanic tribes.

"Hitler believed everything worthwhile in the world had been produced by these people and their offspring. The Jew, on the other hand, had contributed little if anything, and furthermore, the world was in danger of having the Aryan gene pool diluted and eventually contaminated by the Semites.

"The fact is, the Germanic tribes can trace their stock more clearly to the barbarian Visigoths than to anybody else," he said. "But Hitler was not interested in facts that were in opposition to his own ideas. He was all wrapped up in seeing parallels between the culture of the ancient Aryans and the past accomplishments of the German people. He sincerely believed he was predestined to ensure the continuing purity of the German race.

"Hitler liked this kind of convoluted reasoning," Herb went on to say, "And since no one ever questioned him, all but a very few Germans came to accept it as scholarship. Joseph Goebbles, his minister of propaganda, was one of those who knew the truth. But Goebbles saw Hitler's bunkum as an excellent way of uniting the German people against a common cause–namely me and the rest of my progenitors."

Herb paused for a moment to see how his words were being received. Collins was admittedly confused, perhaps because he had not been listening too closely. But Eckert was listening with rapt attention. Herb had not made up his mind about Eckert. Now, when he saw he was paying close attention, as a good student should, he became more impressed with him.

"I did some research and consultation work a few years back for the Simon Wiesenthal Center," Herb paused and then continued. "They were engaged in a study of this very subject."

When Eckert showed no sign of losing interest, he pressed on with his dissertation: "Part of my contribution to the project was a paper on the historical derivation of the mysticism associated with some of the early beliefs of National Socialism. You know, many historians and scholars too, believe the Nazis were almost as much about the occult, astrology, and icon symbolism as they were about a political party. And they believed that much of Nazi doctrine was rooted in the symbols and rituals of certain secret societies; one such was the ancient Knights Templar of the Crusades period.

"Hitler was greatly influenced by some of the German writers of the twenties and their beliefs in the occult. And certainly he leaned heavily on the mysticism of the Eastern religions, namely the Aryans, for much of his religious-like dogma.

"Sometime, if either of you are interested, we can discuss this subject further. You might find it to be very enlightening, as it goes a long way to explain the rapid rise of the Nazi party."

Eckert, who was most familiar with the advent of the Third Reich from his studies at Drexel interrupted, since Herb gave no indication he was going to stop talking. "Weren't the Knights Templar Freemasons while still having sworn an oath of fealty to Richard?"

Herb looked at him, much the way Dr. Zinn the atomic physicist had looked, when he discovered Herb was not an absolute dolt.

"Some authorities believe that's true. They believe Freemasonry began in Jerusalem during the Crusades. However, others don't. They believe it started with the cathedral builders of the Middle Ages in England. But don't get the idea Hitler was any friend of Freemasonry, because he wasn't. The Freemasons were seen by him as being a secret society that had sworn certain oaths to principles that were not always consistent with Hitler's ideas about National Socialism. Then, too, he didn't like secret societies in general, because he couldn't control them and he didn't know what was going on. Having said this, I should qualify my statement by saying that in the beginning Hitler might have gone along with them if they had gone along with him."

"What do you mean?" Eckert asked him.

"Well, for instance, Hitler had them change much of the wording in the craft degrees to come more in line with what he thought was the modern Germany. For example, he changed references to Solomon's Temple to the German Cathedral. And certain references to direct personages, he replaced with certain metaphors he considered less innocuous. I realize I have not made myself very clear, but there are several books on this subject written after the War, which you can read when you get the time. They also explain why the German Grand Lodge acquiesced, and allowed their membership to join the Nazi party. But following this, a circular was written by one of the grand masters, whose name slips my mind. He stated in his letter that he considered them all to no longer be Freemasons. Whatever they were, they were not Masons. They had changed the ancient and accepted ritual to the point where he considered them to be something else. This infuriated Hitler; when he heard about it, he outlawed all lodges in Germany forthwith. There is also evidence that certain of the brethren who went back to the practice of the standard ritual may have been martyred as a result."

Eckert seemed to accept this simplistic explanation of an interesting and complex subject. But Herb realized for the first time the waters of Eckert's mind ran far deeper than he suspected. And he promised himself that in the future, he would allow Eckert more say in the planning of this operation and the one to follow.

Eckert marveled at the depth of Rosenthal's knowledge on such a wide variety of obscure subjects. But when he asked Herb if he had spent much time in the study of Freemasonry, Rosenthal just shrugged his shoulders and said, "No, not much. In fact, not much at all."

"Tell me something," Eckert said, "while we are on this general subject. I heard you mention the Knights Templar. Were they descendant from the Merovingean kings of the fifth century?"

Well, well, I have found me a live one after all. Just when you think universities are teaching little or nothing these days, up pops a splendid surprise. "They were, indeed, old boy. In fact many of the leading families of Europe can trace their blood lines from the Merovengians through the Templars right up to the present day."

"I really would like to hear more on this subject, if you're not too sleepy."

"Not at all," Herb said. As he looked around, he noticed Collins had gone to sleep, but not inside the tent with the girl. "If you're sure you're interested, I can talk on for hours on this fascinating subject? Do you have anything special you want to discuss?"

"Yes, as a matter of fact there is. You say many of the members of Europe's ruling classes were Templars. Does that include those of Hungary in particular? How about the Esterhazy family; are they included?"

"Oh yeah, they're especially included. There is strong evidence the Esterhazy princes, the de facto bankers of Europe, along with the Rothschilds, of course, were Templars. Although I would hesitate to claim that the banking success of the Esterhazy was in any way related to the early business methods instituted by the Templars of the Crusades. But you know, it just occurred to me there might be an interesting parallel. Maybe it had something to do with the oaths of honesty they took, in the same way the Templars promised to treat their fellow man. And maybe some of the teachings of Freemasonry were involved as well."

"Did you mean the prominent Jewish banking houses were Templars?" Eckert asked, confused by part of his last statement.

"No, I meant the Rothschilds shared the distinction of being one of Europe's chief financiers. However, they could have been Templars just as they could have been Masons, but I don't think it likely."

"Is there any evidence some of the Templar wealth remained after the Inquisition instituted by Philip the Fair had the majority of them assassinated?"

"I'm glad you didn't include Pope Clement in your statement," Herb remarked. "You know there are many scholars who believe he was involved in a major way. Clement saw them as a threat to the Church as much as they were to the economic well-being of the Christian world. But I don't agree with this thesis; I mean I don't believe Clement was involved in the attempt to eradicate the Order to the extent that some do."

"Was any Templar wealth salvaged?" Eckert asked.

"Lots of it. Maybe millions of dollars were stashed outside France and England, although it was probably in gold and jewels and not in the coin of the day."

"Could it have been in lose diamonds?" Eckert asked him.

Rosenthal looked at Eckert by the fading campfire–not in the same way he had at the beginning of their conversation, but from an altogether different perspective. When Rosenthal spoke again, it was not with the persona of the teacher. Now he was the interrogator, having discovered that Eckert was fishing for information. But why, Rosenthal did not know.

"Not likely diamonds, because diamonds didn't have the intrinsic value they do today. But they could have been converted from gold much later as a convenient way to stash them." *Eckert, I may have summed you up wrong again.*

"Don't take offense, old boy," Herb remarked, "but you're not the kindred spirit I took you to be. You're not a scholar after all. Something is on your mind besides obscure ancient history. Why don't you come right out and ask me what you want to know? Maybe I have the answer your looking for and maybe I don't. You're looking for something specific, aren't you? You're not interested in the Esterhazy family as some kind of history project. You have me curious. Now I want to know what's on your mind."

Collins liked to listen to Rosenthal. But most of the time he had no idea what Herb was talking about. And this was one of those times. However, he had heard that Herb spoke fluent

Sanskrit, whatever that was exactly. And anybody who could do this had to be smart enough to know where it came from. But true or not, his conversation helped pass the time. And it helped keep his mind off the girl sleeping in the tent a few feet away.

He was tired, but he did not want to go into the tent alone with her.

He had not forgotten Alexi's warning to keep her at a distance and to make sure the others understood. Still he was finding it hard to do. She was young at twenty-six, but she had led a hard and dangerous life; according to Alexi, she had worked undercover in several hot areas of the world. Alexi emphasized the fact that she killed with only the slightest provocation; it had been one of the reasons she had fallen from grace with Alexi's regime. And then she had volunteered for this assignment in order to get back in their good graces. But the thing that really scared Collins was the way she used a knife, which Alexi said she kept concealed at all times.

He thought at the time that Alexi might be kidding him a little; maybe not. But then maybe it was some kind of calculated ploy to keep them all away from her. Everybody knew an operation this far from civilization was doomed if the bunch of them started fighting over a woman.

That was it, he thought. It was just a story. It could have been a scene from one of the Russian classical novelists, everybody out in the wilderness killing everybody else over a woman. It was the kind of Russian romance that would have pleased his buddy Voroshilov, who liked melodrama; but then what Russian did not. Then again, maybe it was the gospel truth; at any rate, Collins was not enough of a gambler to find out.

Rosenthal had been designated as the lead man. Before they boarded the plane, a rough-looking Russian officer from the

MVD gave them a short briefing, which sounded as though it was more a warning than anything else. He stated that any failure to follow orders of the leader-designate would result in them being shot. In fact, if anybody chose not to agree with this officers instructions at this late date, it would result in him or her being shot. The Russian explained why too much rested on this operation for any of them to turn back now. And like it or not, they had all agreed to go. But it appeared to the Americans that this Russian was obsessed with shooting somebody. But then again, maybe it was just the Russian way.

Eckert had been designated navigator. He had been outfitted with an abbreviated set of tables and an American aerial navigator's sextant. It was the same kind of device he had used in Morocco. This apparatus differed from a mariner's instrument in the manner in which it acquired the horizon. The one used by bomber and transport crews during the War did not need a horizon to keep it level, as did the mariners. It was simply aimed at the star or planet, which was superimposed inside a circle. As long as the body was maintained inside the circle, the instrument was level. With the star in sight and the sextant presumably level, the navigator pressed a button, and the instrument automatically registered the angle of the individual shots. It counted up to twenty or so and then it calculated an average. The result was the angle of arc above the horizon of the heavenly body at the precise time the shots were taken. Then, using his tables, the navigator could fix a line of position on his chart. Two more stars were used to complete the exercise. When the three lines were drawn, they crossed, forming a small triangle. The calculated position was presumed to be inside the triangle. A good navigator on a smooth night, with a clear sky, could get within a few statute miles of his position. Eckert, who was standing on the ground, believed he could do even better.

The third night out loomed clear. The moon had not yet risen when Eckert unlimbered his paraphernalia while the rest of them watched. Each offered to help him if help was needed, except the girl, who watched without comment. In fact, she had had very little to say to any of them thus far.

It took Eckert about half an hour to plot the longitude and latitude of the dot inside the triangle.

He called the others over. They huddled around a flashlight brought close so they could see.

"Here is where we are, about fifty miles inside Tajikistan. We are about a hundred or so miles from this river running near the settlement of Hotan. See, here on the edge of the plateau. The river we are interested in comes out of the mountains of the Himalayan chain. Look here, see, the river runs out into the desert and then disappears. About twenty-five miles from Hotan is where the plant is supposed to be located. My plan is to travel in this direction for four days or so until we intersect the river and then head downstream another day or two. I will take a final series of shots when we reach the river to see exactly how far we are from the security fence. Before he could say more about what he intended to do, Rosenthal interrupted him with a well done and a thanks. "I'll take over from here," he said. "Let's get to the point you speak of first, and then we'll decide what happens next.

"But now," Herb said, "I would like to draw your attention to something very important. Note, the girl has gone off to perform her nightly *toilette*. It is just as well, because I don't want her to hear what I have to say."

Looking at Eckert's chart, he began again: "See here. We left Moscow and landed at this large industrial city of Novosibirsk in Siberia. We refueled and penetrated Tibet in Chinese territory about here near Afghanistan. This is where we jumped. And this is where we picked up the tribe. And this is the direction we have been heading. And this is the general direction we are going to exit when we blow the plant on our next trip back here."

Then he looked around; not seeing the girl, he began again: "Listen up close. Collins tells me she is not going to blow the plant on our next trip; she is going to penetrate the buildings where the cooling system is located and then jam the valves, making it look like an accident. By now he was talking in a low whisper to the two hovering around him. Collins, of course, was not hearing anything he had not heard before. But Eckert was as dumb founded as Collins had been when he first heard Alexi tell him about the real plan.

The following morning, early, as the sun rose above the mountains to the east of the Tamarin Pendi, the reconnaissance group broke camp and set out for the power plant. Three members of the tribe, with their wives, volunteered to accompany them. For the first ten miles they were escorted by a contingency of some half-dozen horsemen, who were members of their extended family.

Small boys were already with the flocks. You could see them with their long shepherd's poles and slingshots made from antler horns. Each carried a small bag of stones, which they replenished periodically from the never ending supply lying about the ground. In the distance could be seen flocks of other sheep as they moved across the lush, green grasslands. And occasionally, you could hear the crack of a slingshot, and an accompanying shrill yell of a child's voice breaking the morning stillness as the boys directed their large herds toward the day's pasture.

The tribesman who had volunteered to accompany the group were prancing about alongside their kin, all sitting in high-back saddles on top of colorful saddle carpets of dyed yak hair. They all carried long antique rifles slung across their shoulders, and all sported long swords dangling from leather waist scabbards. They looked to be what they were, nomads who owned the last of the vast open ranges they rode on. And each sat on his mount with a haughty air and the confidence of men who knew they were the best at whatever it was they were doing.

As Rosenthal looked back over his shoulder, he thought the black yak hair tents resembled spiders dotting the landscape. From the tops of the tents he could see wisps of smoke from the dung cooking fires inside.

He thought about the life of these people, seemingly uncomplicated and simple. They were not rich in formal schooling, but each man had a wealth of experiences passed down to him from centuries of ancestors who had learned to survive in this harsh land.

The group had ridden about ten miles when their escort waved and then turned around and galloped away in the direction from which they had come. Collins rode up alongside of Rosenthal. His legs were getting tired, and he wanted to stop. Neither Collins nor Eckert had been on a horse more than a few times, having been raised in the city. And they both were beginning to hurt. Rosenthal, on the other hand, had taken every occasion to ride out into the countryside to watch and record things of interest in his notebook. He was far from an accomplished horseman, but he was far more accustomed to a horse then were either of the other two.

Rosenthal called a halt. Then as if on cue, the nomad women rode back toward the Russian woman, who could just be seen in the distance. The eldest of the nomads dismounted and poured water from goat skin bags for the yaks and then for the horses. He checked the loads on each of the yaks to make sure they were not being chaffed by the hair ropes that held the tent poles and the provisions wrapped in horse hide, inside antique wooden food boxes.

Traveling great distances with animals was what the nomad was about, and Rosenthal was thankful they were not fending for themselves. They had descended from the Steppes, and for the last few miles they were on the flat lands of the plains. Further on, Eckert and the Russian woman would leave the grassy area and enter into the sands of the Gobi. But for now there was plenty of grass for all the animals. And there was plenty of water from small streams, which came from the highlands but originated in the Himalayan range to the south.

This was the rain shadow of the Himalayas, which did not collect much moisture. What was available from the infrequent rains soaked into the ground as rapidly as it fell. Rosenthal was surprised there was as much water coming from the high plateau as there appeared to be.

On the other side of the mountain range to the southeast were the high Himalayan peaks. From the glaciers of these mountains arose four of the world's large rivers: the Yangtze, Ganges, Bramaputra, and Mekong. Herb, consulting his map, was glad they were on the leeward side of the range and did not have to worry about crossing any of them.

When they were underway again, Collins struck up a conversation with Rosenthal, not because he was particularly bored but because something had been bothering him for the past few days. He wanted to know why the nomads were going so far out of their way to assist them. He knew the Tibetans did not like the Chinese, but it was more than that. He knew they were not being paid because money had very little value here. Maybe Herb or the Russians had promised to ship them some horses or yaks or whatever.

"Herb, something is bothering me."

"What?" he asked.

"What is motivating these people to help us–I mean, to the extent they are? I know there is no love lost between them and the Chinese. But that does not account for it all. And it certainly doesn't account for the fact that they're placing their lives in danger."

"You have to understand the geopolitics of the situation," Herb said. "Here we have the Chinese with one of the largest populations on earth. And their land mass, as big as it is, has only a measly ten percent that is arable. But that's not their only problem. A large part of the remainder is being used for industry and urban development. True, they have taken steps to limit their population, but living conditions in the larger cities is getting worse, not better, for lack of living space.

"The Tibetans see this as a red flag. They know as undesirable as their ancestral lands are, they are going to be more habitable than the inner cities in fifteen or twenty years.

"The nomads understand about power plants and what they mean to the Chinese. They figure if the Chinese can bring power to this area, they may be able to make conditions more livable. And then the Tibetans see the teeming masses of the urban areas migrating onto their lands. And when this happens, they will be unable to do anything about it. They will either have to conform or move off, and they have no place else to go.

"Many of them have tried entering Nepal and India illegally. They were treated harshly before being unceremoniously deported. So you see, they want this power plant destroyed, but for reasons different from ours. They don't understand anything about nuclear power plants making plutonium for bombs. And they wouldn't care about it if they did. What they do understand is land, and they are afraid of losing what they have."

They stopped in the early afternoon to eat. One of the women milked one of the yaks, which had not been allowed to go dry after calving. In fact, the young calf was allowed to accompany its mother on the trip. As was the custom, the calf was fed first. Then the remainder of the milk was parceled out to the travelers. What was left over was converted to a kind of stirred cheese.

"You know," Herb said, as he watched one of the nomad women beat the milk into large cheese curds, "the conquering Mongol hoards used to travel with goat skins partially filled with yak milk. They tied the pouch to a yak or to a horse, and the slopping action converted the milk into butter or cheese. They kept a fresh supply on hand at all times. You know, these people do make a solid form of cheese, which they export. It's sought after by gourmet cheese lovers all over Europe. I have tasted some of it and it's good–a lot better than many of our brands. You see, the yak's milk contains about three times the butter fat that cows milk does. And the yak feed on fresh green grass for most of the year. This makes for a kind of sweet, yet sharp cheddar. We haven't been offered any yet, but I'm hoping we will. I'm looking forward to it."

On the evening of the next day, just before the sun set, they came to a rather large stream. They stopped while Eckert and Rosenthal consulted the chart. Eckert was the first to speak: "This is the first of two streams we have to cross before we fetch the main river that runs past Hotan."

Rosenthal had expected to encounter the stream, but by his best guess it was going to be about noon the next day. He waited until they made camp and the cheese ration, along with two cups of milk and some dried vegetables with mutton jerky, were passed around. He waited until the Russian woman and the Tibetans went down to the stream to wash up; then he gathered Eckert and Collins around him. There was still light at this rather late hour.

"Take a look at the chart. The road to Hotan, which we have

been paralleling for the past few days, is north of us about five miles. Instead of trying to swim this stream, which I calculate is about six feet deep in the middle, we're going to stop here. That is, all of us are except Eckert and the girl. In the morning they are going to set out for the power plant."

Eckert was surprised, as was Collins at the change in plans. They both had been expecting the entire group to go as far as about ten miles from the plant along the main river.

"Why the change?" Eckert wanted to know.

"Because," said Rosenthal, "It has occurred to me that just because we have passed for a family traveling to visit relatives of another tribe doesn't mean we can continue to get away with it. I figure the closer we get to the power plant the more security we are going to encounter. Who is going to be fooled by a group as large as ours going down river on a direct course to the power plant? What are we doing there? And another thing, if I were in charge of security, I would use light aircraft to patrol the area. If they spot you and the girl messing around in the trees and shrubs along the river bed, they are going to think less about it than they would if they saw a family headed toward the plant."

Neither of the two onlookers said anything. Rosenthal looked at Eckert before he spoke: "Go north until you hit the road and then cross over the bridge. There has to be a bridge, even if it's not shown on the chart. Move off the highway a mile or so until you get near the next stream. This one is shown as somewhat bigger. Do the same thing. But this time cut north at 45 degrees. I calculate you can make the Hotan river easy by morning if you start out after dark. Go along the riverbed until you are about five or so miles away from the power plant. Then send the girl on forward until she makes contact with the security fence. But under no circumstances let her do her thing. Eckert, I want you to make sure she is not going to be carrying any explosives. We can't tell what she is going to do or what she has been told to do. It's just like the Russians to lay all of this on as a recon mission and then have her blow the intake valves when we least expect it. If she does, you can bet she is going to leave us all to confront the Chinese authorities or to get a dose of radioactivity, which won't do any of us any good."

"Why don't we go ahead and plan for her to do it if she gets the opportunity?" Eckert asked him. "Why don't we play like it's a month or so from now? That way we won't have to repeat the whole thing. As long as it looks like an accident, and as long as we know which way the wind is going to be blowing and can get away, what difference does it make?"

"For one very good reason," Herb said. "The planners need a couple of weeks to set the wheels in motion after they hear from me as to whether it's feasible or not."

"What wheels?" Collins asked him.

"The three of us, including Russia and Briton, want to start a campaign in the United Nations. We want to criticize world policy, which virtually ignores the burgeoning third world nations who are seemingly working toward building a bomb with impunity. At the same time, the President is going to hold several press conferences, wherein he lambastes the world at large and the U.N. in particular for allowing the situation to continue. He will point out the danger of doing nothing and letting things slide as they have. Now do you see, if you bust in there in a couple of days, you are going to spoil much of the shock value."

He paused for a minute to see if Eckert was going to object. When he said nothing, Herb added one last comment: "Your job is to make sure she follows orders to the letter. She may have her own plans, certainly the one Voroshilov told Collins about and maybe some others, too, that we know nothing about. And if she does, your orders are to shoot her."

Two nights later, Collins and Rosenthal were lying in the grass several yards from the stream. They had not pitched their tents. They did not want to be seen. The night was comfortable and the tents were unnecessary. It was not nearly as cool as it had been on the higher plateau. During the day, the group moved into the trees and bushes bordering the stream bed.

"What do you think they are doing right now?" Collins asked Herb.

"What do you think?" Herb asked him.

"If I arrived this afternoon, I know what I'd be doing."

"What?

"Taking a bath and washing these stinking Tibetan homespun clothes of mine." Both of them started to laugh, spontaneously.

"I suspect he is doing the same thing, only he is doing it with the girl."

"Do you really believe she has thawed out that much?" Collins asked him.

"Well, I don't see the two of them bathing in their clothes and then sitting around with them on waiting for them to dry in what is left of the sun, do you?"

"No."

"Well, there you have it then."

"Do you visualize him getting sweet on her, assuming what we're both thinking comes to pass?"

"Yeah, I do," said Herb.

"Then you expect him to shoot her, if need be?"

"No, I never intended him to. I figure this boy/girl stuff we are talking about is going to happen. As far as I'm concerned, it's inevitable. A few hours from now, the last thing from his mind will be shooting her."

Collins started to laugh again and Rosenthal joined him. "He's going to be lucky if he doesn't come out of this adventure married or something." Collins volunteered.

"Just what do you expect from him?"

"I expect him to get close to her so that she takes him into her confidence. Whatever goes on, I want it to be a team effort. I actually expect he will accompany her as far as he can go, and then he will stick around until she comes back. And I want her to actually penetrate the plant to see whether or not she is going to be able to take care of business when the time comes. Also, I want him to come back with a comprehensive report. We don't want any surprises. Eckert knows how to write the report, and he knows what is needed. But he's not going to accomplish much unless he is a best friend with her, because she won't tell him much. She'll save it for her own people. And I still can't get it out of my head that the Russians have their own agenda in this, apart from what Voroshilov told you. I've always thought they were using us, while they suspect us of using them."

"Tell me something," Collins asked him, "How do you know she is technically qualified to analyze the workings of so complicated a bailiwick as this?"

"I'm not as worried about the technical details as I am about other things. We know this plant was copied from one of the CANDU facilities, which you may or may not know was built by the Canadians. They have supplied countries like India, Pakistan, and Korea with plans and technical assistance. The plants in these countries are exactly alike, so we don't think China has done much to change anything. No, I think they have copied everything right down to the last detail. They can be expected to do exactly what all other countries have done who have purchased or misappropriated technology over the years; they will copy it right down to the smallest detail without improving on a thing."

"What do you mean, your major interest is in other things?"

"Well, we pretty much know how things are constructed, and

we know how they're going to be laid out, complete with where the different valves are going to be located. What we don't know is how lax is their security? More to the point, what is the level of their security? Have they adopted our emergency procedures, and do they have a training program. There is a whole host of other things we want her to find out."

"I'm curious about these other things," Collins said. "What are you going to use them for. I mean, if she knows where the right valves are located, isn't that enough to get the job done?"

"There is more to it, much more. What we need are facts we can hand to the U.N. and the world press. We want to make an airtight case against these people. We want to show the world that primitive slip-shod methods of handling volatile nuclear materials are a major danger to us all. If we can show they are babes-in-the-woods, so to speak, without the know-how for this new-age technology, they might be restricted by the civilized world from continuing on unabated. By that I mean civilized like we are, and as civilized as the others are who are members of the nuclear club."

Collins started to laugh when Rosenthal began to smile, as he realized he was discriminating against the Chinese without knowing any more about them than he did.

"Still, the degree of their competency is not the point, although we want the rest of the world to think so. We want China to cease and desist. We don't need another country build-ing a working bomb, because more is not merrier. More simply increases the probability something will go wrong; and as the song goes, *someday we will all be blown away*."

"Where did you get all your information about nuclear plants in general and this one in particular? Voroshilov gave me to understand it was nuclear, making plutonium from natural ura-nium. I don't believe he knew much else."

"He knew," Herb remarked. "And so did McDermott. They have all had their heads together on this for months. McDermott laid it all out for me. They schooled me on this kind of natural uranium fueled facility. Before we started out, I visited the two high-pressure types operating in the U.S. and the one at the Bruce facility near Tiverton, Ontario. Incidentally, we use enriched uranium, the same kind as in an atom bomb. The Canadians and these other countries use the natural uranium with heavy water as a moderator. It's the same principle the Germans tried to perfect during the War.

"There is an added cost of manufacturing heavy water. But over a year or so of operation it pays for itself, because it becomes cheaper than enriched fuel since it lasts a lot longer. That's why we think the Chinese got the plans from Canada, India, or Pakistan and not from us."

Collins looked at him, confused.

Herb could see he wasn't getting it, so he started over. "By natural, I mean the U-235 heating cores are surrounded by heavy water. It functions as a moderator to slow down the neutron activity and prolong the fission process. It also serves to cool the core. But that's not the main cooling principle. There is just plain water from a lake or a stream that circulates through the system. At one point it is heated to pressurized steam. This steam drops its energy across turbines, which makes the electricity. From there the lower-pressured steam is run through a condenser. Then the condensed steam as hot water is cycled through a venturi designed cooling tower before it is returned to the stream or lake. As in the case of the pressurized water reactor, reactor cooling pumps circulate heavy water through the reactor, then to the steam generators in a closed loop. The moderator heavy water system has a separate heat exchanger with a circulation system for cooling the moderator. The heavy water is not highly pressurized, not anything like our two systems. This makes for a much simpler installation, and it's far less dangerous to operate; it requires less training and less experience to operate it safely.

"The cooling towers are venturi shaped. That is, they're narrow in the center like women with hour-glass figures. Something resembling a Gibson Girl years ago. Remember during the War, Army and Navy airman carried an emergency radio shaped like a woman with a narrow waist. They named it the Gibson Girl after the drawings made famous by the artist of the same name.

"The venturi feature, or narrow waist, is like an engine carburetor. It accelerates the air flow across the venturi. The cooling towers work the same way. The cooling air is accelerated across the cooling coils before the cooled water is allowed back into the river. For your information, this facility design is somewhat different than ours. As I said, we use enriched uranium. We use a Boiling Water system or High Pressure, depending on the manufacturer. The Canadian system, using natural uranium, adapts well to the third world countries, who usually do not have the know how to built heavy pressure containers."

"Exactly where is she going to penetrate?" he asked Rosenthal. "I mean, is she expected to wander all over the plant looking for the information you want or is she just going to the one building that houses the valves she is going to sabotage?"

"She has been specially trained by the Russians, who have any number of these kinds of plants. She knows exactly where to go and what to do."

"Tell me again what it is we are trying to accomplish."

"Okay, the plant is harvesting bomb grade plutonium. This material comes about as the U-235 fuel degrades from the fission activity. Now we could blow the plant with delayed plastic explosives and get rid of the plant but not the problem. Although it would get rid of the plant, it would surely be attributed to sabotage. On the other hand, if she shuts down the incoming cooling water to the condenser, the core will overheat. Once this happens there is no way to stop the temperature within the core from rising. There is not any way to shut it down. This type of unit is much more dependent on computers to regulate the valves than are ours. The valves can be operated manually to a certain extent, but not after the system reaches a runaway mode, which proceeds melt-down. What she will try to do in the melt-down plan, which none of us are supposed to know anything about, is set a time-delayed device that will jam the emergency and main cooling valves. At the same time, she will try to set a like device in the switch gear. By switch gear, I mean the automatic system that senses a power interruption and switches to diesel genera-tors for the main power source. Without electricity, the comput-ers will malfunction and try to throw the system off-line. At the same time, the valves will try to fail-safe in the open position. But they'll already be jammed closed. Then it is every man and woman for him or herself."

"You mean like the proverbial Chinese fire drill?"

"Exactly," said Rosenthal, as Collins started to smile and then stopped abruptly as he now more clearly realized the gravity of the situation and the attendant loss of life. Herb had explained to him earlier about the radioactive cloud that would form imme-diately. It could be expected to travel on the wind to the city of Hotan and then rise to the plateau, where it would destroy thou-sands more nomad families.

"Are you really going to let this happen?" Collins asked him.

"No. I want to get rid of the plant, but not the way Voroshilov told you she was going to make it happen. And not the way McDermott and the MVD are planning it to happen either. As far as I'm concerned, they better find another way than the one they're keeping to themselves."

"How are you going to stop them then?"

"I don't know. We're going to take the report back, just as if we knew nothing at all about the real follow-on plan to melt it down. Maybe I'll go to the newspapers or maybe I'll confront McDermott outright. I was planning originally to have Eckert shoot her and leave her behind, and then have him set a charge inside the cooling building. There are several ways to do it, if all we are interested in is destroying the thing and if we don't care whether they find out it is sabotage.

"But I realize that after tonight Eckert will more than likely become attached to her. In this case, his shooting her is out of the question. We have some time to figure out what we're going to do. Got any ideas?"

"Herb, I have heard you discuss before the difference between what is going to happen in a melt-down and what's going to happen if we blow the reactors as we planned. But I would like to hear you expand on what you've told me so far. Voroshilov told me what the Russians think will happen, but what do you think?"

"Voroshilov probably knows more about it than I do. We figure the Russians have experienced dozens of close events, which they've kept to themselves," he said.

"First off, this type of plant has one to eight reactors. They are mounted on their sides, so they can be refueled without going off-line. They have a machine that pushes out one radioactive core and pushes in another right behind it. I suppose however many they have, they'll all be working. This means the plant can be assumed to be up and running at near capacity; this is obviously important when considering the extent of the damage to follow.

"My opinion is based on what I have been told by experts,

plus my own analyses. The difference between a sabotage explosion and a melt-down accident, to my way of thinking, is this: First, an explosion event will blow one or all of the several reactors into fragments. It will scatter radioactive cesium and U-235 along with metal and debris, for at least a circular distance of a quarter-mile, maybe more. It will also level the rest of the plant, spreading hundreds of gallons of contaminated moderator deuterium for hundreds of yards. They won't be able to contain the contamination, short of either cementing it over or covering it over to a depth of ten feet or so using bull-dozers. The site will remain contaminated for many years to come. The river will be contaminated, but since it peters out, according to the chart, in about a hundred miles, and since not many people use it in the desert proper, it can be posted with only a minimum danger to strangers in the area. Innocent deaths can be expected to be held to a minimum. But the big difference is there will be no radioactive debris cloud, as would be the case in a melt-down.

"The melt-down plan will be a catastrophe, and it can be brought about fairly easily. All Russian reactors carry a design flaw, as does this one. And as an interesting aside, I might add, I believe if it's not corrected, someday the Russians are going to experience a terrible disaster on the scale of the one they have planned here for China.

"The flaw, which I'm sure the Russian woman is aware of, will be used to cause the melt-down in this unit unless we can stop them or somehow change their minds back at Langley.

"What will happen is this: When she interrupts the coolant to the reactor core, it will cause a corresponding increase in power output as the reactor heats up. When the operator moves to shut down because of the unstable condition, he will cause a dramatic power surge, one he can't control. Now the emergency system has the flaw. The computers are telling the back-up system to supply more coolant to the reactor. But there is a lag problem, which they are reluctant to shut down the plant to correct. Apparently the fix is not as easy as it sounds, and it will involve a great deal of money. At any rate, when the reactor core overheats, it will rupture the fuel elements. This in turn will release super-heated steam directly onto the elements. Steam is a very poor coolant, and as you can imagine, the problem will become exacerbated. Within a fraction of a second the room will fill with steam under terrific pressure, and the resultant explosion will blow the reinforced concrete roof off the reactor. This will be followed by a gigantic rush of air over the core, which in effect will be a secondary explosion.

"We can expect the two explosions to scatter radioactive cesium, mixed with contaminated debris, for at least a half mile. But the radioactive steam released will form a kind of cloud of contaminated water vapor and minute particles of debris. As I have said, this will be carried for miles toward Hotan and the plateau. I have no way of knowing, but my thinking tells me there will be thousands killed in Hotan as well as thousands more nomads on the Steppes."

A week later, about the time Rosenthal was thinking about giving them up for lost, the two came straggling in. Their horses were almost spent from prolonged riding without adequate forage. And Eckert was so sore he had to be helped from the saddle. Two of the nomad women helped walk him to the edge of the stream, where he was allowed to soak while he was washed from head to foot. He was plied with hot yak butter tea before being helped back to the small campfire. Here he was given fresh *chapattis*, filled with a mixture of dried lamb and rice, ladled from a pot of seasoned stew. *Chapattis*, when filled with this spiced stew, are known as *rhotis* in the northern parts of India and

Tibet. They are eaten like a Mexican *burrito*. In fact, the Asian *chapatti* is made exactly as *tortillas* are made in the Americas. Herb had noted this early on and had made a note to look into the apparent coincidence.

But was it a coincidence? He wondered. Maybe, but no more so than was Swedish anthropologist Thor Hyerdahl's observation that reed boats made at Lake Titicaca in South America were exactly the same as those made on the Nile river. All of which tended to persuade Rosenthal to agree with Hyerdahl's theory that adventurers from the Middle East first settled the Americas.

Herb was on pins and needles waiting to hear the outcome of their lengthy sortie. But Eckert, with his mouthful of much-needed nourishment, was reluctant to talk. His attention was on the food being prepared for him as fast as he could wolf it down. Then he looked up to see the Russian woman watching and waiting her turn to be fed. She would be allowed to fend for herself, but only after Eckert was satisfied. He looked up to see her looking at him with hungry eyes. Then he took the next offered *rhoti* from the nomad woman's hand and gave it to the Russian. Eckert looked at her. And then he stopped eating altogether, long before he was satisfied, and gave her the next one as well.

Herb nodded at Collins, who smiled. But both knew what had happened, and it came as no surprise to either of them.

"It was a snipe hunt," Eckert finally said, as he sipped yet another cup of tea. "Nothing but a damned snipe hunt, and about as much fun. We have been conned. There is no power plant of any kind, and from what we were able to find out in Hotan, there never has been. McDermott has set us up. And the MVD conned Voroshilov, too. I have had a long time to think about it and I am getting really scared. Somebody sent us out here on this wild goose chase for a reason. Whatever it is, I don't like it."

Rosenthal looked at him long and hard by the light of the yak chip fire before he spoke. "Tell me exactly what happened and don't leave out anything. I mean anything of importance."

Eckert blushed. But no one could tell in the dim light. Then he began to speak. The Russian woman drew closer instead of walking out into the shadows, as she had in the past.

"We intersected the river coming from Hotan at exactly ten miles from the coordinates in the Plan. We stayed for about ten hours catching up on sleep, and then she took off for the plant. I decided to go with her. I wasn't accomplishing anything by staying behind, and she needed to know when she was within a mile or so of the security fence. We traveled along the river's edge to keep out of sight.

"We never saw any airplanes or any evidence anybody had ever been there."

"Did you ever see the security fence?" Collins wanted to know.

Eckert gave him a kind of look that begged to know whether or not he might be retarded.

"We saw nothing. I took three sets of shots on the spot where the fence was supposed to be. I verified my fix three different times, and each one of them was no more than a quarter-mile from the river and no more than a half-mile either side of where we were. No, Herb, I had it bracketed. There was no mistake. We were there, right where we were supposed to be."

Then, for some strange reason, the woman drew closer and nodded her head as if confirming the accuracy of the navigation. Rosenthal and Collins both noted that this was the first time on the trip she had shown any kind of interest in any part of the proceedings. Now she looked worried, as though some of Eckert's feelings had rubbed off on her.

"But we didn't stop there," Eckert went on to say, between bites of another pungent *rhoti*. "We went another ten miles down river. And then over the next two days, we went another twenty-five more out into the desert. We followed it until we almost ran out of river. When we stopped and turned back, the river was slowly losing itself in the sand, and was nothing more than a series of rivulets, which I estimate would have reverted to intermittent status in the next ten miles. But the point is there was not enough water to cool a reactor at the point we turned around.

"Thinking we had intersected the river too far to the north, we went back to the place where we camped the first night. We verified this position again and then rode on into Hotan. We talked to several nomads, but no Chinese. None of them had ever heard of a power plant. They had no idea what we were talking about. I tell you guys, something is awful screwy about this."

Then Collins remembered what Voroshilov had told him about there being other plans not known to him. And how Alexi had cautioned him to be on his guard.

I wonder if this has anything to do with what he said. Collins thought a minute before deciding to tell the others. When he told them what Voroshilov had said about other plans, the Russian woman listened intently. She grew pale, but no one could tell it in the light of the campfire. But Eckert knew she was scared to death, and he knew she had been for days.

Rosenthal later asked Eckert if she might have said something when they were alone. He inferred they were now good buddies, and that maybe she had. But he said nothing directly about why he believed this.

"No," Eckert told him, "she doesn't know any more than we do. I know. She was just as surprised as I was when we didn't run into a security fence.

"She did tell me she was in grave danger, and so are we. She said she always suspected the MVD would not forgive her for what she had done. She told me it was just too good to be true when they offered to let her come along, promising to forgive and to reinstate her. She told me she honestly believes the Russians have lured us all away from civilization for the sole purpose of shooting us.

"I told her nothing like this could possibly happen without the approval of our friends in the Company," Eckert said. "But now I'm wondering how good these friends really are. And are we in the same position as she is–unforgivable, I mean..." Is McDermott capable of doing this or maybe he is going to have you or Collins do it. Maybe that's it.

Eckert made the mistake of telling her what he had been thinking on the way back. They had just finished bathing in the stream after a hard day's ride. They were bundled together to keep warm when he told her of his suspicions, which were not suspicions at all, but just the ramblings of a confused and frightened mind.

Then he realized his error. She was drowning, and she saw this as some kind of straw to be grasped. And now, just for a second by the firelight, he caught a glimpse of a kind of Mona Lisa smile. He would not have known what it meant if he had not put the germ of an idea into her head. Now he worried for the lives of Rosenthal and Collins, whom he was sure were not in collusion with McDermott. Now he believed she thought the two of them might kill her. And he was becoming increasingly concerned that she might beat them to the punch. She was afraid. She knew something was far from right. And she had settled in on Rosenthal and Collins; she had convinced herself they were part of the plot to kill her.

"Hello, this is Langley, extension 454. With whom did you wish to speak?"

"Military Operations, for a Mr. McDermott."

"Give code name and telephone number and stand by."

McDermott sleepily said, "Hello, who is this. Rosenthal, do you know what time it is here?" Herb laced into him. He swore a blue streak calling him every name he could think of while McDermott listened passively on the other end of the line.

"Where are you," he said, when Herb slowed up for a minute. "Calm down and tell me where you are."

"I'm in Singapore where I'm supposed to be."

"How did it go?" he wanted to know.

"McDermott, I swear if you were here now, I would shoot you. It didn't go at all. There is no power plant, and you know it."

"Believe me, Herb, I have no idea what you're talking about." Then for the next fifteen minutes, he listened to a very agitated Rosenthal tell him the complete story.

"Look, something is wrong, as you say. Get out of that big hotel where you like to stay and into something less conspicuous. Don't tell anybody in the Company where you are. Stay out of your new place during the day. Act like you work for East India Trading.

"I agree with you, something is wrong and I don't know what. Give me some time to figure it out and I'll get back to you." With that he hung up, leaving Rosenthal as confused as he was before he made the call.

Herb sat down in his favorite bar in the Raffles Hotel and thought. And then he thought some more. And then he convinced himself that in his haste he had made a mistake. He realized he should not have called McDermott. He should simply have vanished after advising the others to do the same.

CHAPTER 18...THE WHITE HOUSE, 1972

The President rose from behind his desk as a few members of his staff filed into the oval office. He walked a few feet and then sat down in one of the sofa-chairs resting on an ornate Oriental rug. The rug itself was covering wall-to-wall carpet. His wife and daughters had picked out the rug, so he had not said anything. But if he had been allowed his choice, he would have chosen something with more of a Western motive, maybe with a little more American Indian design and a little less influence from Bombay. But he realized that would be too non-traditional and would not pass muster. He thought about this often when he was alone pondering some of the imponderables, which seemed to have no solution. The fact that he was ham-strung by tradition and what other people thought of him had always been one of his major concerns—and not just in his presidency, but throughout his long political career as well.

He had inherited Vietnam from Lyndon Johnson, and it was about to destroy him, as it had Johnson. He thought about this often, too. In fact, Vietnam and his re-election were about all he had time for these days.

His re-election was why he had called this meeting this morning.

"I want somebody to come up with some kind of a gimmick to offset the bad Vietnam publicity I'm getting. I won in a landslide, but Johnson and his Asian War is killing me. And I'm going to be lucky if I don't end up going down the toilet, too.

"You know it didn't take the liberal press very long to forget it was a Democrat president who got it started, and the guy who kept it going was Lyndon Johnson. But thanks to him, I'm up to my butt in alligators, in case any of you are interested enough to look around. I need to do something positive, some kind of a public relations thing, something of my own and not tied to Kennedy or Johnson. I'm open for suggestions."

"Mr. President," Henry Kissinger began to speak. Nixon's National Security Advisor and elder statesman of the group was well respected, not only because of the high esteem in which he was held by the President, but because when he spoke he usually had something to say.

"What do you think about China? I mean what do you think about   history recording you as the president who re-established Sino-American relations?"

"What do you think about the voters?" Nixon interrupted him to ask. "I hate those Chinese bastards, but what do you think the average American thinks? Do you think he remembers the Korean War? In fact, do you think he thinks about anything besides his paycheck? I'm not thinking about the students, the ones who go to school and don't work. Not the way I had to, anyway. They have time to protest everything that comes along. And lately they are protesting everything I say or do. I don't worry about them, but I do about their folks, the voters. What do you think they are going to say about it?"

Kissinger began again: "I think any kind of publicity, if it gets their minds off Vietnam, is good. And if we sell it right, like from the economic standpoint, if we tell them we should be trading with China, I mean. We convince them if we don't do it somebody else will. We have to lay on a publicity campaign, and you have to get on television and have a few press conferences to block down-field. I think if it is done right it will turn out a winner."

"How are you going to manage it?" Nixon asked him, as he fidgeted in his chair. "Do you have anything in mind, something that will break the ice with Zhou. The last I heard, he hadn't let any Americans inside his country since 1949, when they went communist, except possibly for that table tennis team.

"He's another one of those thankless bastards who's butt we saved during the War." Nixon did not stop with Zhou-En-Lai and Mao Tse-tung, but continued on with his harangue about Chiang Kai Shek and DeGaulle and then went on to the Germans and the rest of the French before Kissinger gently steered him back to the subject.

"As a matter of fact I do, Mr. President. I mean I am working on a plan."

"Oh, yeah! How much is it going to cost the taxpayer this time?" The meaning of this statement was not lost on Kissinger. Just weeks before, they had argued about the advisability of trying to collect some of the billions of dollars shelled out as Lend Lease. Nixon included the Marshall Plan, which he considered the biggest giveaway in history. He did not mind loaning money for a reasonable interest, but to give it away gratis always rankled him. And then for them all, except Britain, to come back criticizing us the way they had angered him even more. He was aware he might sound as though he was paranoid on the subject. But he was angry with the Chinese and the Russians and the Vietnamese. More than a few times in the past month, he was heard to say about the Asians, "If it wasn't for this country, they would all be Japanese, and it would serve them all the hell right."

"Maybe we have been going at this China thing all wrong," Kissinger said. "Maybe we need a completely different approach. Maybe we need to try and un-thaw them again at the grass roots level, something like that."

"Do you have anything in mind?" Nixon asked him for the second time.

"I might, but it's too early to say exactly what. I have some feelers out and a couple of possibilities in mind. Give me a few days and let me get back to you." Kissinger made the last statement with an air of finality, as if to say that's all the time I have for this subject today. Nixon, quick to catch on and eager to go along with Kissinger, the de facto leader of the group, stood up as a sign the short meeting was over.

Months earlier, Kissinger had started out on a trip to China. The press was told it was some kind of a fact-finding tour. Actually, it was intended as a secret meeting with Chinese officials to discuss a possible presidential trip to Beijing. But on the way, he acquired a stomach bug and they had to layover in Pakistan for two days. By the time he finally arrived, the American press was in position. This did not sit well with the secretive Chinese, who thought it was going to be a low-key meeting between Zhou and Kissinger.

When it did take place, Kissinger lectured Zhou on why a Nixon visit was in the best interests of China. He told Zhou it would be seen by the Russians as the beginning again of American-Chinese relations. Kissenger was not above playing on Zhou's fear of Soviet attack to gain his ends.

What started as a cool reception, gradually warmed up. Zhou seemed amiable enough, but in the end nothing more had been said. And at this point, things had lapsed back to the way they had been before the meeting.

"Special operator, Langley speaking. State code name, branch number, and priority, caller. Stay on line for verification." Thus began the procedure for acquiring the special number at the desk of Ralph Levy, Director of Plans in the Military Operations Division.

One of the staff officers close to the National Security Advisor had placed the call from a pay phone in Washington. He had done so at the direction of his chief, whom he knew had been directed to do so by Henry Kissinger.

"Caller, this is Langley Special Operator... stand by one... hello, caller, operator again. Verify number as pay phone. Address recorded. Recipient advises will contact you at your present location from secure phone in one half-hour. If you understand, hang up now; otherwise, stay on for repeat message. Standing by for a long count. Call is verified as authentic and understood. Langley operator out."

Thirty minutes later the phone rang and the Langley operator advised the staff officer he would be contacted at a coded designation, which, unknown to the operator, was in a small town in Virginia, half-way between Langley and Washington.

The rather elaborate precautions were taken not to prevent information from being intercepted by a foreign agent as much as to prevent interception by agents within the CIA proper.

What the President's advisor had to say he wanted said to one person only in Military Operations. That one man was Ralph Levy, the Advisors trusted confidant.

Richard Morris was a protégé of Kissingers and a friend. He was also a member of an inside clique and he was destined for advancement. He was a career officer in the diplomatic service and had known Kissinger for years, even before Kissinger joined the Nixon administration. Now Kissinger had something of the highest priority and classification he wanted discussed with the CIA. But he wanted to bypass several layers of insulation to deal directly with the man responsible for carrying out his instructions. By "his instructions" Kissinger meant the instructions of the President himself.

To many, and especially to critics who were former agents in the CIA, the CIA was viewed as a special branch of the White House. Not only were they seen as the Agency who kept the President advised of world affairs, but the Joint Chiefs of Staff and the National Security Council as well. But where their mandate was the collection and dissemination of information only, they were being charged by former agents, who had written books on the subject, as the agency who's main purpose was to do the President's bidding, which was clearly outside their scope of operation. But worse yet they were viewed by some members of Congress as a group who often worked hand-and-glove with the NSC on various clandestine operations unknown to all, including the President.

Richard Morris walked into a roadside diner south of Washington. He took a seat in the back and ordered a cup of coffee. He was early. Ralph Levy was not expected for another fifteen minutes. Morris had thought about waiting in the car, but elected to go inside. The weather was brisk for a spring night, and he kept his coat on until the coffee warmed him. If Levy was late, as he had been once before, he could always order dinner. He was hungry, and after looking at the special posted on the menu, decided to order when Levy arrived.

This particular diner had been selected, Morris thought, because it was inconspicuous, and it was located where it would be difficult for somebody to follow either of them from their respective cities.

Morris felt comfortable with the location. As a member of the president's staff, he could have requested another meeting place by a coded designation. Anyplace was all right with Levy, whom Morris thought was easy to get along with and who was not overly suspicious of everybody and everything, as most agents were in his department.

Levy was late, and Morris, who was a stickler for punctuality, having served a hitch in the Marines, was becoming increasingly agitated.

As Levy entered the side door, Morris, in the back, waved to him. Levy smiled a smile of recognition. Then he walked the few remaining yards in his direction and sat down opposite Morris in the booth. The hour was late and they were hungry. They both ordered the special of chicken fried steak.

When the waitress was out of earshot, Morris began to talk while Levy, as usual, prepared to listen to what he had to say.

"I don't know whether you know it or not, but the President has voiced a desire to be the first president to visit China. For some reason he wants to see the Wall. Says he has wanted to see the thing since he was a boy. Strange, because he always uses an expletive when he refers to any oriental. Says they made a big mistake in California when they repealed the Unrah Law. But maybe he wouldn't feel this way if it had not been for Korea and now Vietnam."

Levy nodded his head. Whether it meant he was in agreement or just that he understood, Morris could not say.

Levy was a good listener.

He was one of those executives who had come a long way just by listening and nodding agreement. He believed in the old adage about it being better to keep your mouth shut and be thought a fool than to speak out and remove all doubt.

"Anyway, the election is coming up and Mr. Kissinger wants your help in a scheme he has cooked up.

"We've been working on something for about a year now. We hope we haven't been wasting our time," Morris said. "However, so far so good. At least the Chinese haven't backed off. Sometimes I think we take two steps forward and one back. Somebody started calling it ping-pong diplomacy after Zhou invited the ping-pong team to play in China last year. Then he surprised us all by inviting some of our journalists to come along. He wants favorable press to change world opinion, and he wants us to do it for him.

"This ping-pong thing didn't just materialize out of thin air, Ralph, as you of all people know. Like a lot of things that just seem to happen, a lot of under-the-table work goes on."

Levy nodded his head again as the waitress brought their order. When she left, Morris said. "What he wants is for you to determine whether Zhou is serious about the President visiting China. Ping-pong is one thing, but there was something way more important came out of those games. Zhou was supposed to have told some journalist accompanying the team that he would be amenable to further talks leading toward normalization and a visit by Nixon himself. That is, of course, if Nixon so desires. Well, he desires.

"Specifically, at this point the Security Advisor wants you to check it out. He wants to know whether he can visit beforehand to set it up." *He has switched from the code name to his title, perhaps for emphasis*, thought Levy.

"You know," Morris went on, "Kissinger went there once for a short visit with Zhou, right after the ping-pong team, but nothing ever seemed to come of it. Still, who knows? When he was there they seemed to get along well enough, and we thought it was all set. Now, we think the Chinese want something from us–you know something to show our good faith. They want something to show that we really want to cooperate with them.

"Ralph, we don't want this to get around. If Zhou has changed his mind, for whatever reason, we want to know before the press finds out. You know the President, he has the re-election locked, but he is worried. In fact, he is always worried about something, which usually doesn't amount to a hill of beans. In this case, he thinks if things go sour he will be seen not as the first president to ever visit China, but as the president who screwed it up for others, maybe for the next century.

"There is something else." Morris put his fork down and took a sip of water. "We know how these things work. So far the Chinese have made all the overtures. But then, they have the most to gain. But still, viewed from the long position, it sure would cool the Russians off, especially if they thought it would lead to some kind of non-aggression pact with the Chinese that didn't include them."

Levy, who had been listening but also intent on eating, looked at Morris and spoke for the first time: "What you want from me is some kind of gesture. You want me to play Santa Claus for you. You want me to throw them a sop, something that makes us look as though we're ready to play ball with them right down the line. Something that will prove our good intentions, so we can get our companies in there before somebody else does. Is that about it?"

"You put it so succinctly, old boy," said Morris, affecting the accent of James Bond.

"Of course, nobody is to know about it, right?" Levy formed his statement as a question, but Morris recognized the sarcasm.

"Right," Morris said, as he called for the waitress.

He wanted a lull in the conversation because Levy was looking at him apprehensively. Levy could sense he was about to be put on the spot and he was becoming increasingly unhappy.

Morris could sense Levy's next move, and he suspected he, Morris, was not going to like it. Levy's next statement proved Morris was right.

"This minor miracle you want me to perform is some kind of a dirty trick isn't it?" Levy had pushed his plate aside, a clear indicator he was not comfortable.

"I didn't say that."

"Yes, but that's what you want. I know you guys. You want something they will see as a sacrifice, and knowing the Chinese, it will take something big. And again, nobody is supposed to know, right?"

"Do you have something in mind?" Morris asked him.

"I might, but I'm going to keep it to myself. But suffice to say, if it works it will get you what you want."

"How long is it going to take to set it up?" He asked Levy.

"Not long. Maybe about three weeks. I'll let you know when you can start negotiations with them."

With that he stood up and left a tip on the table. The check he left for Morris. As he turned and started to walk away, Morris could see he was not happy.

He called him back. "Look, Ralph, we owe you one. I'm going to see to it that the people who count in this administration, and the next, know you are somebody who is especially loyal, somebody who can be counted on to do what's in the best interests of the country."

Levy did not say anything. He just nodded his head and walked out. He had an odd feeling in the pit of his stomach; he wished he had ordered a sandwich. He thought, as he started the engine of his automobile that it was not the food entirely that made his stomach queasy. And right now he did not like himself very much for what he was about to do.

CHAPTER 19
RAFFLES HOTEL, SINGAPORE, 1985

Herb didn't call me this time; I called him. That is, I called an operator who called him. She had no idea where he was either, because I asked her. She was an employee of some worldwide answering service out in Texas. Her company had instructed her not to discuss anything about their clients, is the way she put it. I expected as much.

The next day I got a callback from Herb, and this time at a reasonable hour. He asked: "Chris, how goes the book? How are you progressing?"

"Great I guess, but there's a lot I don't understand. What I would really like to know is why all those people were killed and why the bunch of you went out on a wild goose chase and…"

"Look, I hate to bring you back. I know how you hate staying here."

I could hear him laughing, although he obviously had taken the receiver from his ear and turned his head.

"Look Mayo, old buddy. I want to read what you've got so far. I want to see if anything needs to be added. I might want to make some suggestions to really impact the casual readers who might be interested. We don't want to sell it to the avid reader alone; we want to grab hold of the public in general–and particularly the press. I want to make a difference, the way Phillip Agee did. Its not the CIA I am after–the way it was with him–it's certain individuals who work inside, the ones who call the shots–those nobody ever hears about."

I was confused as to why he had not given me all the information I needed to complete the book in the first place. I asked him, and he told me again that it wouldn't have worked out that way. He repeated what he had told me before; if I had known what was going to happen, and had I known it at the beginning, I wouldn't have agreed to be a participant.

Then he told me to bring the manuscript and come to the Raffles as I had before. This time he gave me a couple of days. I suppose the delay was to give him time to get things organized.

My ticket was waiting as usual. I figured he had an efficient secretary working somewhere in the wings. But then, a secretary would have known too much about his business, and that didn't sound like Herb to me.

But then all of a sudden it dawned on me. Now at last, I was sure of what I had long suspected: there were others involved besides the two of us. Maybe one of them was his secretary, and one or more of them had to be rich. I can't say for sure what this means, but I'm not sure I like it. I don't know why, but for a long time now I have felt I was engaged in something a lot bigger than just writing a novel for money or going after a few guys Herb didn't like. And it doesn't take a rocket scientist to see whoever is connected with this deal is going to be in trouble with several agencies–not just the CIA. Still, I figure I'm in too deep to back out now, or am I? No, that's not it at all; I like the good life. And deep down, I like what I'm doing. I like the feeling of getting up in the morning and having something to do. I like the adrenalin rush as I leaf through his papers. I go to bed at night wondering what I will discover in the morning and where it will all lead.

I have learned to play chess. I guess in most large cities they have parks where some of the intelligencia hang out who have nothing better to do–the ones who prefer the company of people with like interests–those who don't care too much for pigeons or sitting around watching mothers with strollers.

Anyway, San Francisco has a few of these parks. I had started hanging around one of them, watching the players. This one guy the other day was waiting for his partner, and he volunteered to teach me the game. He said it was a game that could be learned in a few minutes, and then it would take a lifetime to perfect.

He also explained what a gambit is.

He told me chess calls for the kind of mind that can rapidly think ahead and consider all the possibilities on the board. He said the masters can do it for two moves ahead, although I can't even imagine the kind of mind it takes to do this.

I asked him whether he knew anybody who could play at this level and he told me he didn't, not personally.

Then I remembered a movie. It starred Orson Wells, Jack Hawkins, and Tyrone Power. Hawkins and Power were wandering around Asia looking for fun and profit during the Middle Ages. They met a Mongol chieftain who went around killing people for fun and profit. The name of this picture, if memory serves, was the *Black Rose*.

The Mongol chieftain, who called himself Bayan of the Thousand Eyes, meaning he had spies everywhere, was played by Orson Wells. He finds out Power can play chess to the second move, and he befriends the two of them and then promises to make them both rich. They stick around long enough to make some dough and then they get away from this guy, not wanting to be further involved with all the killing. But the point here is: the Mongol chief tells the Scholar, that's what he calls Power's character, "There is nobody in my entire army who can play to the second move."

Well, anyway, I have a hunch that Herb Rosenthal can. And this thought runs through my head all the time, as I read his notes and piece together his story. I get the idea, now that I know a little about the game, that he is playing a kind of chess game with me. He is playing at a much higher level, though, higher than I will ever be capable of–and at the same time he is playing with me, he is playing with the CIA–and maybe with some other rough characters as well. I have a hunch they're a bunch of sore losers, all of them. And when this book hits the stands, the real game is about to begin. I just hope I'm not one of the pawns who get sacrificed in some opening gambit designed by Herb Rosenthal.

No, I can't quit–not that I want to. And now another trip to Singapore. I'm beginning to like it. What's not to like about the Raffles Hotel?

Herb meets me in the usual place, the so-called Writers Bar. Where else, since I'm masquerading as a writer? And time will tell whether I am or not. But Herb says not to worry about details like this. He says he knows me by reputation. And once on paper, nobody is going to worry much about grammar or sentence construction, certainly nobody in the CIA is going to be interested. He says they'll have their minds on other things. He says not to worry; he says he has a good proofreader standing by, one he can trust. That's what he says, anyway.

I'm in the bar about ten minutes on the second day. He never tells me when he's going to show, and he never has a hotel reservation. He just appears and there he is.

This time, though, it's different. This time he has a woman

on his arm, something really different for Herb. I never thought he cared too much for the company of women. But it just goes to show you how unpredictable he is—or maybe how much I don't know about him.

I stood up as the two of them approached my table. He introduced the woman.

She's dressed in the latest Asian fashion. You don't have to be much of an expert in women's clothes to tell she's loaded. The dress is pure silk brocade. Silk is bad enough, but because of the brocade it has to be woven differently, and around here it costs some big bucks. Either she's as rich as Bim Gump or Daddy Warbucks or somebody who is bought it for her.

I soon found out it's Herb, when next he tells me she is his wife as well as his secretary.

Nobody could be more surprised than I am.

Herb starts talking while I'm still thinking. If she's not loaded, then it must be Herb who has all the money. But where did he get it? Maybe I'm going to find out as the game progresses.

"Chris, you know who this is. This is the beautiful lady you've written about; I guess you have, haven't you." He said this as he reached across the table and handled the manuscript.

"Remember, Helen is the daughter of the herbal medicine physician, the one who played such an interesting game of chess. He has since passed away. But a few years ago, he had his practice not too far from here."

She smiled as she shook my hand, and I could see why old Herb had fallen in love with her.

She said nothing as she bowed and then released my hand with a delicate touch that was almost not there.

Once I had attended a gang interview, back when Herb was grist for the mill of sports reporters—back when he was the darling—the time when he was celebrating his fifteen minutes. Back when he was the best copy, not because he was some kind of standout ball player, but because he was witty. And because he had the ability to string several sentences together in one cohesive thought.

"When are you going to get married?" One of our numbers asked him, irreverently. All of us knew he was a confirmed bachelor. How we knew exactly escapes me now. But we just knew. It didn't need asking, and no one would have been surprised if Herb had not answered. But as I said, he was a good interview; he never refused to comment or to answer most anything asked of him; not like most of the prima donnas nowadays who play the game. Not like those with limited vocabularies who are hard put to remember their names all day. No, not like them. Herb was as unlike any of them as night is from day.

I remember Herb pausing for a minute before answering. Then he replied, "What did you say?"

"When are you going to get married–or are you?" the same sappy voice was asking again.

"Oh! I suppose I will someday," he replied, as he looked out over the group in that seemingly half-baked manner, his exclusive trademark when he was thinking.

"I suppose I will someday, when I find the right woman," he said again.

The same speaker looked up from his notes, which were waiting to be hastily phoned to a rewrite man and then translated into journalistic drivel and featured in the evening blab.

"Oh I suppose I'll get married, 'when I find a woman who is deaf and dumb and over-sexed and owns a liquor store.'" It was all Rosenthal, calculated to tickle the very young among them who had never heard the expression before.

She seemed to be able to speak and to hear perfectly well, so two out of four is not all that bad. But then a second and third look at her dress made me think the store, if she owned one, was doing quite well. Quite well, indeed.

There was a considerable difference in their ages. Even now after several years had passed, she was still quite young, and really beautiful, and certainly very charming. I was fascinated by her. But I was thinking we might not become very good friends–more is the pity. There just wasn't going to be enough time. I suspect this is going to be our first and last meeting. And because of what's written in the book, we might not see or hear from each other again. That is, I'm not ever going to see the two of them again.

"You have no objections if Helen proofreads it, do you?" He held up the manuscript as he said it.

"None whatsoever," I said.

"Good. Then we'll excuse her so she can get started. I'm anxious to finish for a couple of reasons: Our meetings are becoming predictable. It makes me a little uneasy. And to tell you the truth, if we do have to meet again before it's published, I think we ought to do it someplace else. What do you think?"

I'm sure I had no idea what he was talking about, unless it was just more of his need to be secretive, something I now knew was part of his way of life and always had been. I don't call it paranoia or even a compulsive disorder; but then, I'm no psychiatrist. But if I were, I would call it overly precautious. But then I haven't heard the whole story yet. Maybe tomorrow I might think differently about Herb and some of his quirks; maybe I'm about to join him–I mean join him in being quirky.

"Herb, I'm dying to know what the four of you were doing in Tibet, running all over looking for a nuke power plant that didn't exist."

"Oh it existed all right, it sure did. But it was about fifty miles more to the northeast on another river, more out into the Gobi, out nearer to Outer Mongolia." He informed me.

"The problem was with the planning inside McDermott's emporium at Langley. For starters, somebody translated the distance wrong from kilometers to miles, if you can believe it. The starting point was a city in Mongolia designated by the Russian MVD. However, the Russians didn't bother to mention the distance was measured in kilometers instead of miles. And then these same clowns used the wrong kind of chart when they plotted the compass course given them. At any rate, there is a power plant, but it was way off from where we were looking. I always wondered whether it was planned that way.

"I found out the Russians knew of it from the time the Chinese started to build. They hesitated to do anything until Collins found out about it from Voroshilov and told McDermott. That started the wheels in motion, which ended in some kind of an embarrassment for us."

"Were you really going to melt it down and kill all of those people."

"No, I wasn't but they were. No, it was a Ralph Levy operation with another acquaintance of his in the MVD. They figured an explosion was not going to get the required action from the UN. The girl had been briefed to cause the melt-down. We were all to be killed. But the aborted mission caused the president to rethink his position in view of the possibility of getting a meeting with Zhou. And then you know the rest of what happened. The three of us never intended to get involved with any melt-down. We talked it over and decided to blow the plant and then get out of Tibet and away from the Company, and sell our books. We all agreed to write one or have somebody else do it. Different stories, but the same theme—you know about this melt-down thing. We figured we could each sell enough books to live as comfortably as we would have with our pensions. And we would leave the Agency with a relatively clear record, not with all those thousands of dead nomads on our conscience. Ralph Levy was the bad guy–and not McDermott.

"What happened to McDermott? Do you know?"

"You better believe I do. Levy disliked McDermott immensely. He did everything he could to undermine him over the years. He finally edged him out and made him take early retirement. Not early retirement exactly, but he did retire early, still in his most productive years, because Levy closed the door on him. McDermott realized he was going nowhere, so he retired, and Morris made sure Levy took his place. Morris told Levy he owed him a favor and he paid him well. Ralph Levy is going for the top job now, and Morris is still there pushing for him. Last I heard, he was going to make it too, the top spot I mean."

"You mean he was going to make it , if you had not decided to publish this book."

"Yeah, that's what I mean. You see Levy has all the pull in the world. He has friends in high places, in the likes of Morris and a couple of others. Recall, Morris told him he wouldn't forget him. Among politicians, the worst thing you can do is to renege on a promise. And Morris kept his. It all started with Nixon, and Levy has progressed right on up the ladder to the present time. I mean, as Morris has advanced, he has brought Levy along tied to his coat tails.

Levy is known in the Company as one who has special friends, meaning he has high political pull. They have a name for it, which is not shown in any personnel file. Still everybody knows, and the smart ones don't make a habit of crossing people in his position. This gives him clout found only in supervisors at the top level.

"This toadyism is not unique to government agencies. It is

found in the military once in a while and is rampant in industry. Maybe in all walks of life. You see people all the time who get ahead because they have somehow made friends with powerful people."

"Sort of like marrying the boss's daughter," I volunteered.

"Yeah, something like that. But the daughter thing is at least out in the open. These under-the-table friendships can cripple organizations. Everybody is aware of this, but they are hard to stamp out. At least they are in most organizations, most of the time."

"But not this friendship, and not at this time," I said. Herb smiled and nodded agreement.

"Right, not this time, old buddy." Herb paused for a full thirty seconds,   staring into space, savoring the moment by himself someplace. When he returned, he said:

"Yeah, Levy knew what he was doing when he engineered that shoot-up down the street. Job security and advancement weren't the only reasons he set it up the way he did. This guy loves power; I want you to work that part in. I want to make sure everybody understands, especially the members of congressional oversight committees. I want them to know that he is now the head of one of the most powerful directorates in the CIA–and that might very well mean he is one of the most powerful men in government. There is no telling what he might set his hand to next if he's not stopped."

I said: "I think I will put it in the book just this way. I'm not sure I can improve on anything you just said."

I wanted to change the subject: "Tell me some more about the Nugan Hand bank. I understand it was a CIA operation, but I have no idea what part it plays in your story."

"Well, it was the main reason I fell out with the Company. That and the fact I had been skating on thin ice ever since General

Donovan put the hex on me. Recall, he was all but convinced I had given secrets to Heisenberg back in World War Two. The Company has a long memory, thanks to the way they keep secret records. They keep a file or dossier on everybody, including a lot of military as well as civilians who don't work for them. I found out much later that I was being accused of pandering to Heisenberg, when in reality what I told him stopped his experiments in heavy water. He went on with them, but he held back. I convinced him we were going to get the bomb first and blow Germany to pieces, which we would have done if they had not surrendered first.

"Oh, another thing. Remember my telling you how I was so angry at Heisenberg; you remember, when he told me we would have to have a train to deliver an atom bomb to Germany or rope a couple of our bombers together to deliver it. He wasn't a bit scared of the bomb, not really, because he had it in his mind that Germany was safe. That's when I became exasperated at his smugness and told him we had such an airplane. Well, he didn't believe me. That's when I told him—and this is new information—I told him about the then top secret project called *Operation Matterhorn*. It was the code name for the B-29 bomber program, you know, the airplane that was being built to carry the atom bomb. I kind of just blurted it out without thinking; that is how badly I wanted to shut him up. Well, to make a long story short, after the War he mouthed it around about how he knew about our bomb and that he even knew about the B-29 then in construction. Nobody believed him until he told them the classified code name for the project. When they asked him how he knew, he said I told him—suffice to say, he didn't like me and used this information to get back at me. I suspect it was his main reason; that and to still stay in the spotlight growing dimmer by the hour. He wanted to make sure history was aware of the major role he played in stop-

ping Germany's atom bomb project. Nobody believed him. All
he managed to do was get me in more trouble with Donovan, and
this time with Hoover as well."

"How about Nugen Hand, then. You forgot about the bank.
Why was that so much of a black mark on your record?"

"It wouldn't have been if it had not been so serious. I was
doing just what I had been told to do. I set up the bank and
handled much of the CIA's money to get it started. When the
bank began financing drug and illegal armament shipments, I
was suspected of being part of it. Quite frankly, the CIA and the
Australian government never believed either Nugan or Hand had
the connections for money laundering or the know-how for some
of the other things they were later accused of doing. And to prevent a scandal leading all the way back to the White House, the
CIA stepped in before an investigation could get started.

"Australia was pushing for a trial to unravel things. They
were smarting because the bank had been doing a lot of illegal
trading in their country, and the Aussies thought our government
was behind it. This was particularly true after the Vietnam War
went down the drain.

"Students over there were just as radical as they were here.
And the Australian government thought there was going to be a
scandal that was going to reach into their government as well. You
see, we could not have established a bank and then kept it running for some five years without their approval. But at any rate,
when it turned out top aides in the White House, like Halpern and
a renegade agent known as the White Ghost, a.k.a. Ted Shackley
were going to be called as witnesses; the CIA stepped in and put
a stop to any further evidence collecting. They said, and it was no
doubt true, the bank was too closely meshed with CIA activities
in Southeast Asia. They maintained a public look would reveal
their methods of operation, which would expose most of their

undercover operators. All this, to say nothing about what would have happened to all their small contractors."

"So then they blamed you and not Nugen or Hand. They said you knew too much. Your availability to testify was one of the reasons for not going forward with the trial." I commented.

"That's correct. They had to have somebody to blame for the bank's existence in the first place. But I was the guy in the barrel who was also blamed for much of the illegal stuff that came later. Since I was still an officer of the bank, even though I had left a couple of years earlier, I got the blame, just as though I was still there."

"So" I said, "when the trial fizzled out, they figured you were looking around for a platform to get your message across, to vindicate yourself, to clear your name. They figured you were going to write a book and divulge who the real power behind the bank was. Tell me some more about what effect it might have had on the White House if the CIA had not stopped the trial." I asked him. "Did it really spill over that far?"

"You bet it did," he said. "You see, Halpern was a top aide at the time, and he had his dirty fingers right in the middle of it all. The smart money said, if he was there, then so were others next to the President. And it was a short jump from there to the President himself.

"Chris, can you picture the field day the media would have had with this mess if the CIA had not stopped the Secretary of State from going ahead with his pre-trial investigation?"

"Gee, Herb, that was a low blow as far as you were concerned."

"You better believe it. It hurt me deeply. I was innocent, but I was never able to clear my name. Then after I found out I was on their list, I was really bent out of shape."

"Their list?"

"Yeah, they kept a list of potentially dangerous agents. Guys like Phillip Agee, who became disenchanted and quit. Agee later wrote a best seller about the inner workings of the Company. President Bush, who headed the Agency at that time, referred to him as *America's traitor.*

"I had no intention of writing a book, but they thought I did. That's why I ended up on their list."

"You mean you didn't have any plans at the time?" I asked him.

"Not any at all," he replied.

"Then let me guess," I said. "When the Chinese were tipped off and came looking for you in the office of the East India Trading Company headquarters here, and your friends got themselves killed, I take it that's when you changed your mind?"

"Exactly," Herb replied. "What did you expect me to do? But I held off for a long time," he said.

I looked at him, even more puzzled: "Tell me some more about the list. Do I understand correctly that Eckert and Collins were on it, too?"

"You do, indeed," he said. "You know most everything there is to know about Eckert already. But one important thing I might have left out. Recall that he was at Groom Lake. He screwed up big time by getting himself on the record of those who knew about the U-2 spy plane. Not only did he know about it, but he had seen it. They always take the extreme approach to things like that. They never gave him the benefit of the doubt when he said it was an accident. They put it in his file, the fact that he had been arrested and interrogated. That in itself cast suspicion on him. It's like a bad credit rating; you never seem to be able to shake it. They never were sure he had not said something about it to Rowe or to the Countess or to somebody else. When he got in trouble in Morocco and was being investigated for atomic secrets violations, his record of the U-2 incident did not help his case at all. But the CIA knew the score and the Air Force didn't."

"Why was he looking at the airplane the way he was if he didn't have a purpose?" I asked him.

"I don't know why. Curious I guess. But why they put it on his record, inferring he was some kind of agent with an ulterior motive when it was obviously an accident, I'll never know. It doesn't make a lot of sense to me, but it did to the Security people. I guess that's what they get paid for."

"What about the Russian girl?" I asked.

"She was on the Russian version of the List and was transferred to ours at the request of the MVD," he answered.

I asked him if he knew what she had done.

"She had knifed a fellow agent in the field. She was raped and didn't take to it kindly. But the head of her division didn't like losing one of his best men over something he blamed her for. They have their own way of hushing things up, but like us, they also have a long memory. That's the way Voroshilov explained it to Collins, anyway."

"Was there anything between Eckert and the girl?"

"Which girl? Oh, you mean the Russian and not the Hungarian?"

"Yeah, I mean the Russian. But I want to discuss the other one in a minute."

"When I got to know Eckert better, he told me the complete story. There is a lot that transpired between them, which I didn't include in my notes on purpose. I didn't want you to go off on a tangent with a lot of sex stuff and have the reader forget why we're here–to expose a rogue agent in the CIA. Yes, they did all the things people would be expected to do who are thrown together on a long trip. He said he found a soft side to her, no pun intended. He said they fell in love and, by the time they got back, they had planned to get married. They were going to do it as soon as we went back and blew up the real power plant. By marrying her, Eckert would have lost his clearance and any future in the Air Force. And the CIA would have divorced him, too. So I suppose they both wrote fini to their careers. But they both knew this and didn't seem to care. But one thing I don't think they considered; the Agency would not have taken kindly to him marrying her. They would have been suspicious of him revealing classified material and her running back and telling her people. As soon as the Agency found out, he would have been in much bigger trouble than he was in already. But as it turned out, they were already in much bigger trouble than any of us realized at the time. Actually, we all were, thanks to friend Ralph Levy back at Langley."

"You said they intended to provide an income for the rest of their lives from a book sale. Could that be one of the reasons they didn't care whether or not they lost their jobs?"

"I guess so. Not a bad idea, writing a book. Think about it a minute. A husband and wife team of Phillip Agee agents from opposite sides exposing both intelligence organizations. What a gimmick, don't you think?"

"Too bad they'll not be able to make the rounds of all the talk shows starting to show up on television," I commented.

"Herb, could we change the subject for a minute? Would you tell me some more about Edit Esterhazy?"

"Well, for starters, her name was not Esterhazy; it was Eberle. Her mother was an Esterhazy and the title of countess was going to pass to Edit if it had continued to exist. That's one of the reasons she was talking Eckert into getting out of the Service and the CIA. She wanted him to just haul off and take off with her on a big-time treasure hunt. She wanted her treasure and her title. Without the money, it seemed kind of silly wandering around making like you were part of Europe's aristocracy. It would have been kind of pathetic, really."

"Did these diamonds actually exist?" I asked him, commenting as if to voice my own opinion. "It seems to me, Eckert was pretty well convinced they didn't.

"And how did the Hungarian Esterhazy family, who were descendants of Khans and Magyars, get mixed up with Templars who were mostly English and French?"

"First things first," was his answer. Then he said: "Eckert believed her hidden wealth was all a myth at the time she told him her story. He told me in Tibet that he had hardly ever heard of the Templars and the rest of the 'people involved with the rise and fall of this warrior clan. And if he had ever heard of the Esterhazy family while studying European history, he had forgotten about it." Herb paused for a moment, thinking. And then he continued: "He told me he didn't believe any part of it when she told him her story. Talking about secret organizations dating back to the Crusades and millions of dollars in diamonds hidden away someplace–it was too much for him. Then too, there was no way he could immediately leave the Service; he had commitments she knew nothing about. He had a regular commission and had recently been promoted, and he couldn't resign for another two years.

"Oh, there is one other thing he told me about," Herb said. "It might be one of the reasons he never acted on her story and then lived to regret it. He reminded me that after the War, papers and magazines were rife with secret treasure stories and conspiracies. Remember the Reichsbank gold and the stolen *Waffen SS* loot hidden away in a potassium mine? I mean the one General Patton recovered. And then the rumors about *SS* gold dumped into that Bavarian or Austrian lake that never amounted to anything? Well, there were even more. There were unsubstantiated stories floating around all over the place."

"What did Edit mean when she told him she had somebody else waiting in the wings if he didn't want to help her?" I asked.

"Eckert told me she had met an adventurer of sorts," he said. "This guy was a Swede who owned a yacht. He was on some kind of a sail-about. His father was an industrialist and his son was on an extended vacation. I guess she told him the story of the diamonds, and he wasted no time in asking her to get married. Eckert said when he tried to contact her she had left, later settling her parents in Sweden."

"Do you think Eckert made a mistake? Do you think he made an error in judgment? I asked you if you thought the diamonds existed."

"Yes, I do. The reason I do is because of what she knew about this secret society thing.

"I ran across the Esterhazy family when working for the Wiesenthal Center," he said. "The Center wanted to explore all facets of the Third Reich. It was part of an ad hoc study they made to explain what happened to European Jewry. Among other things, they wanted to gather the facts, which would then be used to teach the truth of the Holocaust to the next German generation. We Jews didn't want it happening all over again.

"Well, Edit knew then what I later found out, that is to say, she knew that early members of the Thule Society were a brotherhood rooted in the order of the Knights Templar. By early, I mean before Hitler joined them. We had no trouble finding members of this Society after the War. There were many who had become disillusioned with orders, secret societies, and the like. They were willing to tell us all their secrets. We concluded that the Thule Order, and the Templars had too much in common not to have been connected in some way.

"The Thule's were not Masons," Herb went on to tell me

without my asking. "They had taken similar oaths, but had gone a lot further. They were much less a spiritual organization and more rooted in nationalism. They were more militaristic; they were more interested in promoting their causes through militant rather than benevolent means. She could not have known what she did about all of this if she had not been a member of the Esterhazy inner circle.

"She also knew about Canaris, who was part of the hierarchy of the Thule before Hitler took over. She knew Canaris was a member of the secret inner group after they became the Nazi Party. It is significant to note that Hitler and his close associates never knew the original society remained intact. But Edit did, and she knew Canaris, along with another early Thule member, *Feldmarshal* Erwin Rommel, helped engineer the attempt on Hitler's life later on in the War. But only Rommel knew about Canaris' duplicity in the plot. And recall, the Gestapo had nothing to do with Rommel's suicide. It was strictly the doings of the *Waffen SS*, who had been ordered by Hitler to treat him as the national War hero he was.

"Rommel was never interrogated or tortured the way the other conspirators were. He was not forced to reveal any co-conspirators. On Hitler's orders, he was left alone. They simply gave him a gun and told him to shoot himself. Of course, they promised him his widow could keep his estate if he did. And Hitler gave him his personal assurance that his wife and son would be provided for if he did it without a lot of fuss and bother. Wasn't that generous of him? Who says he never had a heart? Anyway, you can see why Canaris was never found out, why he was one of the few who managed to escape Scott free. But hey! You are not going to find this in the official record. Canaris was supposed to have lost his life, as did a thousand others caught up in the assassination plan. But wait a minute, I'm getting ahead of myself," he said.

"You see, Germany was under the rule of a criminal regime. Opposition by certain members of the Army general staff was a moral imperative, if you believe that basically they were honest men. But their practical chances for a successful coup were nil. They showed by their actions they had no head for conspiracy and no practical concept for Germany's future. They just took it one day at a time. And because they had to watch what they said and whom they said it to, they had a big communication and coordination problem, which doomed them from the start.

"And another thing: Edit knew Canaris had been in touch with Colonel Donovan and Cordell Hull while the War was still raging. She could not have been making up that part of her story. We at the Wiesenthal Center knew, and so did she; Canaris had been hidden by our government right after the War. He was moved to an obscure town in Oklahoma. We know he moved back and forth to Washington, but continued to live out in cow country incognito. After what he had been through during the War, I guess he needed a life-long rest. And he could never be sure somebody was not looking for him–somebody who might have looked on him as a traitor."

"Then what role does this guy Gehlen play in all of this?" I asked him.

"Well, that is the most interesting thing of all, if you are looking for evidence Edit's story was on the level. When Eckert mentioned the name of General Gehlen and told me Edit knew he worked for us, I filed it away in my head. The first chance I got, I looked him up in the classified files of the Company. Sure enough, he had been befriended by Alan Dulles, head of the Agency at the time. After the War, Gehlen and his key assistants were brought to the U.S. and worked for Dulles in the CIA. He worked for the Company all through the worst part of this so-called Cold War–he and several hundred former Waffen SS were known as the Gehlen Organization. Another thing, this guy Gehlen should have been tried as a war criminal for the atrocities he was responsible for on the Eastern front; but he wasn't, because we needed him. Gehlen missed the Nuremberg trials because of his close association with Allan Dulles. As an interesting aside, this guy Dulles was notorious in his own right. I know a lot abut him. Maybe later we will collaborate on another book with him as the central character."

"What did we need Gehlen for?" I asked, getting back to the point.

He answered me by saying: "Immediately after hostilities ceased, we found ourselves at loggerheads with the Soviet Union. The new CIA had no idea what was going on in that country. But General Gehlen knew, and to save himself from a long prison term, he volunteered to work for us. This last thing is not generally known outside the Company. Ask yourself how Edit knew."

"What will happen when this book is published and the world finds out that we hired notorious Nazis like Gehlen?"

"Who knows," he said, with a smile, which indicated he very well knew the can of worms he was opening and the problems his retired enemies were going to have explaining all this away.

"Yes, but what did Eckert think after you found out about Canaris and Gehlen? And then you filled Eckert in on all the historical details, which further corroborated what Edit had told him."

"He changed his mind," Herb said. "Eckert told me he thought he had made a terrible mistake in not trusting her. He thought all along she just wanted to get married to get a passport to go to the States. He told me it might well have been the biggest mistake of his life, not going after the diamonds, I mean. But looking back on it, we both know better. His biggest mistake was getting involved with the CIA in the first place. He should have stuck with what he knew best, the United States Air Force, and left the rest alone."

"Herb, I don't know whether it has much to do with the story about her and Eckert, but I'm curious to know more about this Thule organization that you say ultimately became the Nazi Party."

"Well, it is quite involved, but here is the short version: After Phillip, and to some degree Pope Clement, had most of the Templars murdered, some of the remainder joined up with another sect known as the Knights of Malta or the Hospitaliers. They were another group like the Templars who had also taken certain oaths. Their big contribution to the Crusades was the hospitals they established. They were not wealthy so they were not a threat to Phillip or to the Church. The few Templar survivors journeyed to Hungary, some went to Austria and some to Scotland to get away from Phillip. Those who made it to Hungary and Austria were lost to history for centuries, rising again in the form of the Thule Society.

"The Templars hated the Church for good reason, yet they were still Christians of a sort. Remember, Clement had branded them heretics, for embracing Gnostic views, which he considered to be heretical...."

I interrupted him. "Tell me about these Gnostics. I've heard about them but know nothing at all, really. Who were they? Were they in opposition to the Catholic Church?"

"You better believe they were," he said. Then he began telling me about the history of the Catholic Church, why it was in conflict with Gnosticism, what influence it had on the rest of the world up to the present time, and why the members of the Thule group were believed originally to have been Gnostics:

"You see," Herb said, "one of the problems with the early Church was communication. Its members were scattered all over, located wherever apostles like Paul and Peter traveled as missionaries. They couldn't keep things standardized according to what Jesus' disciples had taught them. Imagine the chaos prevailing when this new organization, with its strange concepts of virgin birth and resurrection, was superimposed on orthodox Jewry. Not only that, but the whole she-bang had to contend with paganism and a whole host of splinter religions in vogue; at times these groups were large enough to pose a serious threat to Christ's young Church. It is no wonder then that some scholars and Christian churches today believe it began to fall away from the teachings of the Apostles almost as soon as it was started. Now enter the Gnostics, who no one knew much about until just recently.

"Over in Egypt in 1947," he went on to say, "near a small town called Nag Hammadi, a young lad, not unlike the one who discovered the Dead Sea Scrolls at Qumran Wadi, found an earthen jar in a cave in the desert. It contained a bundle of codices made of leather."

He paused for a minute, thinking. And then he continued: "These codices were written by Christian Coptics, who are sometimes referred to as Forgotten Christians, that is, they were not tied to mainstream Christianity developing in Rome. The Copts were Gnostics, that is, they used as the basis for their religion certain gospels unlike those featured in the New Testament. The big problem, although they give us another insight into the times from a different perspective, is that their philosophy runs counter to established Christianity. You see, for all their good works the Copts were not looked upon as Christian–they did not believe that the only way to God was through Jesus.

"There were some Coptic writings extant at the time, but they were fragmented and few and far between. Not until the Coptic Library, as the codices have come to be known, were discovered have scholars had a clear picture of this so-called falling away of the early Church. What was known about these people, actually what they had to say about the early Church, was left out of the Bible as it come to be. None of their writings were canonized at the Council of Nicaea in the first decade of the fourth century. Actually, none of them were even considered. This was during the reign of the Emperor Constantine…"

I interrupted him once again, this time to go to the bathroom. But I also wanted to hear more about this guy Constantine. I had heard of him, but like most people, whether they went to church on Sunday or not, did not know the real story about him. When I came back, I found another soft drink sitting in front of me and Herb Rosenthal chomping at the bit; he was spring-loaded in his teaching mode.

"Constantine is sometimes thought of as a Christian," he said. "Nothing could be further from the truth. He was a Roman Emperor, a monster, not unlike all of them down to Caligula in reverse succession. His interest in Christianity was solely to unite the Roman Empire. He made it the official religion, but only because it was expedient to harness the power of its God to benefit the Empire. Even so, he never closed many pagan temples. He did strip them of their wealth, however, and he did give it to the fledgling Christian churches, which might account for their meteoric rise during his reign. In his Legions, for example, he had Christians, Pagans, and followers of Mithra and just plain atheists, who usually kept their non-beliefs to themselves. He was interested in *One Religion, One Emperor, One Empire* or some such catchy saying, according to Pliny, or Eusebius, or maybe it was Tertulian.

"But how to standardize it all was a problem. There were the New Testament Gospels to be sure, but there were also hundreds of other fragments purporting to have been written by one or more of Jesus' disciples. You see, down through the ages, it was not a good idea to be a Christian. You could, through no fault of your own, become the main attraction at the Sunday games held at the Coliseum. If you were taken for interrogation, which I'm told was not the most pleasant way to spend an afternoon, you could escape martyrdom if you recanted your belief that Jesus was the Son of God. You see, the Emperors believed they were also the sons of some god. And they resented a lot of those not *born to the purple* running around professing the same thing. If the interrogating magistrate did not believe you were sincere in your recantation story, you were in big trouble. It helped immensely if you could produce a fragment to recant, and you swore it had been written by one of Jesus' early followers.

"The fragments, written by His disciples, were venerated; so it became a cottage industry to counterfeit them—and literally sell them on the open market. Many Christian families owned a few, against the day they might need to break one out to ensure some family member did not become lion bait.

"Constantine felt it was necessary to hold a convention to decide which of all these fragments were authentic and which were spurious. Those deemed the most nearly scripture were canonized and became the first Bible. But the final document ended up being too large for any practical purpose, and some of it had to be discarded. The first to go was a body of scripture known as the Apocrypha. However, it was included in the Catholic version of the Bible until the time King James had several scholars retranslate the Bible into the scripture that still bears his name. But for purposes of our discussion here, none of the Coptic documents were considered by the convention, because they were branded ahead of time as heretical. Truth be told: as soon as Christianity became the state religion, the new emerging Church sought to purge the scene of Gnostics, as they would later the Templars, and also, a few others along the way who did not choose to worship exactly as the convention perceived things to be. Later, when purging became unfashionable, it was replaced by excommunication, a fate suffered by all protestors or Protestants who challenged the various popes' authority in religious matters. Of course, there were several newly minted organizations that were just not recognized because they didn't believe or teach things according to the way the early Church decided they should be taught.

"But the point is this: the Gnostics were seen as heretical, and all organizations teaching anything to do with them were also considered to be heretics. I believe that's one of the reasons why the Templars were purged as heretics. They had early on abandoned much of their original Christian beliefs for a form of Gnosticism. That's what I think, anyway."

He stopped for a minute with his dissertation before he told me again how much tangible proof he had acquired for the Wiesenthal people. He said there was no question the Thule Society was composed of descendants of Prussian officers, a few civilian diplomats, and wealthy aristocrats all of them having the same interests and goals. He said their oaths and rituals were handed down through generations with their roots in the Templar Order, which did not have Christianity as its basis. And then he said a curious thing: He said he had uncovered writings by supposedly serious historians, who believe the Thule Order now permeates the officer corps of the Allied forces.

"Herb, I have a couple of questions about the ping-pong thing: How come Nixon hated the Chinese so badly, yet he expressed a desire to go to China while he was still governor of California?"

"First off, Mr. Nixon was hard to figure," he answered, with a kind of half-smile. "He had more than a few inconsistencies in his make-up. Maybe this was one of them. But he saw China as a long-time first-class trading partner. But the truth is, we have only been trading with them a few short years and we are running a terrific deficit. Economics is not my field, but where is the sense in this? I can only conclude that Nixon thought they were going to come into the twentieth century slower than they did. And of course, we were supposed to make a lot of money helping them get here.

"But this whole trading scheme of Nixon's is destined to go sour as far as I'm concerned. As a nation, we will continue to do business with them at a loss, but it's not likely we're going to stop anytime soon. What I've never been able to understand is how come our businesspeople can be so sharp as individuals, while at the same time our government is downright stupid when it comes to financial transactions with other countries. I don't know of anyone who things otherwise; I believe we're all united on this point.

"It reminds me of an old joke," Herb went on to say, with a smile on his face, "about the guy who is running a clothing store and is selling clothes at cut-rate prices. His buddy asks him how he can continue to sell clothes at a loss, and he replies: volume, volume. That's what we do best, lose money doing a big time volume.

"I can see now. It is obvious why you're writing the book, and I don't blame you"

"My boy," Herb said, "you have it all figured out do you? Tell me the name again."

"*The Third Gambit*," I said.

"Correct," he replied. "Now you tell me you play the game. So what are the second and third moves after the opening?"

"I don't know. I thought I understood it all, but I guess I don't."

"Well, I'll tell you. I'll tell you what the third move was after the opening:

"Recall how badly the President wanted to be invited by Zhou to go to China. He saw it as a big vote getter in the coming election, something that would offset his bad Vietnam publicity. Well Kissinger knew this, and he made the securing of an invitation his number one priority.

"Now consider this: What if we had gone back the second time and found the power plant and then destroyed it, destroying many innocent lives in the process. And, thereafter, we trumpeted to the world about how China was backward and should not be allowed into the nuclear club. What if this had happened just as they had it planned, right after Kissinger had hatched his scheme to get into China to talk seriously to Zhou about getting an invitation for the President. What do you think would have happened? Do you think Zhou would have had anything to do with Mr. Nixon?"

"I see what you mean," I said.

"So did McDermott actually torpedo the operation as it was progressing just so Nixon could go to China?" I asked him.

"Almost right, old buddy. You were close, but no cigar. But that's the essence of a good chess player. He sets you up and then lowers the boom on you. And that is just what the CIA and the MVD did: they set us all up."

"What did happen then?" I asked him.

Herb sat for the longest time before answering. He even called the waiter over and ordered something to eat. He was not above savoring the moment. He smiled at me before he began to speak again. When the waiter retired, he said: "Recall, Kissinger had sent Morris, his right hand man, to see Levy and not McDermott. McDermott for all his faults was really a straight shooter. But he had gone about as far as he was going to go in the Company. He would have had nothing to do with any dirty tricks. He was not about to jeopardize his pension.

"But Ralph Levy was another matter entirely. He was ambitious. Just as Julius Caesar was ambitious.

"Levy wanted advancement and power, and even though he appeared reluctant to get involved, Levy knew the operation had the attention of the President himself. That's why Kissinger by passed McDermott. He knew Levy was game for anything that would help him up the ladder."

"What did Levy do, Herb. Have I missed something?"

"No, dear boy, you've missed nothing at all. You were not supposed to know that McDermott was a good guy and that Levy was the scoundrel.

"What Levy did was this: He knew the President had changed his mind about blowing the power plant after Kissinger told him there was a good chance he could gain a political coup by being the first president into China. Nixon wanted to rebuild fences, after China cost us thousands of American lives in Korea. He also knew it was virtually impossible to keep China from moving forward with their nuclear power program, and even an atom bomb eventually. France and Canada had sold them advanced equipment after China stole reactor technology from India, so it was almost useless to continue to isolate China. If we did, we were going to let Europe get a strong economic foothold ahead of us. So when he was briefed by the CIA of the first failure to blow the plant, Nixon cancelled the second.

"Our team had been directed by McDermott to stay put in the Company's offices in Singapore. We were calling ourselves the East India Trading Company; Levy knew this, too. He also knew he had to do something extraordinary to impress the Chinese, because they could not comprehend a nation like ours extending a hand of friendship—not so soon after Korea. So this is what

Levy did: he set up what he called a *gesture*. He knew the CIA and the Russian plan called for the extermination of the four of us, who were a thorn in their sides, a la Phillip Agee. And he knew we were in Singapore waiting for the corrected coordinates of the plant before we set out again.

"Now, Levy made an end run around McDermott. He notified Chinese Intelligence through one of his buddies in the MVD. He told the Chinese all about what we had been doing. Then he told them we were planning on trying it again.

"He made sure the Chinese understood our plant blow-up-melt-down thing was not a sanctioned presidential action, but that it was concocted by a few bad asses who had been disenfranchised..."

"Of course, he meant the four of you."

"He did, indeed, mean us. The Russians told the Chinese that the girl was a co-conspirator who went along with it because she was in love with Eckert, and that she was just as guilty of plotting sabotage as we were.

"So," Herb said, "if they, the Chinese, thought their territory had been violated, and if they were seeking some kind of retribution and if they wanted to stop it from happening again, now was the time to make their move."

I said: "I believe I can figure out the rest of the story. Stop me if I'm wrong... The Chinese jumped at the chance to get rid of you, but they never told anybody. They kept it to themselves. But Zhou knew. And that's why he was so cooperative in this invitation thing. Zhou believed Nixon was behind the exposeç of his own people and really wanted to be his friend. What else would he believe; that is exactly how the Communist mind works. That is exactly what he would have done. So you were the chess pieces that were supposed to be sacrificed in the third move of the gambit to gain a better position in the middle game, correct?" I asked.

"Correct," he chuckled, "You might make a player yet, if they let you live long enough."

"Do you really think I'm going to be in some kind of danger?"

"Yes, I do," he replied, "but you needn't worry. You can hide very comfortably someplace in the world. Not here, for sure, but someplace nice where no one is going to look for you. If you want, I'll give you a list of some of the best places.

"And trust me on this, Chris, you're going to have enough money to live well anyplace you want to. Just keep a low profile. We could concoct a *nom de plume* for you and you could go home, but likely as not you would be discovered. We can't take the chance. I have grown rather fond of you. So your best bet is to disappear someplace a long way away.

"The only people who will know where you are living are the three of us, and she won't ever breathe a word about it and neither will I; you know that."

"Herb," I said, "I'm dying to know where you're getting your money and where you're living."

"I'll tell you this much. We're guests of the Sultan of Brunei, where exactly is still my secret. And for your information, since we are blood brothers, almost literally, I'm going to tell you he's bankrolling the whole project."

"That's why you're so generous with the money then. It isn't yours." I said, laughingly.

He smiled at me.

"Why is the Sultan so interested in this book? Apart from the fact he's your friend and he is not going to miss the money, why does he want the book published?"

"Good question," Herb said. "He wants it, maybe not as badly as I do, but he wants it. He has huge investments in publishing houses as well as his other interests. That's why I told you not to worry. You once told me you could write *Gone with the Wind*, and never be able to get it read by most of your friends and relatives let alone a publisher. And I told you to forget that end of it.

"Now suppose the book comes a cropper, which is highly improbable given the volatility of the subject matter; but just suppose for the sake of argument it does. If your cut doesn't make you a millionaire many times over, the Sultan says he will. That's how strongly he feels about what we're doing. He realizes the danger you're in, and he figures, one way or another, you deserve to be compensated. So I guess we can say you're walking in tall cotton."

"Okay," I said, "you can thank him for me for his largess. But why is he doing this?"

"Fair question again. He was agreeable to the project from the first day I approached him. I had been staying at his palace off and on over the years. One night we were playing chess and I told him the story. Not all of it, of course; there was never that much time. But he became interested, and he wanted me to write it all down. One thing led to another, and he suggested we put it in novel form and then publish it to embarrass the CIA and the MVD. And maybe in the end we might get guys like Levy out of the Agency. And if we were very fortunate we might even get a couple of them prosecuted."

I started to ask a question…

"I know what you are going to ask me. You want to know exactly what his interest is in me, other than I play a fair to middling game of chess and on occasion have been known to tell a funny story. The answer goes back to the Nugan Hand bank. The Sultan was most interested in the Vietnam War. He saw Communism as a threat to his kingdom and to his vast wealth, so he was always a Lyndon Johnson supporter. One of the many things he did was to pony up millions of dollars to support arms deals to the South Vietnamese."

"Why was this necessary?" I asked him.

"Because, as the War dragged on, it became increasingly difficult to get appropriations from Congress. The Sultan felt more arms were crucial or we were going to lose, which we eventually did. But at the time he saw his lifestyle, with his concubines and wealth, going right out the window. He believed his fortunes were tied to ours. It didn't happen that way, exactly, but that's what he believed. Now do you see?"

"Yes," I said. "Am I wrong in assuming the Sultan lost a bunch of money in Nugen Hand and was unable to recover much of it because the CIA appropriated all the assets when they closed it down. And I suppose then he was forced to remain silent, which precluded a lawsuit to recover his investments?"

"Something like that. You can write it up almost that way. None of it is fiction. And the Sultan wants the American public to know he was stiffed out of millions of dollars while he was trying to do us a favor."

He stood up, noticing I had almost filled another legal pad with notes. He smiled in approval, as he prepared to leave. As I stood up, he shook my hand and said: "I'll be in touch. I'll leave the edited manuscript with the concierge in a sealed envelope after I've read it. You do the same when you're finished; he'll see that I get it. From time to time I'll call plays in from the bench keeping you posted about where your money is banked, probably in a numbered account in Switzerland. Take care and thanks."

"Say goodbye to the Mrs.," I said. He waved back as he walked away.

I never saw him again, although I talk to him frequently. I'm rich, and I'm living well under a tropical sun. More than that I don't care to say either. Oh! About that other thing in case you are interested, I almost asked him if she really did own a liquor store, but I didn't.

AUTHOR'S NOTE

To insure the accuracy of the physics involved in this story, I consulted the source–the writings of Enrico Fermi, and others who were at the University of Chicago in December of 1942.

The conversations between Niels Bohr and Werner Heisenberg are fictionalized, but are supported in substance by noted play-wrights and reputable historians.

Some of the characters in this work are fiction. Some others are composites while still others lived, and some might be alive today. Also, most of the events occurred–or nearly so.